BLUE
CLASHING COLORS #4

Books in the Clashing Colors series

For the best reading experience and to avoid spoilers, below is the recommended order of the five Clashing Colors books.

BLACK - Clashing Colors #1
VIOLET - Clashing Colors #2
GREEN - Clashing Colors #3
BLUE - Clashing Colors #4
YELLOW - Clashing Colors #5

For a full overview of my books and to be alerted for new book releases, discounts, and give-aways, please sign up to my list at
www.elinpeer.com

PLEASE NOTE

This book deals with the sensitive subject of domestic violence. It's intended for mature readers only, as it contains a few graphic scenes of a violent nature and some inappropriate language.

All characters are fictional and any likeness to a living person or organization is coincidental.

DEDICATION

To my "roomie".
No matter how many books I write...
Our love story will always be my favorite.

Elin

CHAPTER 1
Follow the Fighter

"Geez, are you moving in or what?" my boss asked with a grin.

"You wish." I grinned back at Nigel, and walked sideways down the narrow corridor to avoid bumping my two heavy bags against the wall.

"What do you have in those anyway?" he asked.

"Let's see. In my left hand I have a million bucks in cash, and in my right hand: fake identity papers, traveling documents, and clothing for a warm climate."

"Right, like you would come here if that were the case."

"Maybe I need an alibi?"

"Yeah, or maybe all that's in those bags are your gym wear and those damn psychology books you always read."

My smile widened. "You know me too well."

"True, and you know what, Faith?"

"What?"

"You could use that imagination of yours to make extra money. I know you're always dead broke. Wanna join the dirty talkers?"

"Nah, the concept of horny guys moaning in my ear isn't too appealing." I moved into the small office and plunked my bags down on the floor.

"I thought you were used to horny guys by now."

Picking up the headset, I sat down in front of the computer. "This is different. Setting up appointments between the girls and their clients is not the same as phone sex."

1

"Whatever you say. I still think you would be amazing at it, and think about it – no one would ever see your face."

With my identical twin sister one of the biggest stars in Hollywood, discretion was key to me. I couldn't let the press know my involvement with an escort service, although there was nothing illegal in it.

My sister, Chloe, aka Cleo, was already on every front page for her own turbulent life. I wasn't going to contribute more headlines suggesting that Cleo's twin sister was involved in prostitution.

I wasn't!

Sadly, people just confuse call girls and escorts all the time.

"Thanks, but no thanks," I said to end the topic.

"Okay. Maria will be here at eight. Can you hold down the fort until then?"

"Don't I always?" I said with a smile.

Nigel put on his pilot jacket, the one that looked too small on his corpulent torso. The guy used to work in security and had the height to show for it. But his body-builder muscles had turned to fat over the years, and now he looked like a middle-aged guy stuck in the Eighties.

"See you, Faith."

"Yup, enjoy your evening and say hi to Angie for me."

"I will." He clapped twice on the doorframe and looked back. "She's making meat loaf tonight; my favorite."

The sound of an incoming call made me turn my attention to the caller. "Blue Ribbon Escort Service, this is Mary, how may I help you?"

It was a regular client, and setting him up with his preferred escort took less than a minute. Four more calls came in over the next twenty minutes, and then it was quiet for a while.

I got my book out and started reading up on Jung's archetypes, making notes on the side. If I was lucky, it would be a slow night. Those were my favorites, as it meant getting paid while studying. If all went according to plan, I would graduate with a major in psychology next summer.

My sister had offered to pay for my schooling, and at first I had gratefully accepted. But after two years of her using it against me in every argument, I had refused to take any more money from her. Now I got by on two jobs, and a talent for using as little money as possible.

This job was ideal; it was flexible, paid well, and allowed me to study when the phone wasn't ringing.

My other job as a cheerleader for the Seahawks was a more glamorous one. Twelve years of dance lessons, and good genetics, had secured me that job.

A new incoming call made me press *answer* and put on the fake Southern accent I used to disguise my own voice.

"Blue Ribbon Escort Service. This is Mary, how may I help y'all?"

"Ehhm, hello, I dinnae know how this works, but I wish to book an escort girl for tonight." The man had a deep voice with a distinct Scottish accent.

"Sure, honey, do you have any preferences?"

"Nah, I dinnae know any of the escorts."

"All right, not a problem. If you tell me what you're lookin' for, I'll match you up with the right one."

"Okay, I just want a lass who's kind."

"And by lass, you mean girl, right?"

"Aye, sorry, I try my best to use American words when I speak."

"Don't be." I chuckled. "I always knew readin' Highlander novels would come in handy one day. All right, honey, so you're lookin' for someone kind and...?"

"And, ehm..." He thought about it. "Not too young."

"Ohh, do you want someone older?"

"Not old. Just mature, I suppose."

"What age range are you interested in?" I asked.

"Mid-twenties and up."

"And what are you into? White, Asian, or African American?"

"I dinnae care about that. As long as she's not easily scared."

My brows furrowed, but I kept my tone light and flirtatious. "What do ya mean, handsome? Why would she be scared of ya?"

"I'm not handsome. And I just meant that she needs to be able to handle that."

"Ohh, don't worry, honey. This isn't a beauty pageant. All our girls are warm and lovin' women. They don't care about your looks. You'll be fine."

"Are ye sure about that?"

"Absolutely, and ya know, with that deep voice and sexy Scottish accent of yours, I envy the girl who gets to go out with ya."

"Aye, right." He said it sarcastically. "Ye say that to every customer."

"Not everyone has a sexy accent." I laughed.

"I meant the part about being jealous." His tone was soft and pleasant.

"I most certainly don't." I laughed again. "Now, tell me a bit about yourself. If you were to tell me three words that describe you, what would they be?"

"Three?"

"Yes, just three words."

"I'm smart."

"Yes."

"And I'm a fighter."

My eyes widened. A fighter with a strong accent. Only three months ago I had been at a party where Violet, a psychic woman, had predicted my future in what seemed

4

to be a confusing riddle. Now, however, the words spoken between her and me that night ran through my mind.

"Someone with a real accent is going to change your life," she told me.

"In a good way?"

"Follow the fighter, and you'll find out."

"You're being mysterious."

"I'm sorry but all you need to know, I've already told you. The rest you need to experience; and luckily for you, you won't have to wait long."

"Look how the hairs on my arms are standing up." I reached out both my arms to show her.

Violet smiled. "That's because your soul recognizes that I've just predicted your future."

"You did?"

"Uh-huh."

"But I didn't understand much then."

"You will. Trust your instinct and know this: Sometimes it takes a drowning person to bring out the hero in another."

"Okay."

"Remember what I said."

"I will," I told her.

A deep male voice cut through my memories. "Are ye there?"

"What, sorry, what did you say?"

"Ye wanted three words, and I said the last word is ugly."

I shook my head. "Don't say that about yourself."

"Why not? If ye could see me, ye would agree."

"People define beauty differently. I might think you're gorgeous."

"Only if ye're blind. I was, ehm, in an accident, and there are scars," he said in a low voice.

5

"Well, personally I always find scars intriguin'," I told him firmly. "There's a story behind every one of them, like a mystery to be solved."

He chuckled. "Ye're not serious?"

"I am, and some scars can even be sexy."

"Huh. If ye feel that way, maybe I should take ye out."

I grinned out loud, uplifted by the flirtatious connection between us. "I wish, honey, but I'm not one of the escorts," I said.

"Why not?"

I used the phrase that I had been trained to use. It worked every time. "The escorts are all beautiful and athletic. You'll be really glad you went for one of them and not me. I'm on the chubby side, short, fuzzy hair, and the type to wear peeling nail polish, you know?"

"Doesn't sound too scary."

I arched a brow, impressed that he wasn't turned off. "Aww, you're too sweet, but I got just the right woman for you. Her name is Charlene, she's thirty-two, five foot seven, and she's got long brown hair. Charlene is fond of animals, she's got a great sense of humor, and she loves to travel.

"Okay, if I cannae meet ye, I guess Charlene will have to do," he said in that Scottish brogue that made me a bit giddy.

"Great, where would you like to meet her and what time?"

"Can she come to my apartment?"

"If you become a regular, that will certainly be possible, but our policy is that our escorts always meet a new client in a public place. Is there a bar close to your home, or maybe a coffee house, or a library?"

"There's a bar around the corner called 'Trolls and Dolls.'"

"And what time should Charlene meet you there?"

"How about nine?"

6

"Sure. Can I get your name?"

"It's Logan."

"And your last name?"

"MacKay."

"Logan MacKay." It had a nice ring to it.

"So, Logan MacKay," I said flirtatiously. "To help Charlene find you in the bar tonight, I need you to give a few pointers on what you look like."

I never asked clients how they looked. Charlene would get his cell phone number and call him when she arrived. My question was only to satisfy my own curiosity. I imagined him as a tall Highlander with long dark hair blowing in the wind, a muscular torso, and large battle scar across his cheek.

"I'm blond," he said.

"Okay."

"Short hair."

I frowned as my Highlander fantasy evaporated.

"I'm six-one, and I'll be the ugliest guy in the bar."

The way he said the last words in a low mutter made my heart ache for him. All my life I had been blessed with beauty; I could only imagine what it would be like to feel ugly.

"Hey, Logan," I said with sympathy.

"What?"

"You know what is much more important than beauty?"

"What?"

"Humor and a good heart."

"Riiight." I could almost hear him roll his eyes.

"No, really, think about it. We all grow old and ugly with age, so the only part that remains attractive all your life is your personality."

"Hey, what happened to yer accent?"

Shit! I had spoken without my Southern cover accent.

"Whatevah do y'all mean?" I said, putting it on thick again. My hands nervously moved papers around on the desk.

"Ye just sounded different for a minute."

"Did I?" I chuckled. "Oh well, never mind about that. Yo're set to meet with Charlene tonight at nine, and all ya have to do is give me yo' cell phone number, so I can send ya a link to get the payment outta the way."

"How much is it?"

"It's two hundred an hour with a minimum of two hours."

"All right..." He paused and I sensed there was something he wanted to add.

"Yes?"

"Will she kiss me?"

"That's up to her. Most girls don't mind a bit of intimacy, but remember, Charlene is not a call girl and sex isn't part of the deal."

"But my colleague said that he went out with a girl and they had sex. He was the one who gave me your number."

I wrinkled my forehead. "Maybe he was braggin'. We are a non-sexual escort agency and our girls offer companionship, not sex."

He sighed. "It's okay. I wasn't looking for sex anyway."

"Good."

I should end the call and get back to my studies. But there was something about Logan that had me interested and curious.

"But you want her to kiss you?" I asked, hoping he wouldn't find it odd that a simple booking conversation took this long.

"Yes and no..." he trailed off and sighed. "Mary, the truth is that I haven't been with a woman since the accident. I'm hoping Charlene can help me overcome some of my fear of being touched."

"You're afraid of being touched?"

"Aye. And I'm aware of the ugliness of my scars."

"Is that why you're coming to a professional instead of going on a normal date?"

"Aye."

More than ever, I wished I could meet Logan in person. There were a million questions burning on my mind.

"Last year my therapist told me that this would be a good idea. It's just taken me a long time to actually come this far."

"Do you live here in Seattle or are you just passing through?" I asked.

"Why?"

"For no reason."

"I told ye I had an apartment, which would indicate that I live here, would ye know think?"

"It could be rented for the week; how would I know?"

"Hmm," he muttered.

"So how long have you lived here?"

"Five months."

"And you're from Scotland, right?"

"Nah, why would you think that?"

My eyes closed and I felt stupid. Had I confused his accent with an Irish accent?

"Ireland then?" I asked.

He laughed. "Ireland. Nah, I'm just messing with ye. I'm as Scot as they come."

"Hey, that wasn't nice, I felt really stupid for a second."

"Sorry." He had the most amazing deep and masculine laugh.

"And what brought ya here?"

"My job. I work in the tech industry and was offered a good deal."

"Nice. So you're a programmer then?"

"Of sorts. And you, Mary, how long have ye lived in Seattle?"

"Oh, you know. A while." My computer showed an incoming call.

"Logan, I'm afraid I have to get another call, but it was a real pleasure talking to ya, darlin'. Is the number you've called from your cell phone number?"

"Aye."

"Good, I'll send you the payment link then, and I wish you a wonderful evening with Charlene."

"Thank you, Mary, take care." He sounded so lovely.

"Bye now and call me again soon."

"Hey, if ye wanna talk, ye have my number – I'll welcome yer call," he said with a smile in his voice.

I smiled widely when I ended the call and pressed to answer the next one.

"Blue Ribbon Escort Service, this is Mary, how may I help y'all?"

All the while I helped set up the next client, my head kept thinking about Logan.

I wondered how old he was. How bad his scar was. If his smile was as warm as I imagined.

Follow the fighter with the accent, Violet had said, and before my shift was over I had made my decision.

I needed to see Logan MacKay for myself.

Charlene had never met me in person, which meant I could easily blend in with the crowd in a bar. Logan and Charlene would never know I had watched their first meeting.

CHAPTER 2
Trolls and Dolls

Logan

I had to force myself to enter Trolls and Dolls and take a seat at the bar.

The fear of being rejected and humiliated sat deeply ingrained in me. Kenna, my long-time girlfriend, had made sure of that when she left me after the accident.

Of course, she blamed my mood swings, but the hurtful comments she made when we fought had slowly broken me. I could still hear her say she was repulsed by me, and feel the pain of being rejected sexually. I still thought daily about her comment that "no woman would ever love a man this ugly."

She had tried to take her words back, but I still saw disgust and pity in her eyes.

But then again, I saw pity in most people's eyes. My family, my employees, and my friends – they all felt bad for me. It was a constant reminder that I was changed.

The handsome, happy, and adventurous lad I had once been had died in that accident. All I was left with was this bitter, ugly version of myself.

"What would you like?" the bartender asked and dried the bar off with his cloth. I avoided eye contact with him and simply pointed to the sign behind him saying Carlsberg.

"A beer, please."

"Coming right up."

It was tempting to pick up my phone and disappear into my newsfeed, but I forced myself to look around.

A few groups of people were lounging around but the place wasn't too full.

Scanning the room, I caught a blonde woman meeting my eyes. As always, I looked away to avoid her reaction to my scars. She was probably just morbidly fascinated like most. A few minutes later I looked discreetly over again.

Barbie. It was the first word that came to mind. She was reading, which gave me a chance to study her a bit. This woman looked like she had just stepped off the set of a commercial for natural beauty. Flawless pale skin, straight nose, perfect arch of her eyebrows, full lips, and high cheekbones. Of course her classical beauty was topped with long golden hair that rested over her left shoulder in a thick braid.

Had I seen her somewhere before? Recognition sparked in the back of my mind. A TV host maybe?

Seeing a truly beautiful woman like her used to brighten my day. Now she was nothing but a painful reminder that the only way I would ever get intimate with someone like her was to pay her for her time.

Back in Scotland I'd seen a therapist who told me I could overcome my anxiety around women. I wasn't sure, because it seemed that my social skills were seriously uncalibrated. Either I got terribly shy around women, or my insecurities manifested as rudeness.

Charlene was late. It was already ten past nine, and I wondered if she had blown me off. Maybe I shouldn't have told Mary that I was ugly.

Mary. My lips pursed upward. She had been flirting with me. Even though I knew it was her job, it had felt good to have that energy pulsing back and forth between us.

There had been such kindness in her voice; I wished I was meeting with her tonight. To me it was all about a human connection, and not some beauty ideal the bureau had for their escorts.

My eyes moved to Barbie, who was reading a thick book. *Who the hell brings a book to a bar?*

Maybe she was trying to send a signal that she was not only pretty, but smart too. *As if she needs more than those long legs to get a man's attention.*

Nah, a girl like her didn't need brain or personality; she would never be lonely like me.

I frowned when she lifted her gaze and looked me straight in the eye.

Did she just smile at me?

I looked down at my beer, wondering if it had been spiked or something, and then it hit me that there was probably someone behind me that she had smiled at.

Turning in my chair I searched for the person she would have smiled at, but there was no one.

I slowly turned to look at her again, but her eyes had returned to her book.

Before I had a chance to think more about it, the door opened and a woman walked in wearing high heels and a long black cotton coat. Everything about her looked expensive and fashionable.

Charlene!

Her eyes scanned the five people in the bar and zoomed in on me. I swallowed hard and held my breath. She was seeing me from my left side. My good side.

"Logan?" she said with a smile and walked toward me.

"Charlene." I got up from my chair to greet her.

She stopped an arm's length from me, her eyes widening.

My jaw clenched. This was exactly what I hated most. The slight frown on her pretty face and the hesitant handshake as if my ugliness was contagious.

"Thank you for coming," I said politely.

Her smile was forced. "Of course."

I gestured for her to take a seat next to me and watched her sit down with stiff movements.

"Would you like me to hang up your jacket?" I offered.

"No." she pulled it closer around her slim body.

"Are you cold?"

"No." She shook her head, her eyes landing on my bad side and then darting around the room, looking anywhere but at me.

"Can I get ye a drink?" Most of all, I wanted to get up and leave. If I wanted to feel rejected, I could have approached any normal woman.

"Mary didnae warn ye about my scars?" I asked in a low voice.

"Yes."

"Then what's the problem?"

"I don't have a problem," she said and faked another smile.

I knew better than to smile back; it only made my face look more grotesque.

"Listen," Charlene finally met my eyes. "I like to be upfront."

"All right."

"You told Mary you wanted kissing."

I frowned.

"That's not happening." There was a hint of disgust in her tone.

It felt like a physical slap in my face. "I think we're done here." My pride was wounded and I had no intentions of sitting through another minute of this humiliation.

Charlene didn't try to stop me when I threw money on the counter and hissed at her, "Thanks for nothing."

I could feel eyes on my neck when I stormed out the door, but I didn't stop to look back.

CHAPTER 3
Stop!

Faith

I arrived around a quarter to nine and bought myself a cup of overpriced coffee. Trolls and Dolls was a wine bar with a cozy feel to it. No doubt this place would be crowded on the weekends, but today was Wednesday.

Since I knew the meeting between Logan and Charlene would take place at the bar, I strategically chose to sit in a chair by the window, which offered me a perfect view.

"I'm sorry, but could I get your autograph?" the bartender asked with a shy smile when he brought my coffee.

"I'm not her," I said patiently, because this was a question I got all the time. "I'm not Cleo."

"Oh, sorry." He nodded and retreated to the bar.

With my cup in hand, I looked out the window, spotting a man pacing the sidewalk with his head down. He was tall and blond. *Bingo!* That had to be Logan MacKay.

I was so focused on the way he clenched his fists, as if pumping himself up to enter, that I accidently spilled warm coffee over my hand.

"Augh." I scrunched up my face and sat the cup down, my eyes flying back to the man on the street while I used a napkin to dry the table.

Show me your face, I willed, but he had his back to me. "Come on," I muttered under my breath, afraid that he would chicken out and not go through with the meeting.

"That's it," I mumbled in a low tone when he straightened up and took a deep breath, placing his hand on the door handle.

Quickly, I pulled my thick book up to my face, sinking low in my chair, ready to spy on the man.

Holy moly. How in the world could this man describe himself as ugly? He was the complete opposite! But then again, from my angle I could only see him from his left side.

With a solemn expression Logan steered straight for the bar and ordered a drink before he began to look around.

Turn your head, I willed him, *let me see those scars you talked about*

When he finally did look my way, I almost leaned forward with eagerness.

Ohh, shit. Even from the quick glimpse I got, it was easy to see that the right side of his face was disfigured. There was a dominating scar by his eye that cut through his eyebrow. But the worst part was the lower part of his face and neck, where his skin was marred by several angry red scars, one making his lips asymmetrical.

I could see why some women would be turned off by that, but I wasn't interested in him romantically and only felt empathy well up in me.

The more I looked at him, the more intrigued I felt. *How did he get those scars?*

Sure, some women would be scared off, but those were women who cared about beauty and superficial things. Why would he want to be with a woman like that anyway?

The right woman would quickly digest the initial shock and start to find all the things she liked about him. *It wouldn't be difficult at all,* I thought. *He's tall with wide shoulders and looks reasonably fit, and that thick, curly, blond hair looks good on him.*

16

As if he could hear me evaluate him, Logan looked over and this time I smiled at him.

It was sweet to see him turn in his seat, as if he was unsure that I was actually smiling at him.

Internally I scolded myself for connecting with him. After all, I was only there to observe and nothing else.

Charlene finally arrived, ten minutes late.

I talked to the escorts on the phone all the time, but I rarely met them in person. It was fascinating to see this side of the business, and I discreetly followed the way she entered with a breeze of elegance. Charlene used to be a model, and her regular clients included successful businessmen and other rich guys who enjoyed her company.

That was why I had chosen her.

With the demand for her, she had to be kind and sweet. Still, I crossed my fingers under the table, praying that I had made a good match tonight.

It was like being in the front row in the movie theater, following the first meeting of two people you want to like each other.

I'd sensed the pain and loneliness in Logan when we spoke on the phone. He deserved a night of fun.

But something went wrong. Only two minutes after Charlene entered, Logan got up with anger emanating from him.

No! This wasn't how it was supposed to go at all.

I watched in horror as Logan stormed past me and left the bar. My first instinct was to confront Charlene and demand to know what she had said to upset him like that. But on second thought, I picked up my things and chased after Logan. He lived close by and I needed to act fast to stop him.

Damn it! He had trusted me to set him up with a kind woman, and I had promised him that he had nothing to worry about. I had to fix this somehow.

It was late September and drizzling with rain, but I ran without putting my jacket on.

"Stop! Logan stop!"

I could see him further down the street, speeding away. *Shoot* – he had just rounded a corner.

"Logan!" I shouted and ran after him.

With my jacket and bag in one hand and my thick psychology book in the other, I turned the corner running full speed and collided with a wall of man.

"Whoa, whoa, slow down."

I would have fallen if he hadn't steadied me, but now I was panting for breath while Logan scowled down at me.

"Who are ye, and why are ye following me?"

"I'm... I'm..."

A thousand thoughts were running through my mind. Should I tell him I was the woman he knew as Mary? And if I did, would he discard me as a liar? I had described Mary as chubby and short. I was neither.

"Answer me," he demanded and shook my shoulders.

He looked grim with the rain running down his face and anger marring his features.

"I'm Faith," I cried out, because I'm really bad at lying.

"How do ye know my name and why are ye following me?" he demanded to know in that Scottish accent.

Frantically thinking of the right thing to say, and coming up with nothing, I fell back on a classic. "I just wondered if you would have coffee with me."

"What?" He pushed me away.

"I saw you in the bar, and I was just about to approach you when your friend came in."

His nostrils flared when he scoffed. "She's no friend of mine."

"I could tell, and that's why I was hoping maybe you and I could..." I blinked, not sure how to finish that sentence.

Logan glanced up and down the street. "Ye ran after me to have coffee with me?" His tone was incredulous.

"Uh-huh," I said, knowing how unlikely it sounded.

Logan shook his head and dried rain off his face. "I'm going home."

Guilt filled me as I watched him walk away. I had just made him even more confused.

"Logan." I ran up to him again.

"For the last time, how do ye know my name?" he asked without slowing down.

"The woman back there called you Logan, I heard her."

He didn't respond, and in desperation I placed my hand on his arm.

"Dinnae touch me " He angrily shook his arm free.

I had once seen a documentary about a great lion who had been injured by humans. After that he was grumpy and aggressive toward everyone, even the people who brought him food. Logan reminded me of that lion. He didn't trust me.

"How about that coffee?" I asked bravely.

He stopped abruptly and spun around to stare me down. ""Look, *Faith*. Ye dinnae want to have coffee with me."

"Why not?"

"Do I look like good company to ye?"

"You did, until you got angry."

Logan narrowed his eyes. "Do I know ye from somewhere? Ye look familiar."

"My twin is an actress; you've probably seen her in movies. Does the name Cleo ring a bell?"

The expression on his face softened a bit. "Aye."

For a long second we locked gazes, and I had a feeling he was testing me; waiting for me to back off.

"I use milk in my coffee," I said and gave him a probing smile.

19

Logan had paid for two hours of female companionship. I was determined to make sure he got value for his money. Plus, I was curious about him. What if Violet had been talking about Logan when she said, "Follow the fighter with the strong accent"?

He moved back to let an older man pass us, and shifted his balance with a grim expression. "Ye're really serious?" he asked.

"Why not? Do you have somewhere you need to be?" I asked, knowing the answer already.

"Ye want to come home with me and drink coffee?" he asked slowly. Clearly he found the idea strange.

"Uh-huh... or we could just find a coffeehouse. Either way."

"Why?"

I shrugged. "Because it beats getting wet and cold in the rain."

He hesitated for a second, probably debating with himself whether or not to walk away, but finally he grumped, "All right then."

We walked in silence for a minute until he pointed to the other side of the street. "That's my building. Last chance if ye want to change yer mind."

"Why? Is your coffee bad?"

I think his grimace was an unwilling smile.

Once we entered his apartment he kicked off his shoes and went to the kitchen. He was wearing a dark suit and loosened his tie after removing his wet jacket, while I left my shoes by the door and followed him inside.

"Nice place you have here," I said to be polite, but in reality the place was sparsely decorated and looked like he hadn't fully moved in, with the walls bare and a few boxes in the corners. "Did you just move in?"

"I moved in five months ago."

"Oh, okay."

20

"Faith, come here." Logan pointed to a chair by the kitchen counter.

"Since you ask me so nicely," I said sarcastically and moved closer."

"Who are ye?" he asked with a scrutinizing glare at me.

"I'm Faith. I'm twenty-six, and a psychology major at UW."

"UW?" he asked.

"University of Washington."

"Ohh, right."

"I'm also a cheerleader for the Seahawks – you know, the football club?"

He nodded. "Yeah, I know what the Seahawks are. I'm foreign, not from a different planet."

"You're Scottish?" Of course I already knew that as Mary, but Faith wouldn't know.

"Uh-huh."

"So what brought you here?"

"Work. I sold my tech company, and part of the deal was that I would stay on board for two years."

"And do you like it here so far?" I smiled.

He shrugged non-committedly. "It's all right."

"Augh…" I chuckled, trying desperately to loosen him up a little. "Maybe you haven't met the right people in Seattle yet?"

"Maybe."

"Have you made many friends?"

"Nah."

I stepped forward and reached out my hand to him. "Then let me officially welcome you to Seattle. I hope we'll be great friends."

Logan arched a brow and took my hand. "Ye are the strangest lass I've ever met."

"Doesn't lass mean girl? I'm twenty-six, so more like a woman, wouldn't you say?"

21

"Woman then." He prepared the coffee and handed me a cup. "How much milk do ye want in yer coffee?"

"You remembered the milk. Thank you."

"Say stop," he said and poured slowly.

"Stop."

Logan put the milk back, grabbed his cup, and moved to sit on his brown leather couch.

"This is a Chesterfield, isn't it?" I said and sat down on the armrest of the couch.

He nodded and took a sip of his coffee, observing me closely.

I pointed around the room. "If you need a bit of the female touch to make your place more welcoming, I could help you out."

Logan looked around. "Why, what would ye change?"

"A few paintings on the wall. Maybe unpack your boxes, and buy a rug to give some warmth and color in here," I suggested.

He shrugged. "I've been busy. I think what I need most is a housekeeper."

"A housekeeper?" I snickered and took a seat. "You don't need a housekeeper."

"How would ye know?"

I slid down on the seat of the couch, my back against the armrest. "You live here alone, right?"

"Aye."

"Are you saying that housework for one person is too much for you?"

"I dinnae like to cook, clean, or shop. And I dinnae have time for it."

"How big is this place?"

"It's three bedrooms, two baths, and this living area." He looked around.

"Why do you need three rooms?"

"A guest room, an office, and a bedroom," he said as if my question was stupid.

A brilliant idea hit me. From our conversation, I knew he had issues with women. As a psychology student I was already diagnosing him and trying to find ways to help him. People like Logan were the whole reason I'd wanted to become a psychologist in the first place. He was hurting, and I was naturally drawn to help.

"You don't need a housekeeper, you need a roommate," I said with conviction.

He choked on his coffee.

"No, seriously, think about it. If you get a kind female roommate she'll help you make this place nice. And if you don't need the money, you can have her pay rent by cooking, shopping, and cleaning. *Plus*, you would get a friend here in Seattle. It's brilliant, don't you think?"

Logan put down his coffee and crossed his arms. "I just told ye that I already use all three rooms."

"Just combine the office with the guest room, and rent out the last room."

"Not a chance. I'm not getting a roommate," he said firmly.

"Then think of it as a live-in housekeeper-slash-friend."

Logan shook his head. "Under no circumstance will I have a woman move in with me."

"Why not?"

"It wouldn't work with a woman; if anything it would have to be a man."

"Why?"

"Faith, believe me it just wouldn't."

"That's sexist. At least make a valid argument."

He puffed out air. "I'm no good with women."

"Says who?"

He frowned. "It's a fact."

"*I* could be your roommate," I said with my heart starting to thump faster.

"No." He shook his head. "Don't be stupid, ye don't even know me."

"I didn't know my current roommates before I moved in either. Sometimes, you just gotta take a chance."

"Did yer parents ever tell ye not to go home with strangers? I'm surprised ye're still alive with yer disregard for common sense."

"Hey, I have excellent people skills, and I can tell if a person is good or not. And for your information, I don't normally go home with strangers."

"Then what made ye come here tonight?"

Again, I left out the truth. "Let's just say that I find you fascinating. And about that roommate thing; it really would be a win-win."

"How so?" he asked.

"I'm trying to get through school without too much debt, and I'm good with housework. Living here and working for the rent would be perfect."

"It's not happening, Faith, I dinnae know ye. Ye could be a crazy person."

"*Or* I could be your first friend in Seattle," I said with a bright smile. "A friend who can help you get some decent food, and have a nice home."

Logan groaned. "I'd said no."

"Will you at least think about it?"

He didn't respond.

"I'm taking your silence as confirmation."

His lips pursed. "Let it go, Faith. I'm an introvert. I'm not good with people."

"That's okay. We would hardly see each other anyway. You said you work a lot, and so do I."

"But ye just said that ye're a student."

"Yes, but I also work two jobs to pay for college. So you see, with work and my lectures you would hardly ever see me. I promise that I'd study in my room and not bother you."

"But why would ye want to live here?" he asked skeptically.

"You want the truth?"

He nodded.

"Okay, the thing is that I live in a two-bedroom apartment with two roommates. My bed is the living room couch and one of the girls has a boyfriend that stays over a lot."

"And ye dinnae like him?"

"Dennis is nice, but I'm tired of hearing them fight or have sex when I'm trying to sleep. And it's impossible to study because I have no desk and people are always noisy there. Sharing a bathroom with two other women and a guy isn't ideal either. Let's just say that stressed people get in a lot of conflicts."

"And how much do ye pay to live there?" he asked.

"Five hundred a month. That's cheaper than living on campus."

"And ye're willing to keep this place clean and do the cooking if I let ye live here for free?"

My heart was hammering. This was just what I needed. If I didn't have to pay food and rent, I could start paying back my loan.

"If you pay for groceries, I'll do the cooking. I travel a lot on weekends during the football season, but I'll fill the freezer with homemade food for you. I'm a good cook, and if you let me live here for free, I'll do the cleaning."

Logan rubbed his forehead. "I cannae."

"Please?"

He got up. "Listen, ye're probably a really nice person and all, but I'm not letting a stranger move into my apartment."

"But then get to know me before you make up your mind." I stood up too. "How about I come by on Friday and help you make this place cozy? We could order a pizza and get to know each other."

25

Logan wrinkled his forehead as if he was trying to make sense of me.

"Look," I said and held out my hand to placate him. "I know I can be a little over the top, but you'll get used to me, and I'm sure we'll be great friends before you know it."

"Actually, I was warned that Americans can be over the top, but so far ye're the worst." There was a slight twinkle in his eye that I hadn't seen before and it gave me hope that I was starting to crack his hard shell...

"Right, but it comes with being a cheerleader. We learn never to give up and to stay positive."

"And do cartwheels," he added dryly.

I pointed at him. "Exactly, and you know what is a bonus feature if you choose me as a roomie?"

"Nah."

"I can give you a private tour of the Seahawks stadium, and introduce you to some of the players."

Logan gave a tiny smile. "Wow, lucky me, but I'm afraid I wouldnae know any of them. I've never watched a game."

"What?" I said in a high pitch. "Then it's about time someone taught you about American culture. Wait, you *have* tasted a burger, right?" I said with blatant irony.

It tingled in my toes when he played along and said, "A what?"

"A burger."

"What are those?"

Boy, was I good. This man had been so full of anger when I met him half an hour ago, and now he was joking with me.

"I'll cook some for you if you agree to let me move in with you."

"No way, Faith." This time it sounded softer and less convincing.

"All right, I won't push more tonight." We stood facing each other, and my social cues told me it was time for me to go. "But promise you'll think about it. You might not know any of the football players, but I could introduce you to a lot of hot cheerleaders too."

The minute I said it, I knew it had been a mistake. Logan looked away, his lips pressed into fine lines.

Shoot, this guy truly had issues with women. Maybe I had just reminded him of what had happened tonight with Charlene.

"Or maybe not," I said, low.

I left his apartment with a foul taste in my mouth, thinking like crazy about how I could make things right.

Because the evening ended kind of awkward, we hadn't exchanged numbers, so my options were limited.

I had his number, of course; it was on file at the office, but he would think me a stalker if I called him up. He was already suspicious of my motives for wanting to be friends with him.

If I couldn't call him, what could I do?

A wide grin spread, as an idea formed in my mind.

CHAPTER 4
Compensation

Logan

It was the strangest Thursday, with me walking around in a bubble of unanswered questions.

Yesterday I went to meet an escort, but somehow ended up with a cheerleader in my home instead.

It was the last part that I still didn't understand.

Women like Faith weren't interested in me.

That was a fact!

Part of me wanted to write her off as a hallucination, but I wasn't taking any medicine, and had no history of hallucinating.

Besides, her coffee cup was still there this morning when I left for work.

I looked at the clock in the low corner of my computer screen. It was already seven thirty and like most other nights, I was alone in the office.

When my phone rang I picked it up with a short. "MacKay speaking."

"Oh, hey, darlin', this is Mary."

My brow flew up. "Mary?"

"Yes, remember me from yesterday?"

"Ehhm, yes, hi."

"I talked to Charlene, and she said you weren't a happy camper last night. What happened? I can't tell ya how sorry I am that it didn't work out between y'all."

I leaned back in my chair. "Not a happy camper?"

"Right, it just means you weren't a happy client."

"I guessed that much."

"Logan darling, I can't tell you how it breaks my heart that I failed to give you a good experience."

It's not yer fault. Blame Charlene."

"But I feel responsible, and I want to make it up to you."

"Really?"

"Absolutely! We pride ourselves on excellent customer service, and it's my job to make sure you get value for your money."

"And how do ye plan to give me that? I'm not interested in meeting with any more of yer escorts."

"Are ya sure?" she said in that cute Southern accent.

"I'm sure."

"All right – well, unfortunately I'm not authorized to give you a refund, but I could give you three hours o' phone time, if you like."

"Phone time?"

"Phone sex. We operate a phone sex company too."

I grinned. "Phone sex with ye?

She broke into that heartfelt laughter that I remembered from the first time I spoke to her. "No, silly, with a phone sex operator o' course."

"But what if I only want you? Ye have the most amazing voice and that sweet Southern accent of yers is doing funny things to me." I don't know what it was about Mary, but she brought out the old me. Talking to her felt amazing because not only did I like her, but I liked me too. With her I was confident and humorous – something I hadn't been around any woman since the accident.

I flirted with her and didn't worry that she would see how ugly my mouth looked when I smiled or grinned.

With Mary, I held nothing back.

"Oh." She laughed nervously. "No, I'm afraid I wouldn't be any good at that sorta thang. I'm just the phone lady."

"But ye said it's yer job to make sure I get value for my money, and then ye offered me phone sex. I'm willing to accept yer offer, but only if I can talk to you."

I could almost hear her flush red through the phone.

"Logan, honey, it truly would be a waste of your time. I'm not exactly the kind of woman you would consider sexy."

"Yer voice is sexy."

What I didn't tell her was that it really wasn't about sex to me. I just wanted the connection with her.

"Have ye ever had phone sex?" I asked.

"No," she admitted. "I wouldn't even know where to start."

"Ye could start by telling me about yer first time." I said in a low voice, knowing full well I was pushing her.

"My first time?"

"Uh-huh."

"Ehm. Okaaay." She hesitated for a second before she spoke. "I was seventeen."

"And?"

"And he was my boyfriend."

"How old was he?"

"Nineteen."

"Were ye nervous?"

She sighed. "Very. But we had been together for almost two years, and I was deeply in love with him."

"Was it his first time too?"

"Yes. He was a sweet boy."

"Tell me what happened."

Mary sounded more relaxed now. "We had been talkin' about it for a long time and then one night my parents left to visit friends."

"Uh-huh."

"He came over and we kissed until my cheeks were red. Then he asked me if we could try to have sex..." She trailed off.

"Did ye like it?"

"We were young and fumbling in the darkness. It was over before it began."

"So not a good experience then?" I asked sympathetically.

"I wouldn't say that. I didn't regret it, because I wanted him to be my first."

"How long were you together?"

"Almost four years." I traced sadness in her voice.

"Tell me about the hottest sex ye've ever had in your life."

"Ehhm, wow…"

"Don't worry, you never have to see me, remember?"

"Right. I think it was the time we had sex in the forest behind his house. We did it in the afternoon when someone could have seen us. It was risky, but we were crazy for each other."

"How did ye have sex?"

"How?"

"I meant what position?"

"Ohh." She hesitated again. "He took me against the tree from behind.

Her silky voice and that charming accent felt so soothing to me. I should be working but there was a strange kind of connection between Mary and me.

"Mary?"

"Yeah."

"When did ye last have sex?"

There was absolute silence.

"Mary?"

"Yes, I'm still here."

"Did ye hear my question?"

"I did. But do I have to answer that?"

"Nah."

"How about you? When did you last have sex?"

I sighed. "It's been two years."

31

"And how old are you now, Logan?"

"Twenty-nine. And you?"

"Thirty… one."

I laughed. "No ye're not. Ye just made that up."

She laughed with me. "Hey, it doesn't matter how old I am, and in Georgia, where I'm from, a gentleman never asks a lady her age or her weight." "I never claimed to be a gentleman, so how much do ye weigh?" I grinned loudly and felt elated when she didn't get offended, but rolled with it and said, "Let's just say that I'm generously proportioned."

"Good, I prefer my woman curved. What color is yer hair?"

"It's brown. Kind of dull actually."

"Am I right in assuming that ye haven't had sex in a long time either?" I asked.

She took a deep intake of air. "Yes."

I got up and closed the door to my office. There was no one outside my door and everything seemed quiet, but I wanted to be sure no one heard me.

"Mary, ye can't see me, and I can't see ye, but I think we should do it."

"Do what?"

"We both haven't been with anyone for a long time. Why not help each other out and have sex?"

"Real sex?" she asked in a whisper.

"Phone sex, Mary," I whispered back and smiled. She was innocent in a charming way.

"But I thought we were already having phone sex."

"No, sweetheart, we were only having foreplay."

"I don't understand."

"We were getting to know each other and getting comfortable. Now, it's time to take it a step further."

"How?"

"I just locked the door to my office and I'm sitting back down in my chair. Are ye somewhere where ye can have privacy?"

"I'm alone in the office. My colleague is next door, but I can hear her talking."

"Why don't ye touch yourself for me, Mary?"

"Ehhm, okaaay," she said, drawn out.

"I'll do the same."

"Logan, I don't think I can do this. It's awkward."

"Trust me, I've had phone sex many times," I said. "Just go with it."

"All right."

"Are ye touching yerself, lass?" I asked her with a teasing smile and picked up a pen to draw doodles on my paper pad.

"Uh-huh."

"Tell me."

"I've opened my shirt and I'm caressing my nipple."

"Good, how big are yer breasts?"

"Bigger than I would like them to be."

"Mary, I'm sure they're beautiful, and I would like to play with them myself. Are they bigger than a handful?"

"That depends whose hand you mean. Bigger than mine, but if you have big hands..."

"I do." I smiled. "And ye know what else I have that's big?"

"Your heart?"

I chuckled. "I was referring to something a bit sexier. Something that will feel good inside ye."

"There's nothing sexier than a good heart."

I was shaking my head, swallowing a grin. Mary was terrible at phone sex but she was cute.

"Keep touching yerself. Are ye wearing pants or a skirt?"

"Pants."

"Open them."

33

"Okay. I just did."

"Good, I'm opening my pants too." I drew another doodle.

"Now what?" she asked.

"Now touch yer clit and tell me how moist ye are."

"Okay..."

"How does it feel? Are ye wet for me?"

"Kinda. I like the sound of your voice and your accent. It's sexy."

I smiled. "Good, now be a good girl and slide yer finger over your clit and play with yerself."

"Logan." Her voice suddenly sounded small.

"What's wrong?"

"I can't do this. It doesn't feel right."

"Why? Did I say something wrong?"

"No, but I told you, I'm no good at it, and I feel stupid."

"Hey, don't worry about it. Ye did fine."

"Can't we just talk about other things than sex?"

I felt bad that I had pushed her so far out of her comfort zone. "Of course. Tell me about yerself."

"Actually, I was hopin' you would tell me what happened between you and Charlene yesterday. Was she rude to you?"

I took a deep breath and exhaled. "Remember when I told ye I needed an escort who wouldn't be easily scared?"

"Yes."

"Charlene got scared. Her expression was one of disgust, and she made it clear from the start that she wouldn't be kissing me."

"Wow, I'm surprised to hear that. She seems like such a nice person."

"I told ye, I'm ugly."

"And I still don't believe you," she said in a silken caress. "Haven't there ever been any women who weren't scared off by your scars?"

I rubbed my nose. "Actually, something strange happened yesterday after my meeting with Charlene."

"Yes?"

"There was a blonde woman who came running after me when I left the bar. She wanted to have coffee with me."

"See, I knew you were exaggeratin'. How many men have women chasin' after them?" She broke into a melodiously chuckle.

"I brought her back home and we had coffee."

"Nice. And what did you think of her?"

"I dinnae know."

"Well, was she kind?"

"Aye. But she talked too much and she seemed a little crazy."

"In what way?"

"I cannae even begin to describe how bizarre it was."

"Try."

"All right, first she runs after me in the rain. Then we go to my place and the next thing I know she wants to decorate my place and move in with me as my roommate."

"Ohh..."

"I think she's lacking some social filter or something."

"Really? Maybe she was just an exceptionally warm and open person."

"Aye, maybe, but what are the odds that an extremely attractive woman would move in with a stranger like me? I mean if ye think Charlene is good-looking ye should have seen Barbie."

"Barbie?"

"The blonde."

"So you found her attractive, but I thought you said you preferred your women with curves?"

"Aye, why are ye assuming she had no curves?"

"Because you said Barbie, and Barbie is slim."

"True, but this woman looked healthy."

"Healthy?"

"Aye, hips, breasts, and a really nice arse. She was beautiful in an unapproachable way. I wouldn't go near her."

"Why not?"

I scoffed. "It would be like a bad joke. Ye know, Beauty and the Beast."

"Hey, I'm going to start referrin' to you as handsome to counterbalance all the times you put yourself down."

"Ye're doing the exact same thing, Mary. Maybe that's why I feel safe with ye. We're the same."

"Really? You're an American woman too?"

I grinned. "No, I meant we're both imperfect."

"Everyone's imperfect."

"Not Barbie."

"You just said she was socially inept."

"No, I didn't say that. Just lacking a filter. Ye know, a bit strange and pushy."

"See, that doesn't sound perfect to me at all. And besides, aren't you a little socially awkward yourself?"

"Only around women."

"Maybe she's only awkward around men."

I snorted. "I find that hard to believe."

"Have you ever wondered if bein' pretty makes her feel objectified and stigmatized?"

"Nah."

"You don't know this woman, but she was brave enough to run after you – doesn't that count for somethin'?" Mary argued, in what I assumed was some kind of sisterly solidarity.

"I guess."

"So what's stoppin' you from lettin' her move in with you?"

"Mary," I groaned. "Not you too."

"Why not? I like you Logan, but you need to grow your confidence around women. Isn't that why you called the escort agency in the first place? What better way to get comfortable with women, than to live with one?"

"But..."

Mary cut me off. "Trust your instincts. If you think she's crazy, then tell her no. But if you think she's a good person, then take the chance and get to know her better."

I sighed. "I dinnae want or need a roommate."

"Then what do you need?"

I frowned at that question. "That depends who you ask. My mum thinks I need a wife. My therapist thinks I need a lover."

"And what do you think?"

"I think I like talking to ye."

"Aww, thank you, I enjoy talkin' to you too, but I'm at work, Logan, and my colleague is probably wonderin' why she's the only one takin' calls."

"When do you get off work?"

"In two hours."

"Ye could call me then, or better yet give me yer number so I can call you. Ye did promise me three hours of phone sex and we've only spoken for..." I checked my phone. "Twenty-nine minutes."

"I'm not giving you my private number. It's against our company policy."

"Okay. But at least promise me that ye'll call me again soon."

"Hmm... what are you doing tomorrow night?" she asked.

"I don't know, probably working."

"It's Friday."

"So?"

"You should be at home chillin'."

"Maybe I will be, if ye promise to call and talk to me."

"Okay, sugah, so this is the plan then. You'll plant yourself in your couch tomorrow night with a glass of wine, and I'll do the same on my end and then we'll talk for two hours and thirty-one minutes."

"Deal."

"Until then, Logan."

"Until then, Mary."

As soon as I hung up, I missed the sound of her calm breathing and silvery voice. I had friends in Scotland that were easy to talk to, but there was something about Mary that was different. Like a friend from a past lifetime.

I didn't want to think too hard about it. The important part was that talking to Mary was the most fun I had had in months, and tomorrow I would talk to her again.

CHAPTER 5

Womb Mate

Faith

The last two hours of my shift were endless.

My conversation with Logan kept playing in my mind. I should have told him "no" when he suggested phone sex. That had been so embarrassing.

I cringed inwardly from the mere thought of the things I had told him.

On a positive note, my main purpose for calling him had been achieved. He had told me what happened with him and Charlene, and as "Mary," I had even been able to support the idea of my moving in with him.

The thought of living rent-free in Logan's apartment became ever more appealing when I came home late to find Dennis and Tanya fighting again.

I slammed the door hard to make them aware I was home, but I should have known it took more than that to break up a loud argument between them.

"I didn't flirt with him. I was just being friendly," she shouted.

"Then why is he texting you?" Dennis roared back.

They always fought about the same thing: his jealousy.

Ignoring the shouting coming from her room, I pulled out the sofa bed, and went to brush my teeth. By the time I was done, their fight had morphed into sex, as was their usual pattern.

The squeaking of the bed, the loud moans, and the bumping of the metal frame against wall, were all reminders why living here wasn't working for me. Pulling my blanket over my head, I closed my eyes.

The first time my phone rang, I ignored it since I didn't recognize the number. I don't have time for telemarketers.

When it called again, I sighed and pressed answer.

"Hello."

"Hey, Sis, it's me."

"Chloe? Why aren't you calling from your own phone?"

"This is my phone, but I'm calling through Skype. I'm still in Germany."

"Is everything all right?"

She was quiet, and my trouble-barometer went through the roof.

"What happened?"

A small sniffle warned me that this conversation might be *one of those.*

"What did he do this time?"

"I don't know how to tell you, but..."

"But what?"

"My agent just called me, and it's going to be all over the news in a few hours. Last time, you said you preferred hearing it from me and not the press, so that's why I'm calling you."

I covered my eyes with my hand and prepared myself for this month's scandal.

"Apparently some paparazzi got a picture of me and Jason kissing. Now they're running with a story that I'm unfaithful to Niko."

"Jason – your co-star?"

"Yes."

I controlled my voice. "And *did* you kiss him, Chloe?"

"Just a little."

"I take that as a yes."

"Excuse me for not being a nun like you, but Jason is smoking hot, and it's not like I slept with him or anything."

"But the papers will speculate that you did," I said dryly, knowing the drill too well.

"Uh-huh."

"And Niko Did you talk to him?"

"I tried calling him, but his phone is turned off. I think he might be on his way to confront me."

That raised my hackles. "You have security with you, right?"

"He's my boyfriend, not some dangerous stalker," she protested.

"I don't trust him after that incident with the gun. If he's high on something, and fired up with jealousy, you might be in danger."

"It'll be fine. I can talk him down." She didn't convince me.

"Just make sure he's not carrying any weapons and that your security is always close by."

"Yes, I already promised Mom that too. Please don't give me a hard time about this, I'm stressed enough as it is. You have no idea how hard my life is."

I rolled my eyes. "We all make choices, Chloe."

She started crying. "You want to swap? Sometimes I think you're the lucky one. The pressure of being perfect is hard, you know?"

I loved my sister but she could be draining with the constant drama that surrounded her. Expertly I changed the subject.

"Are you coming home for Thanksgiving?"

"No, I'll be on set, but I talked to mom about us having it a little early this year at my apartment."

"But we always celebrate it at Mom and Dad's. You know how Mom loves to cook."

"So? She can cook at my place if she wants, or we can order food and let her relax. Either way, it'll be October twenty fourth."

"You said a little early, that's a whole month early."

"So?"

"Okay." With Chloe, it was all about picking my battles, and this one I wasn't interested in.

"What's that noise?" she asked.

I held up the phone to let her hear the orgasmic screams from the bedroom. "That would be Dennis and Tanya reaching the finish line in their make-up sex."

"Wow."

"I know. It's getting ridiculous."

"Then why are you still there? You have the key to my place, so use it already."

"Chloe, sweetie, you know I love you and you're my womb mate and all. But I already told you that I'm never taking any money or favors from you again."

"Because we fought?" She smacked her tongue. "But all siblings fight."

"We've been through this. You threw me out the day before my exam."

"I was momentarily crazy."

"It wasn't just that. It was your constant threats of throwing me out when I wouldn't let you control me."

"But don't you see that it makes me look bad to have you living in poverty? I don't want a headline calling me stingy."

"Hey, I'm a college student, not a homeless person."

"But you work two jobs and sleep on a couch. That's kind of pathetic."

"Maybe, but at least you don't get to boss me around," I retorted.

She blew out air. "You make me sound like a monster."

"No, you're just a diva."

Chloe smacked her tongue loudly again. "Whatever. I just wanted to warn you about the headlines."

"Thanks, and just for the record, I think you should go for Jason. He seems much nicer than Niko."

"Jason is married, Faith."

"Oh, but then why is he kissing you?"

"It just happened, and the good thing is that it offers exposure to the movie."

I shook my head "Are you saying it was all a media stunt?"

"No. I was just being flirtatious and in a good mood, and then we kissed a bit on the balcony. You should try it some time."

"What, kiss a married man?"

Chloe snorted. "I don't care, as long as you kiss *someone*. Hell, you could try kissing a woman if you want. The point is that you can't avoid love and sex forever. Allan isn't coming back."

"I know that," I muttered.

"It's been six years, sweetie."

"Seven," I corrected her.

"Okay, seven then. It's time to move on."

The door to Tanya's room opened and she came out.

"I have to go, Chloe – take care of yourself, and promise to stay close to your security," I said into the phone.

"All right, Sis. I'll see you soon."

Tanya stopped next to my bed. "Was that your sister?"

"Yeah."

"Is she in danger? What did you mean 'stay close to your security?' Did something happen?"

I yawned. "You can read about it in the paper tomorrow."

"Okaaayy," she said, drawn out. "But hey, I need to tell you something.'

"What is it?"

"Dennis got thrown out of his apartment, sooo..."

I finished her sentence. "So he'll be moving in with you?"

"Yeah. You don't have to move out right away or anything, but…"

"But it's gonna be cramped."

"It's just that he likes to play his Xbox at night and the TV is in here." She gave an apologetic shrug.

"I see."

I yawned again and turned my back to her, signaling that I wanted to sleep. Without a word, she moved to the bathroom and turned on the water to take a shower. *Christ, really?*

A minute later, I buried my head under my pillow, trying to block out her annoying humming.

I needed to find somewhere else to live, *fast.*

CHAPTER 6

Pizza and Wine

Logan

For someone who had been declared clinically depressed, I was in a surprisingly good mood. The prospect of a Friday night talking with Mary made me feel good inside.

For the first time in five months, I was home before seven o'clock pouring myself a glass of wine, and setting up the sound system that I hadn't unpacked until now.

The boost of hearing music again made me feel even better, but then the doorbell rang.

I hadn't invited anyone and logically assumed it would be a neighbor a sales rep, or a religious person trying to save my soul.

"Damn music," I muttered because it revealed that someone was home.

The doorbell rang again. Long and insistent.

"All right, all right." Already prepared to reject whomever was at my door, I strode down the hallway and opened up.

"Hi." Faith stood outside with a pizza tray in one hand, and a big smile on her face.

My eyes narrowed in confusion. "What are ye doing here?"

"Did you forget?"

"Forget what?"

She tilted her head. "You said you wouldn't consider me as a roommate because you didn't know me, and then I said that I could come by Friday and help you make this place cozy and we could eat some pizza."

"I can't tonight."

45

Her face fell. "Why not?"

"I'm meeting with a friend."

"Oh, are you going out?"

"No, she's..." I trailed off, unsure how much to tell her. "I'm, ehm... expecting a phone call."

Faith's eyes drifted to the pizza in her hand. "Couldn't we at least eat the pizza before it turns cold? I promise to leave as soon as your friend calls."

I drew a heavy sigh and shifted my balance to the other foot.

"Come on, Logan, it took me thirty minutes to get here, and a guy almost ran me over on my bike."

"Ye biked here?"

"Yeah. I bike most places. It's the cheapest transportation there is."

This woman puzzled me, and I didn't understand why she was here. Her story of seeing me at the bar and finding me interesting seemed fabricated to me.

"Are you just going to let me stand out here?" Her voice cut through my ruminations.

Curious to see what she was up to, I stepped to the side and let her in.

"Thank you." She followed me into my living room and placed the pizza on my coffee table. "I hope you like pepperoni," she said in a chirpy voice.

"I'm not hungry." A paranoid thought hit me that she could have spiked the pizza. This was America after all, and crazy shit happened in this country all the time. If her motive was to rob me, I wouldn't make it *that* easy for her.

"Would ye like a glass of water?" I offered politely. "Or wine perhaps?"

"I'll have whatever you're having."

"Then wine it is," I said and poured her a glass.

"Did you have a nice day at work?" she asked from the couch.

46

"Uh-huh."

"What is it you do again?"

"I'm in the tech industry."

"Right, but that's a wide description. What do you do?"

"Software."

"What kind of software?"

"The kind that helps big companies keep track of their money."

"Okay. And do you program or manage?"

"A bit of both. I used to program, but now I'm stuck in a lot of meetings."

"And you don't like that?"

I shrugged. "It's part of being a manager, I guess."

"So how many people do you manage?"

"Why?" I asked and got her a plate for her pizza.

She tilted her head. "Because I'm trying to get to know you?"

"Why?"

"Hey..." Faith gave me a reproachful glance. "I'm trying to be your friend here, but you're not making it easy."

"Listen. I dinnae mean to be unkind," I said and handed her a glass of wine. "But yer story doesn't sound plausible to me."

"What? That I'm a cheerleader? That I biked here? What?"

I gave her a direct glance. "That ye want to be my friend."

Faith gaped. "Wow, you haven't met a lot of friendly people, have you?"

"I have friends back in Scotland, but not a single one has ever behaved the way ye do. It's like ye're skipping all the initial steps."

Faith got herself a slice of pizza. "You can't compare your Scottish friends to me. I'm American, we do things differently here."

"True, but yer behavior is abnormal even for Americans," I argued.

"So?" Faith took a big bite, and used her fingers to catch some strings of melted cheese.

"So what do you really want from me, Faith? Are ye hoping to get money?"

She shook her head. "You're new to this city, and I feel obligated to be welcoming."

I didn't buy it, but an idea suddenly hit me. Maybe I could get her to show her true colors if I pushed her.

If she was planning to use her looks to get money from me, there was only one way to find out.

Pumping myself up, I buried my fear of rejection, and moved to sit next to her with a calculated glance at her cleavage.

"And how welcoming do ye intend to be?" I asked rudely.

Faith snapped her fingers. "Hey, sailor, my eyes are up here."

I lifted my gaze.

"I'm offering you my friendship, not my body."

"No, of course ye aren't," I said, tight-lipped.

Faith took a sip of her wine. "You can wipe that expression off your face and stop feeling sorry for yourself. It has nothing to do with your looks; I'm just not looking for anything sexual, *with anyone.*"

"Is it a celibacy thing?" I asked and moved out of her personal space.

She shrugged. "Sort of... it's a long story."

I observed her eating the pizza. "Are ye some kind of religious nutter? If ye're part of a sect I want ye out of my apartment."

"Geez, Logan, take a chill pill, will you?"

48

Puzzled, I sat back in my couch silently watching her and trying like crazy to understand what her motive was.

"Look, you're right, I do want something from you," she said and put down her pizza.

"And what is that?"

"At first, I thought you looked like a really interesting guy and I was curious about you. But then when we talked about you needing a roommate; I saw that as a great opportunity."

"I never said I needed a roommate. Ye said that," I corrected her.

"Exactly," she exclaimed and tilted her head. "Think about it. You definitely look like someone who could need a little cheering up, and where else are you going to find a happy cheerleader who will also cook and clean?"

"Hmm. Ye know what they say: when something seems too good to be true, it usually is," I told her.

"They also say that good things happen to good people," she answered and smiled at me.

"I think it's obvious that ye and I see the world very differently," I remarked dryly.

"Don't be so negative. What are you afraid of anyway? If it really came down to it, you're taller than me, and probably a bit stronger too."

I raised a brow. "A *bit* stronger?"

"Uh-huh." She pushed out her chest. "Being a cheerleader requires a lot of strength. Do you have any idea how many pushups I do a week?"

I scoffed. "Faith, be serious. If it came to a physical confrontation between us, ye wouldn't stand a chance. I'm six feet one and *much* stronger than ye. What are ye? Five-two?"

"Five-four," she said and sat up straight. "And for your information, I've taken down some pretty big guys before."

"Really, and why is that?"

49

She shrugged. "Some men don't respect a no, and in some cases I've had to fight them off."

I frowned, not liking the idea of anyone harming a female. "Well, dinnae worry, that's not going to happen with me."

"Good, but still; I could fight you off if I had to."

"Tsk... Ye couldn't even win an arm wrestle with me."

She narrowed her eyes. "Oh yeah? Are you sure about that?"

"Oh, come on, look at those little sticks ye have for arms. I would break them if we arm wrestled."

"Game on!" She shot up from the couch.

"No." I shook my head in disbelief when Faith stomped to my dining table, sat down, and placed her elbow on the table with a thump.

"Are you coming or not?"

"This is bonkers," I muttered but took a seat across from her.

"Okay, since you're so damn sure of yourself, then let's do it this way. If I win, I become your new roommate and I get to live here free of charge. You pay for all groceries and I do the cooking."

I raised a brow. "What about the cleaning?"

"And the cleaning too..." she repeated.

"And the laundry?" I added.

"Honestly," she said. "Are you completely incapable of doing anything yourself?"

"Nah, but I told ye; I dinnae have time for house chores."

She rolled her eyes. "Fine, I'll do all the house chores, but then you have to pay me two hundred dollars a month."

"Two hundred dollars? That's robbery. I could take my clothes to the cleaners for that money."

"Then take them to the cleaners."

Slowly I wrapped my hand around hers in a firm grip. It was warm and when she squeezed my hand, heat spread from our joined hands down my arm and into every corner of my body. This was confusing and stirring things that were better left alone.

"It doesn't matter, because I'm going to win anyway," I said.

"Okay, and if you win, what do *you* want?"

What did I want?

I wanted to say, "For ye to stay away from me," but that wasn't true. I was entertained by this enigma of a woman, and beneath my scars I was still a man and Faith was drop-dead gorgeous.

"What do you want?" she said impatiently.

"Let me think." My brain was in a freeze. *What did I want?* If she stood up and left right now, would that be a good thing? The resistance in my stomach told me "no."

"Ehhm..." I mumbled.

"How hard can it be? What do you want?" she asked.

I want to see where this goes. That was the conclusion that I came up with. "Okay." I cleared my throat and squeezed her hand. "If I win, I get my apartment to myself. But if ye win, ye get to move in."

"Deal!" she said and started counting. "One, two, three."

With her left hand gripping around the edge of the table, she put all her strength into her right arm and pushed my hand toward the table.

My eyes widened in surprise. I hadn't expected her to be this strong. Pride kicked in and I used my superior strength to wrestle her hand all the way to the table.

"Hmph," she said, annoyed and slightly out of breath. "Best out of three."

"Tsk," I scoffed. "Ye just lost, admit it."

"No, with arm wrestling it's always best out of three. Everyone knows that."

I smiled smugly. "Sure, whatever ye say."

It was fun to see her put all her energy into it. Her face was tomato red from pushing so hard. My respect for her grew as I realized that she was a fighter like me, and probably just trying to get by. From what she had told me about her crappy living situation I didn't blame her for seeing a free room as a golden opportunity. And from the way she was almost popping a vein to win, I would say that she *really* wanted to move in here.

Yesterday Mary had told me to follow my instinct regarding Faith, and my instinct told me she was a strange but good woman.

I made it look as realistic as possible when I let her win the second round.

"Yes!" Her hands went up in the air. "See, not such a weakling, am I?"

"No, yer stronger than ye look."

"*Again!* And this time I'm gonna win, so you better get used to having a new roommate."

I laughed on the inside and put on my poker face when I clasped her hand again. "All right, the winner takes it all."

"Yup, prepare to give me your guest room."

"Not happening, Faith," I said.

But of course it did.

Faith was practically dancing around my living room while I pretended to be upset about it and crossed my arms with a scowl.

"Ye cheated," I accused her.

"I did not," she said offended. "I told you all those pushups would come in handy."

"Yeah, maybe I should do some more myself."

"Maybe, but you know what this means, right, Logan?"

"That I have a roommate now?" I said with a brow raised, and felt a bit of panic creep up on me. *Why the hell*

52

did I agree to this? Part of me was scared and the other part excited.

"That's right, baby, I'm your new roomie. And you're going to get homemade pies and a ton of other good things. I promise you'll love having me around."

"We need some ground rules," I grumped.

"Okay, sure." She smiled, still high on her victory.

"No friends over."

She nodded. "That's okay. I just need the room until I graduate next summer. Then I can afford a place on my own and throw as many parties as I want."

"Right, and no waltzing around half dressed. I'm a guy."

"What's that supposed to mean?" she asked. "Are you saying you couldn't control yourself if you saw me half naked?"

"Nah." I held up a hand. "Of course not, I'm not a rapist."

"Then what?"

"It's just that I...' I looked away, unable to tell her that I found her extremely beautiful and that seeing her flaunt what I couldn't have would be torture.

"What?"

"I think it's fairly self-explanatory and since I'm setting the ground rules, you'll make sure that you're dressed when we're together."

"All right. Anything else?"

"Nah, not for the moment, but I reserve the right to add rules as we go along."

Faith lit up in a smile and stretched her hand out to me. "All right, then let's shake hands on us now living together."

And that's how I found myself shaking hands with Faith, agreeing that she'd move in with me.

"So." Faith smiled at me. "Can I please see my new room?"

I nodded and led her to the guest room. The room was pretty standard with a built-in closet, a twin bed, two side tables, and a dresser. The window offered a view of the street.

"It's not very big," I said, comparing it to my master bedroom.

"Are you kidding me? It's perfect," she said and twirled in the room.

"Are ye always this happy?" I asked with fascination.

"Tonight I am." She grinned.

My phone vibrated in my pocket and remembering my "phone date" with Mary, I pulled it out eagerly. It was a text from an unknown number.

Hey, Logan, I'm sorry. Have to attend to a family emergency. I'll call you tomorrow or Sunday. Please don't be mad. Love, Mary.

CHAPTER 7

Moving Out

Faith

Seeing the disappointment on Logan's face made me feel awful. It had taken me only ten minutes this morning to learn how to send anonymous text messages. And the feature to send the message with a delay meant that I could stand here while "Mary" texted him.

"What's wrong?" I asked with sympathy and cringed inwardly when he said, "I was expecting a call, but she had something come up."

"Sorry about that."

Logan turned around and walked back to the living room with me on his heels.

"Does that mean you have time to help me get my stuff?"

"Yer stuff?"

"Yes. From the apartment. I thought that if you have a car maybe you could help me out."

Logan raised his brows. "Ye want to move in *now*?"

"Of course."

"Ohh…"

"What did you think?"

"I don't know. I thought maybe ye needed a few days to pack yer things."

I shook my head. "There's not much to pack. I live in a suitcase."

"Then why do ye need my help?" he asked.

I smiled. "Because biking with a suitcase might be too difficult, even for me."

"Right." After a bit of hesitation, Logan went to pick up his car keys and jacket. "Let's go then."

A smile beamed on my face, and twenty minutes later when we arrived at Tanya's apartment, I was still babbling happily.

"It'll just take a minute for me to pack my things, come in." I held the door open for Logan to enter.

Tanya's place was small and cramped, and his eyes darted around with his brows creased closely together.

"You sleep here?" Logan asked and pointed to the old pull-out sofa. I bit my lip seeing all the books and papers stacked on the floor, the clothes in the corner, and my laptop on top of a paper pile. For someone who wanted the role as a "live-in housekeeper," this wasn't good advertising.

"I promise that I'll be tidy at your place," I said.

"Hey, Faith." Tanya came from her room and stopped to watch us. Her eyes hardened when she saw Logan.

"Tanya, this is Logan. Logan, this is Tanya. She's the one who owns the apartment," I explained to him.

"Nice to meet you," Logan said politely and offered his hand to Tanya.

Tanya stared at Logan's scars, and the slight wrinkle of her nose didn't escape me. No wonder he had issues with women, if they all behaved like this.

"Tanya, remember what you said about Dennis moving in, and me having to find a different place to live?"

"Uh-huh," she said distractedly without taking her eyes off Logan.

"I'm here for my stuff. I'm staying with Logan from now on."

Her eyebrows shot up. "You're staying with *him*?"

"Yes."

"I've never heard you mention a Logan before."

"That's because I haven't known him long."

"But..." Tanya gave Logan another scrutinizing glance before turning to me. "I'll still need rent for October."

"What? No way. It's September 21st and I've paid for the whole month. That's ten days more than I'm living here. I'm not paying you for October."

"You have to, it's in the contract. One-month warning, remember?"

I took a stance, hands on my hips and chin pushed out. "I'm not paying a dime. Ask Dennis to pitch in with the rent. That's only fair since he'll be the one living here."

Tanya scrunched up her face. "Don't be a bitch about it."

My body tensed. "Did you just call me the B word? That's nice, Tanya. Real nice." With harsh movements I threw my things in the suitcase that functioned as my improvised "closet." With all my books and clothes, the damn thing wouldn't close. Not even with me huffing and puffing on top of it.

"Here, let me help," Logan offered, pushed me gently aside, and took on "project suitcase."

"I'm keeping this until you pay me the five hundred dollars for October's rent."

Logan and I both swung our heads around to see Tanya standing with my laptop pressed against her chest.

I gasped. My computer was my life. I couldn't leave without it.

Before I had a chance to react, Logan spoke.

"Ye could choose to keep Faith's computer," he said slowly and calmly while at the same time moving closer to her.

"I *am* keeping it." she said firmly.

"Tanya, what do ye do for a living?"

"Why? What does that have to do with anything?"

"She studies economics," I said behind him.

"Really?" Logan had a sly sparkle in his eyes and kept his eyes on Tanya only. "And do ye intend to get a job after you graduate?"

"Of course."

"A simple question then." He tilted his head and narrowed his eyes. "Do ye think having a criminal record will improve yer chances of getting yer dream job?"

She snorted. "I'm within my rights to keep Faith's computer until she pays up."

Logan nodded slowly. "Maybe ye are. Or maybe what ye're doing is defined as theft. I'm not a lawyer, but I have one working for me."

"So what?" Tanya said with a sassy attitude.

"Personally, I find lawyers tiresome," Logan said in that wonderful accent of his. "Ye talk to them for a few minutes and they charge you a leg and arm. How many hours of legal counseling do ye think ye can buy for five hundred dollars?"

Tanya blinked a few times.

"Of course, Faith doesn't have to worry about money."

"Ha, is that supposed to be a joke?" Tanya looked at me. "Faith is always worried about money."

Logan shrugged. "Aye, but dinnae forget that her sister is a millionaire; surely *she* can sponsor a good lawyer."

"You clearly don't know Faith very well. If she was willing to take money from her sister, she wouldn't live on a couch with me, would she?" Tanya snorted. "I bet you don't even know that Cleo has an apartment down by Pike Place Market and that Faith has the key, but never goes there."

Logan took a second to ponder what Tanya had said. "Ye're right, I dinnae know Faith very well, but I do know that if someone took my computer, I would see red. In fact, I'm so sympathetic to Faith's predicament, that I'm happy to pay her legal fees if it comes to that."

Surely he was bluffing. But I admired his calmness.

There was an iron will behind his words when he reached out his hand, palm up. "The best economists make decisions based on cool rational. The worst make decisions based on emotions. Which type are ye?" he asked Tanya.

I was used to fighting my own battles, and it baffled me that I'd allowed him to step in and take over like this. The only way I could explain it was that Logan radiated such strength and authority that I was a bit awestruck.

My diagnosis of him had been hasty. There was *much* more to this man than a wounded soul who needed fixing. He might be awkward around women in general, but I'd bet he was hardcore at his job.

Logan gave her time to respond, and when she didn't, he simply turned to me. "Are ye ready to go? I think we need to make a stop at the nearest police station and report Tanya for theft"

"You wouldn't," she sneered at me.

"Here, let me get that," Logan said and squatted down. Together we managed to finally zip the suitcase closed.

My arms were full of bags and we had made it to the door when Logan turned to Tanya.

"Oh, before I forget. What is yer last name, Tanya? We'll need it for the police report and I'm sure my lawyer will ask me that, when he starts building a case against ye."

Tanya huffed out air and stomped over to us. "Here, take the stupid computer," she said and handed it to me with a sardonic sneer, "I hope you'll be happy with Scarface."

God, I wanted to hit her but held my tongue, afraid what poison I might spew at her.

Logan was quiet too, his face cut in stone when he walked out the apartment with my suitcase in hand.

For the next ten minutes we didn't talk.

We silently drove through the city, passing people with umbrellas who hurried down the street. It was close to nine and the stores were closed with only their window displays lit up.

"Thank you," I said softly. "For sticking up for me."

"It was nothing," he muttered without taking his eyes off the road.

"I'm sorry about her calling you Scarface."

He said nothing.

"You know what I thought, the first time I saw you?" I said, hoping to distract him from Tanya's harsh comment. "I thought you looked handsome. Tall, strong, and super badass with those scars."

"Badass?"

"Yes. You know, one of the bad boys that mothers warn their daughters about." I laughed a little. "And then it turns out that you're a computer whiz who probably hasn't been in a single fight in your lifetime."

"Ye say that as if it's a bad thing."

"Not at all. It's just not very *bad boyish*, is it?"

"Depends. There are criminal computer hackers and programmers too. Are they considered badasses?"

"Why? Are you one of them?"

"If I were, do ye really think I would admit it?"

"Anyway, I just wanted you to know that I thought Tanya was rude to you and that you're wrong if you think all women find you unattractive. Personally, I think some will be attracted to you *because* of your scars, you know?"

Logan gave me an incredulous look. "Ye don't really believe that, do ye?"

"I do," I said and thought about it. "But it's not necessarily a good thing."

"I'm not following."

"If someone is attracted to you because they think you're a badass, then what happens when they realize that you're a genuinely nice guy?"

"Wouldn't that be a bonus?" he asked.

"Maybe," I speculated. "But people have different kinks, and a woman who's into bad guys is looking for something specific that you can't provide."

"Ye dinnae know how bad I can be," Logan said.

I pointed. "Weren't you supposed to go that way?"

"Shite." He shot me a small scowl. "Ye're distracting me."

"Hey, don't blame me for not paying attention to where you're driving." I defended myself. But for the rest of the drive, I kept silent and considered how lucky I was that from tonight I would be sleeping in a real bed and have my own bathroom.

A quick side glance at the large man beside me brought a surge of excitement in my belly. Logan was a good man and I would help him deal with the anxiety he had around women. I would fix him!

A smile erupted on my lips at the thought of Logan and his future wife inviting me to their wedding and thanking me for fixing him. Maybe his wedding would take place in an old Scottish castle and the men would be wearing traditional plaids. That would be so much fun.

I was still smiling when Logan parked the car and turned to look at me. "Why are ye smiling like that?" he asked suspiciously.

"Because I'm moving in with you," I said with a happy grin.

CHAPTER 8
The New Rule
1 Month Later

Logan

Another look at the clock told me it was half past midnight.

Living with Faith this past month had involved a roller coaster of emotions for me. At the moment, the predominant feeling in my body was fear. *Why isn't she home yet? Where is she?*

Faith had been right. With two busy schedules, I didn't see her much. It was football season and that meant she practiced during the week and cheered on the weekends. Sometimes in town, sometimes out of state. Three evenings a week, she worked as a telemarketer, and then there were her studies. I didn't understand how she had time to do all the house chores. But she did.

My freezer was now full of portion-sized home cooked meals that tasted amazing.

My laundry she placed neatly folded on my bed. And most evenings I came home, I would find a note from Faith telling me that she had placed food for me in the fridge and wishing me a nice evening. I was even beginning to smile at the little positivity quotes she left me. Today's note said,

On particular rough days, I like to remind myself that my track record of getting through bad days so far is 100%, and that's pretty good.

Another glance at the clock. 12:36.

Where are you, Faith?

I looked down at the phone in my hand. She hadn't answered the three text messages I had already sent. *Something is wrong.* Usually she only worked until ten p.m. and was home by ten thirty. I kept pacing in my room. How the hell was I supposed to go to sleep, knowing she was two hours late? *And what if something has happened to her? Who will tell me? Does her family have my number? I should ask to have her family's number.* I knew so little about Faith and hadn't met any of her friends.

12:43 p.m.

Come on, Faith... walk in the door. Please!

My mind was racing with worst-case scenarios and at ten to one, I called her up.

There was no answer, and with a frustrated growl I threw the phone on my bed.

Should I call the police? What if she'd been run down on her bike, or robbed on her way home?

If I dialed 911, what would I tell them? I had no idea where the telemarketing company was located. I didn't even know the name of the place.

The only thing I could do was wait or drive around searching for her. *Maybe she's sleeping at a friend's place? Or maybe she's on a date and it turned into more?* That last thought didn't sit well with me. With a knot in my stomach I lay down on my bed.

That night, I drifted in and out of sleep, waking up to check if Faith was home yet.

She hadn't returned when it was time for me to leave for work the next day.

Like a worried parent, I cancelled my morning meeting and stuck around the apartment, hoping she would walk in any second now.

It was almost eleven o'clock before I heard a key in the lock. Without hesitation, I jumped up and moved to see that it really was her.

"Hey, Logan," Faith said with the biggest smile on her face. "I didn't expect you to be home. Shouldn't you be at work?"

Stay calm, I told myself, but my blood was boiling. Clearly, Faith hadn't been the victim of kidnapping, stabbing, rape, or any of the awful things I had worried sick about.

"Aye, I should be at work!" I said curtly and returned to my office, slamming the chair against the table and gathering my things. God, I could just scream at her.

"What's wrong?" she asked from the doorway.

"Nothing," I sneered and zipped my bag.

Faith stood in the doorway when I wanted to pass. "Excuse me," I said without looking at her. I was too mad to talk.

"What's wrong?" she repeated and didn't budge.

My nostrils were flaring and my hands squeezed the bag in my hand. "Where were ye?" I asked without looking at her.

"I slept at my sister's place. She's back in town. Why?"

At last my eyes landed on her. "I'm making a new rule."

She frowned.

"From now on," I started. "Ye will call me when ye're not coming home for the night."

"Why?" she asked.

"Because I worried something bad had happened to ye."

"You worried about me?"

"Aye." I didn't tell her that I hardly slept or that I had cancelled two meetings today already.

"Aww, that's sweet," Faith said and placed her hand on my arm. "You're like a protective big brother. I always wanted one of those."

"I'm not yer brother," I said stiffly. And thank God for that. If I were, the fantasies I'd been having about her would make me a pervert.

"I know. But you get my meaning, right?"

With a raised brow, I pushed past her. "I'll be at work."

"Okay." she called out behind me. "And don't forget to call me if you come home later than eleven."

Whipping my head in her direction, I grumped, "Why would I call ye when ye dinnae answer anyway?"

She pulled back and before I closed the door, her smile had vanished.

$\langle\infty\rangle$

Faith

It shocked me to see Logan so angry with me.

To be honest, I hadn't even considered that he would lose a minute of sleep if I didn't come home. But plugging my phone in the charger, and seeing his missed calls and worried text messages, told a different story.

He had called me throughout the night, which meant he hadn't slept much.

"I'm sorry," I texted him, and hoped he would forgive me for being so thoughtless.

Five hours later a reply ticked in, saying, *"I'm just glad you're okay."*

My mind kept running over ideas on how to make it up to him. I could make him a cake, but he didn't seem to have a sweet tooth. Of course, I could buy him something nice, but I didn't have much money.

With a sigh I returned to my studies, reading up on new research from Europe on ways to boost the human immune system through therapy.

And that's when it hit me. My answer was right there in the article. I *could* do something for Logan that wouldn't cost me any money! Something that would benefit his health and happiness, and serve as a perfect part of my plan to fix him too. I just needed to find a way to make him agree to it.

CHAPTER 9

Skin Hunger

Logan

When I came home that night, I was tired. No wonder, since worrying about Faith had kept me up the night before.

A lovely smell of garlic, spices, and something sweet met me, and I stopped to stare when I found my living room lit in candlelight.

"Hey, rocmie," Faith called out from the open kitchen and smiled. "I've made you a feast to apologize for my thoughtlessness."

"Okay," I said and looked around. "What's with all the candles?"

"I wanted to make it cozy and nice."

"But isn't candlelight related to romance?" I asked, a bit dumbfounded. *Is she trying to tell me something?* I immediately dismissed that thought.

"It can be, but it doesn't have to be," Faith said, which only confused me more. "I've been keeping dinner warm for half an hour, so it might be a bit overcooked, but I made you a sheep pie."

My eyebrows shot up. "A sheep pie?"

"Yes," she said and carried a tray to the table. "I Googled what people in Scotland like to eat and this came up."

"I've never heard of sheep pie," I told her.

"Oh... really?" She had a cute frown on her face.

"What's in it?" I asked and walked over to sit down.

"Lamb and potatoes."

I studied the dish and took another whiff of air to detect what Scottish secrets she had uncovered.

"Do ye mean shepherd's pie?" I asked.

"Shepherd's pie... yes, that's it."

I smiled at her briefly, before remembering that my smile only distorted my face.

"Bon appétit," she said after placing a large portion on my plate.

"Thank ye."

The first bite was really good and with a nod of approval, I said, "Not bad, Faith."

"You like it?" She lit up. "Is this how it's supposed to taste?"

"Aye, it's really good."

"Thank you. I'm so glad you like it. I made you a traditional Scottish dessert too."

"Really... and what did ye make?"

"Clootie dumpling, it took forever but I'm not sure I got it right. It looks a little funny."

"Ye went all in, huh?"

She bit her lip. "Yes. I feel bad about last night. I should have texted you that I was staying at my sister's place. Which reminds me: she wants to meet you."

"Excuse me?" I squeezed my fork and knife tighter.

"Yes. She's in town for our 'early Thanksgiving'." Faith stopped talking and looked up at me. "Wait a minute, would you like to come?"

"I don't celebrate Thanksgiving," I said matter-of-factly.

"But Logan." She put her fork and knife down. "Thanksgiving is a big deal. You should celebrate with me and my family."

"Faith," I said softly, feeling touched by her kindness. "I've never celebrated Thanksgiving in my life. I assure ye it means nothing to me."

"Why?" she asked with her eyebrows raised up in astonishment.

"For the same reason that I haven't celebrated the Fourth of July. It's a North American thing."

"Right, of course. But do you celebrate Christmas at least?"

"Aye."

"Ohh, good." She nodded. "Still, I think you should join me and my family for Thanksgiving. Think of it as a cultural experience, and that way my family can meet you."

I hesitated, feeling my heart pound faster and my neck flame up. It was one thing to be around someone like Faith, but Cleo was a whole other ball game. After I met Faith I had done my research.

I knew Cleo had been named the sexiest woman alive this year, and that she had won an Oscar. From the pictures I had seen, she looked like a goddess.

My anxiety kicked in and I pulled at my shirt, feeling suffocated by the collar.

"I dinnae think that's a good idea," I muttered and took a big swig of my glass of water.

"Hey, what's wrong? Why are you getting so flushed?"

"Yer sister..." I greedily drank more water, my mouth suddenly dry as the Sahara Desert.

"Yes. What about her?"

I shook my head and Faith made an "ohh" sound, as if seeing my predicament. "She makes you nervous?"

"Meeting the world's sexiest woman would make most guys a tad nervous," I said with forced humor.

Faith crossed her arms and tilted her head. "Need I remind you that you live with her identical twin?"

"I've seen her pictures," I said and physically felt the "flight response" set in. My body was telling me to get away from the perceived danger.

"So? What are you afraid of? You're not going on a date with her. She's got a boyfriend, you know."

I rolled my eyes at that ludicrous remark. Me on a date with Cleo!

"You have nothing to fear. My sister isn't scary at all. Once you meet her in private, you'll see that she's sweet and a little fragile."

"Fragile?"

"Yes, I love my sister, but she's far from perfect." Faith lifted her shoulders in a small shrug. "You'll see for yourself. And my parents are really nice people. So will you come?"

When I hesitated, Faith pinned me with a long gaze. "Don't tell me you're afraid of going to a dinner party. I thought Scots were brave people. Aren't you all descendants of warriors and rebels?"

"We are!"

She arched a brow. "Good, in that case I'll inform my family that you'll be joining us for Thanksgiving tomorrow."

I was silent for a few minutes, thinking hard.

"On a different topic, there's something I wanted to ask you," she said, drumming her fingers on the table.

"What is it?"

The way her blue eyes shone made me suspect she was up to something, but I tried to focus on eating my food.

"There's a new trend. You know the Tinder app, right?"

My head popped up. Yes, I knew Tinder. My brothers used it to hook up with women, but I would never use it myself. With my face, every woman would wrinkle her nose and swipe away from my picture.

"Yeah, what about it?"

"Well, a lot of singles use it for quick hookups because it's an easy way to satisfy a physical need."

"What's your point?"

"My point is that they're working on a new app which is similar but for cuddling instead of sex."

I laughed.

"What's so funny?" Faith asked.

"Let me guess, a woman came up with that idea?" I joked.

"I don't know, but hear me out because the reason is valid." She leaned forward. "Did you ever hear about skin-hunger?'

"Nah."

"It's a real thing. Humans need to be touched. When we don't get touched it affects not only our immune system, but our mental state too. Lack of human touch can cause depression."

"Go on," I said, intrigued by where this was going.

"Yeah, so the app is designed to find people to cuddle with. No sex. Just human touch. It's an alternative to professional cuddlers."

"Professional cuddlers?"

"Yes." She nodded firmly. "You can find them in most big cities now."

"Interesting," I agreed. "And what's your question then?"

"When I read about it today, I thought about you. How much human touch do you get?"

I leaned back, not sure how to answer.

"Do you have anyone you go to for your physical needs?" she asked slowly.

"Are ye asking me if I see a hooker?" It came out harsher than I intended.

"No." She flushed red. "I didn't say that. I just wonder if you have someone in your life that you..."

I cut her off. "Are ye asking me if I have a fuck buddy?"

"No."

"Do you?" I turned the question on her.

She frowned. "I told you, I'm not interested in sex."

"So there's no one?"

"No." She shook her head. "I'm talking about touch, not sex."

"Listen, Faith, I'm not sure what ye want to ask me."

"Isn't it obvious?" she asked. "I'm offering you human touch. I could massage you or we could cuddle up and watch a movie. You know, for the benefit of your physical and mental health."

I stared at her, my anxiety setting in. "Ye want me to cuddle with ye?"

"Yes," she said and nodded seriously.

"No." It didn't take two working brain cells for me to think this one through. "Not a chance."

"Why not?" She looked hurt.

"Only a woman would come up with a stupid concept like that."

"What do you mean?" she asked and threw her hands up. "It's brilliant. There's no sexual complications, only wellness and touch."

I narrowed my eyes. "I have the perfect name for that app. They should call it Blue Balls, and I'm sorry to say this, but I hate that idea."

"You don't want to be touched by me?"

"Are ye daft?" I gave her an incredulous glance. "What ye're asking for is crazy."

"How so?"

I changed my voice into a mocking one. "Here you go, lad, let's go look at the candy. Wanna touch it? Ye cannae have it... put it back. It's not for ye."

She stared at me with wide eyes.

"Do ye get my point? I dinnae want to touch ye because if I do, I'll be stuck with the biggest boner in my pants and no release."

"But Logan..."

"No, Faith. It's out of the question."

"Honestly." She stood up and carried her plate back to the kitchen. "I don't understand you. Surely you can be around woman without being sexually attracted to them."

"Of course."

"And you do understand that it would benefit you, right?"

"Aye, I heard, but my immune system is fine."

"Don't you think you're making a bigger deal out of this than it is? If we watched a movie together and I stroked your back, you would be okay, wouldn't you? I mean I'm not asking you to touch me if you don't want to, but at least you could let me touch you."

I counted to ten in my head and took some deep breaths as my therapist had taught me to do when I felt the anxiety coming.

"Are you okay," she asked.

I wanted to say that I was fine and retreat to my room like the moody dick I was, but I forced myself to stay and confront her.

"No, I'm not fucking *okay*. I'm confused."

"I'm sorry." She leaned over the table and placed her hand on top of mine. "I'm just trying to help."

I pulled my hand away. "Help? How is this helpful?"

"I just thought that since you admitted to feeling awkward around women, well..."

"What?" I moved in my chair, impatiently.

"I'm your friend, and if you can learn to be comfortable around me, maybe it will build your confidence around other women too."

Or maybe I'll be comfortable around you, and suffer when you hook up with someone else and forget about me. I didn't say that last part, but it worried me, especially with the dread I had felt last night.

"So we're friends, are we?" I asked while looking deeply into her eyes.

"Yes."

"Then tell me this. What happened to ye?"

Her head tilted slightly. "What do you mean?"

"Ye dinnae have a boyfriend, why is that? And why live in celibacy? Did someone hurt ye?" I had wondered about this and feared that behind that eternal smile of hers, there was a story of abuse.

Faith looked down and seemed to be thinking for a while. I held my breath, hoping I hadn't upset her by asking. "Is it a secret?" I asked.

"No, it's not a secret," she said when she finally met my eyes. "I just don't talk about it very often."

She paused and gave me a small nod. "You really want to know what happened to me?"

"Aye."

"And I really want to make it up to you for keeping you up all night, so how about this: I'll tell you while we cuddle."

I took a deep breath and let air out slowly.

"Come here," she coaxed, reaching her hand out to me. Even though my sanity was screaming, "Don't go into the candy shop," I got up and followed her to the couch.

Faith took a seat, her back against the armrest, and then she patted the couch. "I want you here in front of me." It felt strange to sit down between her legs and lean back against her chest.

"Relax," she said and started slowly massaging my scalp. "Are you comfortable?"

My body was tense but I lied and said, "Aye, I'm comfortable."

"Okay, good." And then she started telling her story. "When I was fifteen I fell in love with Allan. We were together for four years." Her voice was soft and full of emotions. "Allan was my first love, and we promised each other that we would stay together and start a family someday."

I was worried that I was crushing her, but she stroked her fingertips down my face and massaged my shoulders in calming movements. This position offered an intimacy that I hadn't shared with anyone in years, but it felt good and I started to relax a little.

"Allan was older than me by two years, and I absolutely adored him. He was handsome, and smart," she said in a dreamy voice. "Every girl at school envied me."

"Did he sleep with someone else?" I asked, because that seemed a plausible reason why her heart had been broken.

"No," she exclaimed in a gasp. "Of course not, we loved each other."

"Okay, but then how did he break yer heart?"

Her hands weaved through my hair, and she took a minute before she answered.

"One night Allan went to a party without me. I had just started college and he was on his third year. He called me in the middle of the night, drunk." She paused again. "We spoke and he told me the party was boring and that he wished he was with me instead."

I opened my eyes and tilted my head back to see Faith's eyes glazed with memories.

"The next morning his mom called me up and told me he had been in a car crash." Unshed tears welled up in her eyes. "He had borrowed a friend's car to come see me, but ended up in a ditch instead."

"He died?" I asked quietly.

"Yes. After three days on life support, the doctors told us there was no more hope. His parents had to give consent to turning off the machine."

"Och, that's awful."

"Uh-huh. I was there holding his hand, kissing him, and telling him that I would always love him." She dried tears off her cheeks.

"And you kept that promise," I concluded softly and went to get her a paper towel to dry her eyes.

Faith looked small and fragile as she sat on my couch, her knees pulled up to her chest, her arms wrapped around her legs.

"I loved him so much," she said with such sadness.

I didn't know what to do, except sit down next to her.

It surprised me when she wrapped her arms around my shoulders and scooted closer. Anxiety raced around my body, making it hard to breathe, and when she crawled onto my lap, I sat stiff as a mannequin with my hands folded into fists by my side. We sat like that for a long time, with her head resting on my shoulders.

Breathe, just breathe. You can do this, I kept telling myself and searched for an appropriate response to her grief.

"I'm sorry, Faith," I whispered into her hair. "Allan sounds like an amazing guy."

A loud sniffle erupted from her and then she whispered back. "Will you please hold me?"

I hesitated, still stiff and tense from her closeness.

"Please, Logan, I need a hug."

Swallowing hard, I forced my arms to lift up and wrap around her. The quick pat on her shoulder made the hug more like a man hug, and I'm sure she found it as awkward as me.

"Hey," I asked, trying to find a way to lift her spirit. "What about that dessert ye promised?"

She lifted her head. "You wanna try it?"

"Clootie dumpling? Yeah, I think my grandma once made it."

"And did you like it then?" she asked hopeful.

I wrinkled my nose a little. "Not really. It was so heavy and stayed in my stomach for a week. But I'm sure yers will be much better."

She dried the last tears away with her palm. "Right. Well, let's give it a try then."

We both stood up and moved to the kitchen.

"Are ye okay?" I asked with concern.

Faith turned around and looked at me with her beautiful moist blue eyes. "Thank you, Logan. You were a really good friend for listening."

"Any time," I said and nodded sternly and tried to suppress my thoughts. *Don't fall in love with her. You're doomed if you do.*

CHAPTER 10

Role-Playing

Faith

I knew Logan didn't like the dessert.

Neither did I. One bite was enough for me to give up, while he was polite enough to eat most of the clootie dumpling on his plate. He even told me it was better than he remembered it.

I suggested we cuddle some more, but Logan insisted he had work to do and retreated to his office on the other end of the apartment.

"Hey Logan," I called after him when he left. "About those rules of yours."

"Aye?"

"They go for you too, right?"

"What do ye mean?" he asked.

"If you decide to stay out for the night, you'll tell me."

He nodded. "If ye wish."

"Good, and don't go walking around half naked either."

He tightened his jaw.

"What?" I said with an arched brow. "You don't want me to tempt you, so it's only fair that you don't tempt me either."

"Is that a joke?" His scowl told me he didn't find it funny at all.

"No. I may have chosen to stay away from men, but I'm not a robot."

His confused expression before he turned and walked into his office was hilarious. I felt better about myself already. I would help this man heal. I might not have my license as a psychologist yet, but I would build his confidence, and help him find love with someone special. He would be my first triumph and he would thank me for it.

The double life I led was both challenging and exciting. As Mary I spoke to Logan often and met a different side of him. On the phone he was playful and flirtatious. In person he was reserved, although tonight had been a breakthrough. I was truly pleased with myself for getting him to accept my touch. The fact that I had enjoyed his masculine perfume and closeness was just a bonus.

My mission was clear.

First step was to help Logan overcome his anxiety around woman by getting him used to me.

Step two would be to empower him to start dating again. Hopefully, he would find someone special that would love him.

I should be respecting that he had to work, but I was so set on my mission to help him that I retreated to my room and called him up.

"This is Logan," he said in that deep sexy voice I loved so much.

"Hey, sugar, it's me, Mary," I flirted with my fake Southern drawl. Thank God he was a foreigner or he surely would have known by now that I wasn't really from Georgia.

Afraid he would hear me talking on the phone from his office, I lay down on my bed and pulled the cover up to dampen the sound.

"Mary, how are ye? It's good to hear yer voice."

"It's good to hear your voice too," I said softly. Logan was easy to talk to and we usually laughed a lot together. Last time we spoke had been Sunday night and it had lasted hours, with long talks about his work, his childhood, and my fictional life.

"So did ye think about it?" he asked.

"Yes, I did."

"And do ye wanna do it?"

"But I've never done role-playin' before," I argued just like I had the first time he brought it up.

"I know, but it'll be fun. Ye tell me one of yer sexual fantasies and we play it out on the phone."

I laughed softly, intentionally keeping my voice down. "I already told you my fantasy."

"Aye, but I want ye to tell me again."

I blushed a little, my heart pounding fast with excitement. Talking with Logan was always unpredictable and fun.

"Okay," I sucked in air. "You know how I told you I love Highlander novels."

"Aye, ye did..."

"Right, so I figured, with your accent, you could be that fierce Highlander laird who kidnaps me and brings me back to your clan to wed me. You know they forced women back then, right?"

Logan laughed. "And ye know this how?"

"The novels."

He laughed loudly.

"What's so funny?"

"They are pure imagination, Mary. I doubt my forefathers forced women to marry them."

"They did!"

"All right, so for the sake of the argument we'll say that ye're right. So what am I? A fierce, dirty, smelly laird who rapes ye?"

"No, of course not."

"But ye just said..."

"You're not dirty or smelly. And no, I don't want it to be rape. Just forced."

The humor in his voice was clear. "Isn't forced sex the definition of rape?"

"But you would make me like it once you got started. I would fight against you, of course, but you would insist that's it's your right as my husband and take me anyway."

"All right, and who are ye again?"

"I'm Mary, an English noblewoman, who despises the Scots, but I got separated from my protectors. Now I'm bathin' in the pond when you find me and you're completely bewitched by my beauty."

"Am I? Or am I just horny?" he said and laughed again.

"Logan," I said reproachfully. "You were the one who wanted to do this role-play."

"All right... I'll be a rough laird for ye. How do I look?"

I thought hard. "You're tall and strong, with long hair, and you've got scars that tell stories of battles and blood."

"Hmm..."

"So how do we do this?" I asked a bit uncertain.

"Close yer eyes," Logan instructed. "Imagine yerself bathing in the pond. The water is cold and yer nipples harden. And then ye hear sounds from the forest that make ye look up."

"All right," I said. "I'm so scared and I cover my chest, lookin' around to find the source of the noise."

"Aye, but everything is quiet again and, frightened, ye decide to come out of the water and cover up. And that's when I grab hold of ye."

"Let go of me," I said in my best imitation of a fine British accent, while at the same time trying to hide my snicker.

"Why would I let go of such a bonnie lass?" Logan had a thick brogue in his voice.

"You're hurting me," I exclaimed.

"Then stop fighting, and I'll make it feel guid."

"I'll never stop fighting. Get your vile hands off me."

81

"Lie down, woman."

"No."

"I said lie down." Logan grunted. "Are ye married?"

"No, but you *will* leave me alone."

"Will I?" Logan gave an evil laugh. "Not a chance. I'm bewitched by yer beauty and ye belong to me now."

"I most certainly do not."

"We Highlanders dinnae ask permission, and I just decided ye'll be my wife."

"You cannot just decide that. You'll need my father's consent."

Logan scoffed. "Yer father will give his consent when I tell him I already bedded ye. That makes us man and wife in the eyes of God. And now I'm forcefully pulling ye down on the ground and placing myself on top of ye, pushing yer knees apart.

"Stop it," I whined. "You cannot do this, I'm a virgin."

Logan gave a hard grump. "Not for long, ye're not! Do ye feel that? That's my large erection pressing against yer."

"No..." I pretended to cry. "Help."

"You can't shout any longer, I just covered yer mouth with my large hand, and I'm thrusting all the way in, bursting through your hymen."

"Hmm... I would have thought I was too dry for you to do that?" I said with another smile. This was fun.

"Right, on second thought," he said, "I want to taste ye first."

"Taste me?" I made a mock sound of shock.

"That's right, I'm pushing yer legs up and burying my head between them, making ye squirm in delight."

"Stop it, sir, what are you doing to me... it feels so..."

"Lie still and enjoy this, wife."

"I am *not* your wife."

"Aye, ye are my wife. And I'm placing a hand over yer mouth now and sucking yer nipples while pleasing you with my other hand," Logan said.

"Do you feel me arching up against you? I don't want to like it, but all these sexual emotions are new to me, and I'm so confused." I swallowed a grin.

"I do feel it. Ye're a wee wanton lass, aren't ye, my bonnie love?"

"I want to object, but with your hand on my mouth, it sounds like this." I placed a hand over my mouth and made muffled sounds of resistance.

"That's good lass, now ye're going to take all of me, and yer virgin blood will mix with my strong Highlander semen. Soon my son will grow inside your belly and we'll have wee bairns of our own," Logan told me.

"It hurts," I whined.

"Ye'll get used to it, love. We'll be doing it three times a day from now on."

"Three?" I said with my brows arched.

"Uh-huh. In the Highlands we don't have much to do after dark; that's why bed sport is our favorite thing to do," Logan said with pretend seriousness.

"But I don't want to be your wife."

"Too late – I'm already pushing my hard cock inside ye, making ye mine."

"Only a priest can do that," I objected.

"No, lass. This isn't England. In the Highlands a man can marry a woman by claiming her and taking her. Ye belong to me now. I'll protect ye and care for ye."

"Oh..."

"Do ye like this, wife? Me thrusting inside ye, teasing yer nipples?"

"Uh-huh... it feels strange, but good."

"I'm kissing ye now, Mary, long and greedy."

"And possessive." I added.

"That's right, Mary, ye're the laird's wife now and ye'll be living in my castle, warming my bed, and giving birth to my babes. Do ye understand?"

"Yes."

Logan was pretty good at staying in character and just for the fun of it, I went with it. Enjoying the sound of his thick brogue in my ear telling me how good it felt to bury his large cock inside me and how I would have to please all his needs from now on. Every day, whenever he wanted me. My fingers found their way to my clit, and maybe he could hear in my breathing what I was doing, because his breathing changed too.

"Mary, tell me ye like what I'm doing to ye," he ordered.

"It feels so good inside. I've never felt anything like it. The warmth of you and the way you press down on my chest, forcing your will on me. I have no choice but to surrender myself to you and accept that I belong to you."

The last sentence came out breathy as my fingers expertly rubbed my clit. The sound of Logan's heavy breathing was turning me on big time. Knowing he was in his office just down the hallway, pleasuring himself to the sound of my voice, was exhilarating. He had no idea he was having phone sex with his roommate.

"Aye, ye *do* belong to me, wife," he muttered. "And I'm never letting ye go."

I felt a wave roll in, making my insides retract in small cramps that left a smile on my lips. "Ohh, that feels so good," I said honestly and heard the sound of him breathing loudly into the phone.

"Aye, it does, Mary. It feels fucking amazing."

He came. I'm sure of it.

It was my first time doing anything like this. Never had I imagined that non-physical sex could feel this intimate. I closed my eyes and imagined Logan on his bed, breathing heavily, his eyes closed, and the phone to his ear. We had just had sex. A strange sort of sex, but nevertheless a very arousing and exciting form of sex.

It wasn't that I had been a complete nun after Allan died. There had been a few guys, but every time I let another man touch me, I felt horrible for betraying Allan and the love we shared.

This was different. Logan hadn't touched me. He didn't even know he had shared this experience with me. I felt no guilt and made a happy sigh.

"That good, huh?' he chuckled.

"It was fun."

"Sure was."

"So now that we've done my fantasy, how about yours?" I said.

"Ehm... that's okay, ye dinnae have to do that."

"Why not? Is it very perverted?" I asked playfully.

"Maybe. Depends who's judging."

"Okay, Logan McKay, tell me, darlin', what turns y'all on?" I exaggerated my Southern drawl.

"Normally lots of things, lately only one thing."

"And what might that be?"

He hesitated.

"No judgment," I said. "And hey, I told you about my Highlander fantasy. I doubt yours is more pathetic than that."

"It is," he muttered. "It's a god damn cliché."

"Okay, spit it out, handsome."

"All right, but remember; no judgment."

I bit my lip. *Please don't say anything about diapers, animals, or children,* I thought.

"I fantasize about having sex with a cheerleader."

"Ohh." My jaw dropped. "What kind of cheerleader?" I asked slowly. "A high school cheerleader?"

"No, she's, ehm..." he trailed off. "It's my roommate. She a professional cheerleader."

"Ohh, wow. Are you sayin' you fantasize about your roommate?" My heart galloped and I frowned.

His voice fell to a low mutter, "Yeah, me and every other male who sees her."

I had to know, so I closed my eyes and asked, "Are you in love with her?"

"Noo." He said it with a laugh.

It was what I wanted to hear, but the way he said it made me a little cross. "You sound like the idea is ridiculous."

"It is! The woman is annoying on so many levels."

Did he just call me annoying?

"Why do you say that?" I was trying to keep my voice calm.

"She talks too much, and she thinks she can push me around. Definitely not girlfriend material. Still, she's every man's erotic fantasy."

Not girlfriend material?

For someone who wasn't interested in a boyfriend, I got pretty offended by that comment.

"Ye know, she asked me to come to one of the games and see her cheer," Logan continued.

"Let me guess; you said no?" I remembering how disappointed I had felt.

"Yeah, it's hard enough to see her fully clothed, I didn't think seeing her in a small uniform would help. But then one day at work I was stupid enough to look her up on their website."

"And?"

He gave a hard scoffing chuckle. "Now, I'm cursed with these sexual fantasies about her in her wee uniform."

"And what does she do in those fantasies?" I asked, still annoyed with him, but also driven by a perverted need to get inside Logan's mind and understand what turned him on."

"Different things. Sometimes I fantasize that I wake up with her on top of me, riding me in her uniform. Other times, she asks me to see a new routine and when she bends over, I see that she has no panties on and then she looks back and winks at me, encouraging me to take her."

"And do you?" I cleared my voice. "Take her, I mean."

"Mary," he sighed. "I've had so many sexual fantasies about my roommate that it's disgusting. Even to me."

"Why?"

He cleared his throat. "Somedays I can't even look her in the eye, knowing what I've done to her in my fantasies."

I tilted my head and narrowed my eyes. "Why? Are you abusing her in your fantasies?"

"Depends what you consider abuse," he said slowly. "I can be pretty dominant, and I love to imagine her on her knees with my cock in her mouth."

I was silent for a few seconds, remembering the fascinating class I took on clinical sexology. I could use this information to help him, couldn't I?

"Right, but you've never acted on it, have you?" I asked.

"God no. But the fantasies are horrible. Sometimes I cannae sleep, knowing that she's in the other room."

"And?" I probed.

"Mary," he sighed. "I dinnae know why I'm telling ye this, but ye have to promise that ye willnae hate me for it."

"I promise," I said firmly, my heart hammering.

"I've had disgusting thoughts about touching her in her sleep. It grosses me out that I can even think it."

"What do you mean, touch her in her sleep?"

"Ye know... go to her room when she's sleeping and remove her blanket, just to see her or touch her. Sometimes I fantasize about her waking up with me on top of her and she smiles at me."

My brows creased closely together. "Do you think you would ever do it?"

"Of course not, I'm not a creep. But it's hard to look at her the morning after those thoughts. If she had any idea how many times I've undressed her in my mind, she wouldn't want to live here."

I could tell he was beating himself up for having these fantasies. "Did I ever tell you that one of my friends is a psychologist?" I said.

"No... why? Are ye saying I need to see a psychologist?"

"Definitely, but not because of your sexual fantasies. You need help with your anxiety– I already told you so."

"I did get help, back in Scotland," he answered. "But what was yer point about yer friend?"

"Just that she once told me about a patient of hers."

"Is she allowed to discuss her patients with ye?"

"No, but she didn't mention names and it was someone from her early years as a psychologist."

"All right."

"Anyway, this guy had some disturbin' fantasies that freaked him out and he came to her."

"What kind of fantasies?" Logan asked.

"Rape, incest, cheatin'. Basically everything forbidden and disgustin'. The man was tormented by these thoughts and didn't understand how he as a good Christian, and normal workin' family man, could have these unwanted dreams and fantasies."

"Uh-huh," Logan said.

"So my friend explained to her patient that he wasn't alone and that all people have forbidden thoughts that freak them out."

"Hmm."

"Trust me, Logan, there's a huge gap between fantasies and reality. Most people wouldn't like to act out their fantasies, even if given the choice," I explained. "At least not if those fantasies clash with their values, morals, and ethics. It simply violates what they stand for, and ultimately that's why they're so disgusted with havin' the fantasies in the first place."

He kept quiet, so I continued, "Like me; I might like the sexual fantasy about surrenderin' to a strong Highlander, but in real life, I would run away screamin' or try to kick his ass."

"I hope so," he said.

"Psychology tells us that suppressin' forbidden thoughts is actually hurtful. Have you noticed that the biggest sexual scandals are often related to the most holy of people, or people who try to convince others they are good?"

"Aye, it's the truth."

"How many times have we heard about politicians who promote family values but are caught cheatin', or priests who claim to be holy, yet sexually abuse children," I said solemnly.

He made a sound of agreement.

"Right, it only shows that the more vigorously you try to suppress and deny forbidden thoughts, the more power they get over you. It's impossible to enhance the front side of a coin without enhancin' the back side too, you know?"

"What do ye mean?"

"Just that everyone has a shadow side."

"Okay," Logan muttered. "That makes sense."

"So what I'm tryin' to say is that you shouldn't judge yourself for having forbidden fantasies."

"Are ye sure?"

"Yes."

"Your friend told you this?"

"Who?"

"The psychologist."

"Right. Yes, she told me that all human bein's have unwanted forbidden fantasies. The people who deny it probably have the worst ones."

"So what you're saying," Logan said slowly, "is that you can think it, but you can't do it."

"Exactly! You can fantasize about hittin' your boss but you can't do it in real life."

"That's lucky for me, with hundreds of employees."

"Exactly. But think about the irony of bein' human. A few hundred years back it was considered civilized to duel a man to death if he offended you. In fact, you were considered a coward if you didn't defend your honor, whereas today you would be considered primitive or mentally unstable if you used violence to solve your problems."

"Right, I get that," Logan said. "But surely, it's not okay to fantasize about molesting yer roommate?"

"You want to *molest* her?" I exclaimed with my eyes wide open.

"I told ye, I fantasized about touching her in her sleep. I even fantasized about making love to her and waking her up that way."

"But you said that in your fantasy she smiled at you?"

"Aye."

"I'm confused." My heart was hammering in my chest. "How does your fantasy differ from the role-play we just played out? Didn't your Highlander alter ego just take me by force? Does it make me a pervert to find that thought arousin'?"

"Mary," he said in a breathy sigh. "Ye're fantasizing about some fictional historical Highlander, I'm fantasizing about my roommate, for fucks sake."

"So?"

"It's different. My scenario is more real."

I rubbed between my eyebrows. "Have you been listenin' to me at all?"

90

"Aye, I'm listening."

"I don't think you are. Logan, let me ask you this. If you fantasized about stealing a million dollars, would that make you a thief?"

"Nah," he said drawn out. "Not unless I actually stole the money."

"And that's your answer. End of discussion," I concluded.

He was quiet for a few seconds and then asked, low:

"Do you really think everyone has dirty fantasies, Mary?"

"Of course they do. Nasty ones that leave them feelin' dirty. I think that's why they're called *dirty* fantasies." I gave a small laugh.

"Tell me yer worst ones, then," he coaxed. "Come on. Ye and I share secrets, remember," he said softly.

"Okay, first of all, I've had sex dreams about the strangest people. And by dreams I mean wakin' up confused, because I certainly didn't want to have sex with them in real life."

"Who?"

"My volleyball coach, a strange guy from class... and once I fantasized about sharing a guy with my sister."

"How old is yer sister, Mary? I thought ye said ye only had a brother."

"She's my, ehm... stepsister," I said quickly and added, "She's one year younger than me, and I never told her."

"Is she sexy?' Logan chuckled. "Geez, Mary, that actually sounds kinda hot."

"Incest sounds hot to you? How about you and one of your brothers then?"

"Eew." He made a sound of revulsion.

"Exactly! I felt so icky and dirty after that fantasy, but you're the first one I ever told about it.

"Besides, did ya know that incest is legal in several countries."

"No way."

"It's true. You can have sex with a family member as long as they're old enough. I think Japan, Belgium, Portugal, and India are some of the countries that allow it."

"Shit. I had no idea," Logan said. "That's crazy."

"Maybe, but it just shows that what is dirty in one part of the world is acceptable in another."

"You're just saying that to make me feel better. I'm not convinced that this happens to everyone. Maybe ye and I are just both perverts."

"We're not." I grinned. "It's just that no one talks about these thangs openly. I wouldn't admit all of this to you if we were face to face."

"Ye're probably right, but still, I really want to meet ye," Logan said softly.

"Even after what I just admitted?"

"Aye, even more than before. I mean it, Mary, at least give me yer number, and the things we spoke about..." he trailed off, then: "It has to be our secret."

"Of course. It's good to have someone to share secrets with, isn't it?" I said and ignored his request for my phone number.

"Aye, it is. I've never talked about this openly. Not even with my girlfriend."

"You have a girlfriend?" I asked and frowned.

"Kenna. She was my girlfriend for five years, but we broke up about two years ago, after the accident." He was quiet for a minute. "We never talked about dirty fantasies."

"Probably because most people are terrified, and judgin' themselves and others harshly."

"Aye, me too. My roommate would be disgusted, if she knew."

Maybe not."

He snorted. "Aye, a hundred percent."

"But you said that she's a cheerleader."

"Aye, she is."

"And do you honestly think that a cheerleader has no idea that men fantasize about her?"

Logan scoffed. "I don't think any woman thinks like that."

"Oh, come on. Don't be so naïve. A cheerleader knows she's a sex symbol. "My guess is that your roommate wouldn't be offended as long as you behave civil around her."

Logan stayed silent, clearly contemplating my point of view. "Ye know, Mary. Something strange happened tonight."

"What?"

"I came home to a candlelight dinner."

"Okay."

"As if that wasn't strange enough, my roommate told me she wanted us to cuddle. It confused the hell out of me. Why would she do that?"

I rubbed my palm against my forehead. *Shit,* when he said it like that it made me feel bad. I had wanted to create a cozy welcoming atmosphere, and the cuddling was part of my plan to make him feel comfortable around women.

I sighed. "She was probably just tryin' to be nice."

"Hmm."

"And you said it yourself: you don't want her anyway."

"When did I say that?"

"You said she wasn't girlfriend material."

Logan muttered, "True. And sleeping with her would be stupid anyway. I would miss her cooking and her cleaning when she moved out."

"Excuse me," I exclaimed, and almost forgot my fake accent. "Are you saying that you would sleep with her and throw her out afterward?"

"Mary, why are ye raising yer voice at me?"

"Explain yourself."

"I'm just saying that sleeping with her would make everything more awkward than it already is. She wouldn't want to stay, and I would miss her cooking and cleaning. That's why I wouldn't touch her with a barge pole."

I didn't know what to say.

"Mary, are ye there?"

"You would miss her cleanin' and cookin'. But not *her*?" That stung.

"I dinnae know."

I was quiet.

"Listen," he sighed. "My roommate is nice, but she's not ye. Ye know?"

"What is that supposed to mean?"

"With ye I can be myself. We laugh and joke together. My roommate isn't like that. I dinnae think she has much humor and I dinnae feel relaxed around her, it's more..." he paused. "It's more forced and draining to me."

Wow. I felt like he had just smacked me in my face. *I'm easy to talk to, socially intelligent, and funny as hell.* How could he not see that?

"Soo..." He drew out a sigh. "Since ye're apparently not appalled by my sexual lust for my roommate, do ye wanna do the role-play?"

I blinked a few times, trying to stay in my character as Mary. "Sure, honey, what's her name? If I'm playin' your roommate, you need to tell me her name."

"Faith, her name is Faith."

CHAPTER 11

Thanksgiving

Logan

Thursday morning, I woke up thinking about the role-plays Mary and I had played out last night. Just the thought gave me a hard-on.

Mary was incredibly easy to talk to and I had even admitted to my fucked-up fascination with Faith. It was ridiculous! Still, going over the role-play that I had shared with Mary gave me a quick release in the shower.

After the shower and a shave, I went in to the kitchen and found Faith eating breakfast.

"Hey," she said without looking at me.

"Hey," I replied and joined her at the table, pouring myself a bowl of cornflakes. "Did ye sleep well?" I asked.

"Uh-huh," she muttered but still didn't look at me.

We ate in silence before she disappeared into her room, leaving me with a weird feeling that I had done something wrong.

I went for a long run, and worked in my office until it was two in the afternoon and she popped her head in.

"Hey," she said and kept her hand on the doorframe. Her hair and make-up were styled, and she wore a cute blue dress that made her blue eyes stand out more prominently. Over the five weeks she had lived with me, I'd noticed that her eyes changed color depending on the light. Outside in the sunlight, her eyes had an almost turquois color. This morning they had been the color of a bright summer sky, but now they were a dark shade of blue that made me think of the ocean.

"Hey," I said.

"Can we take your car?"

"Ehhm… ye mean for the Thanksgiving thing?"

"Yes."

"Is something wrong, Faith? Ye seem different today."

She shook her head, but the fact that she couldn't look me in the eye told me something *was* wrong.

"I'm fine," she lied.

"Look, if I said something wrong or did something to upset ye, please tell me. I cannae read your mind."

She lifted her shoulders in a small shrug. "No, it's not you. I just have a lot on my mind."

"All right. Look, I'm happy to give ye a ride, but ye really don't have to include me in yer family dinner."

"I already said you were coming," she said determinedly. "We leave in forty minutes."

My mind was searching for a reason for Faith's bizarre behavior. I had never seen her so withdrawn. Yesterday, she had been talkative and open. Today she was quiet and reserved. *What happened?*

Different theories played in my mind.

Maybe she got her period and it's hormonal.

Or maybe she received bad news of some kind.

Maybe she doesn't look forward to spending time with her family.

Maybe telling me about Allan yesterday has brought her grief. Or maybe she regrets asking me to come.

I was quiet on our way there, blaming myself for going in the first place. I didn't even like turkey that much.

"Logan, this is my dad, Spencer," Faith said when we arrived at the address by the Pike Place Market.

Spencer was a handsome man around fifty who gave me a bright smile and shook my hand. "So glad you've come to my rescue. It can be a bit much with all the females in my family," he jested.

I nodded at him. "I'm pleased to be of service."

"And that's my mom, Marianne." Faith pointed to the open kitchen, where a tall woman stood over the stove. She brushed her hands on her apron and came to shake my hand.

"I'm glad to meet you, Logan, we've heard so much about you."

It was easy to see where Faith got her looks from and I felt my heart race a little faster, waiting for Marianne's reaction to my scars. There was none.

Faith must have prepared them, I figured.

"I hope you're hungry, because there's plenty of food," Marianne said chirpily and went back to the stove.

"How can I help?" Faith offered and went to wash her hands, leaving me and Spencer in the open-space dining room.

"Chloe's is in her bedroom, talking to her boyfriend; she'll be right out," Spencer explained and picked up a bottle of wine. "Care for a glass?" he asked.

"Yes, please."

"Faith told me you work with computers," he said and poured a generous amount of red wine into the large glass.

"That's right. And you?"

"I'm a plumber." He nodded to the kitchen. "Marianne works as a hair stylist now, but she was a stay-at-home mom until the twins turned twelve."

"Thank you," I said and took the glass he held out to me.

"We met in high school," he added and shot a smile in his wife's direction. "Marianne caught my eye during lunch one day; the rest is history."

A loud bang made us all turn toward the closed door, which I assumed was Chloe's bedroom.

"Don't mind that," Spencer said with a small frown. "Chloe has a temper and she and her boyfriend don't always get along."

"That's an understatement," Faith interjected from the kitchen. "The best word to describe their relationship would be 'toxic.'"

A few minutes later, Chloe came out with a strained smile plastered on her face.

"Oh, hello," she said in her signature British accent and came to shake my hand. It was like looking at Faith, except Chloe used a lot more make-up and had on tight leather pants and some sort of black corset top that resembled lingerie. With her impossible high stilettos and voluminous hair, she reached my eyebrows where Faith only reached my nose in her pumps. Chloe was beautiful in pictures, but in person she was sex on legs.

"Hi," I muttered stiffly. My neck and back prickled like someone had dumped a glass of fire ants down my shirt.

Her reaction to my scars was less dramatic than normal, but she still stared a little and her nostrils flared the way they do when someone is trying to suppress their reaction. Quickly she looked away and broke into a tirade about her boyfriend Niko.

"Can you believe he says that I'm overanalyzing everything? The woman sent me a transcript of their sexting – how can he not apologize for writing those things?"

To my astonishment Spencer and Marianne didn't say anything. Only Faith sighed deeply. "Drop him. How many times do you have to hear me say it? The guy is a psychopath, and not only is he playing you, he's controlling you too."

"You just said the exact thing Niko told me you would say." Chloe rolled her eyes. "We all know you never liked him."

Marianne cut in. "How about we have a nice Thanksgiving dinner?"

Faith, who had her mouth open to respond to Chloe's accusation, closed her mouth and nodded. "Yes, let's."

"Come, Logan," Chloe took my arm and gave me a sugary smile. "I want you to sit next to me and drizzle that amazing Scottish charm all over me."

The fire ants crawled to my face, and I think I looked like I had eaten a raw chili when Chloe nudged me toward the table, leaned up against me, and said in a silky voice, "Faith told me it makes her panties wet to hear you talk, you know?"

My eyes shot from Chloe to Faith, and I saw her move closer with tensed jaws.

"I never said that," she corrected her sister. "I told you to be nice to Logan, and the first thing you do is embarrass him – that's nice, Chloe."

Chloe touched my shoulder, making me look back at her. "Don't mind Faith, she takes everything much too seriously." She lowered her voice to a conspiratorial whisper. "Yesterday she chastised me for changing back to my blond hair color; she doesn't like it when we look too similar."

"I can still hear you, you know, and all I said was that it's better when people can tell us apart," Faith interjected.

Chloe arched a brow and looked directly at me, "See what I mean? She's always so critical, but I'm sure you're a big guy who can handle a small female like myself, aren't you?" The way she batted her eyelashes flirtatiously was playing tricks on my sanity.

"Ehm…"

Spencer took a seat at the table. "Chloe, leave the poor man alone. He's here with Faith – show some respect."

"I *am* showing respect," she pouted.

Marianne came in carrying a turkey on a big platter. Faith carried mashed potatoes and vegetables.

Soon we were all seated at the table with a feast in front of us. The conversation was casual and polite with questions about Scotland, my work, and background.

"How did you get the scars?" Spencer asked and took a sip of his wine. "Or am I not supposed to ask that?" he added when Faith shot him a dirty look.

"No, it's fine. Ye can ask," I said and squirmed a bit in my seat. Faith had never asked me directly and I had never offered her an explanation.

"I was in a plane crash five years ago," I said.

I had their full attention.

"My family lives up in the Scottish Highland and flying has always been a passion of mine. This particular day, my sister Patricia came with me." I wet my lips and fiddled with my napkin.

"It was a small two-person Cessna and when the engine failed I tried to find a place to land, but we were flying over forest at the time and the only place was a lake."

"So you crashed into the lake?" Faith whispered with wide eyes.

"Aye." I looked down.

"And your sister?"

My hands formed into fists under the table. "The plane broke in parts and my Patricia..." I cleared my throat. "She was stuck and I struggled to get her out."

"Did you?" Marianne asked breathlessly. "Get her out?"

"Aye, but the autopsy showed she died from the impact."

Chloe's hand flew to her mouth and tears welled up in her eyes. They were all watching me with silent sympathy.

"I'm sorry that I asked," Spencer said low. "I didn't mean to bring up painful memories."

"It's okay," I reassured him. "I don't talk about it often, but my therapist said it's better to be honest about it."

"How old was Patricia?" Marianne asked.

"Sixteen."

"So young?"

"Aye, she was from my father's second marriage."

"Were you close?"

"I loved her very much," I said softly.

Chloe leaned closer. "Can I hug you?" she asked and spread her arms to me.

I pulled back a little, but she still hugged me. My eyes shot to Faith, who lifted her shoulders in a small apologetic shrug.

By the time we reached dessert, three bottles of wine had been emptied and funny stories from the girl's childhood were being shared.

"And then Faith tried to explain to Chloe that they had both been inside Marianne's belly at the same time," Spencer boomed with a smile. "And then Chloe looks at Faith and says in all her childish innocence, 'But I didn't see you in there.'"

I laughed.

"Remember the time the girls decided to dress up as fine ladies?" Marianne asked her husband and turned to me. "I was always at home with the girls, and then one day I ask Spencer to look after them while I go somewhere. Imagine me coming home to a house with two girls screaming and Spencer shouting."

"Because they dressed up?" I asked.

"No, because they had found my red nail polish and applied it as lipstick, rouge, and eyeshadow."

"I couldn't get the damn stuff off," Spencer said forlornly.

"The whole house stank from the turpentine he was using and the girls were sobbing." Marianne's eyes were shining with humor and she used her whole body when she spoke. No question, Chloe took her acting skills from her mom.

"And how old were the girls?" I asked her.

"Three."

Chloe spread her arms. "We wanted to look pretty."

"You still do," Spencer said with a loving wink to Chloe.

"I know," she said and winked back to him before putting me on the spot with her question, "Do you think we're pretty too?"

"Ehm," I muttered and felt that damn anxiety kick in again. Why did it matter what I thought? Wasn't it enough that she had been voted the sexiest woman alive? An acute dryness developed in my throat, making me reach for my glass and emptying it in one long gulp.

"Well, do you?" Chloe whispered against my ear.

Her closeness made me jump in my seat and I mumbled a short, "Aye, ye're both bonnie women."

"But who do you think is prettier – Me or Faith?" Chloe said teasingly and made a pose to present herself from her most favorable side.

"Chloe, this is your last warning." Faith waved a finger at her sister and resembled a strict schoolteacher. "Be nice to Logan, or we're leaving."

"Tsk." Chloe smacked her tongue and got up to take her plate out, placing it harshly in the sink.

"And you can quit shaking your head at me, like I'm some kind of crazy," Faith complained.

Chloe rolled her eyes. "Geez Louise, will you calm the fuck down?"

"Chloe, watch your language," Marianne interjected but Chloe was speaking over her: "Logan's a grown man, Faith. I doubt he needs or wants you to be his bodyguard."

"See what I mean?" Spencer told me and shook his head. "It's all them damn female hormones."

"Estrogen," I added.

He nodded. "Yup. I love my girls, but I hate the drama."

Ten minutes later I was checking my phone in the kitchen while Faith disappeared into the bathroom and their parents shared a romantic moment on the balcony. That's when Chloe snuck up on me.

"So tell me, Logan," she said and moved close. "What is your relationship with my sister?"

"Relationship?"

"Are you her lover?"

"No!" I said firmly. "She's just my roommate."

Chloe tilted her head and bit her inner cheek, making her lips skew to one side. "Are you in love with her?"

"Nah!"

"Shoot... I was hoping she was finally moving on from that dickhead."

My eyes grew big. "What dickhead?"

"Allan."

"Allan? The one who died? But he sounds like an amazing guy."

Chloe rolled her eyes. "So she told you?"

"Aye."

"Listen." Her eyes darted to the bathroom door and she lowered her voice to a whisper. "Faith might romanticize him, but the guy was a jerk and they fought all the time. He smoked too much weed and it's no coincidence that he died in a car crash. Did she tell you he already had a DUI?"

"No."

"He was her first love, but not half as perfect as she remembers him." Chloe pointed to her chest. "*I* remember all the fighting – and there's so much she doesn't know about him."

"Like what?"

"Like the fact that he cheated on her several times."

I frowned. "Are ye sure?"

"Yes, I'm sure. He even tried hitting on me, and when I told Faith about it, the bastard convinced her that he'd simply confused me for her."

She waited for me to speak, but I honestly didn't know what to say.

"I wish she would just move on already," she whispered.

The sound of the bathroom door opening made both Chloe and me step away from each other. Faith creased her brows but didn't say anything.

"How about we play a game?" Chloe asked in a cheerful voice and went to fetch Spencer and Marianne.

Faith wanted to play cards, but Chloe insisted on playing charades and enlisted me and her parents.

"I'm with Logan," Chloe declared and gave me a beaming smile. The woman was stunning and her white teeth flawless. I tried to act cool, but her attention made me nervous and flustered.

"No, Logan is with me," Faith said.

"Don't be stupid. I called dibs first," Chloe dismissed Faith, and I got the feeling that she was deliberately trying to provoke Faith.

"And who am I supposed to partner up with?" Faith asked in exasperation.

"We can be partners," Marianne said and smiled. "Your father won't mind being an observer in the first round."

"How about *I* just observe?" I suggested, hoping to get out of it.

"No way, Highlander, you're mine to play with," Chloe said with a playful grin and grabbed my hand, pulling me to the couch.

Faith scowled at her but we never got to play before Chloe's phone rang.

"What do you want, Niko?" she said in a harsh tone before she walked back into her bedroom and closed the door behind her.

"Are you okay?" Faith asked me.

I nodded. "Aye, I'm fine."

"Good. I'm sorry about Chloe," she said apologetically. "Told you she was fragile."

When I frowned in confusion, she continued. "Her need for attention makes her overstep people's boundaries, but I'm sure you've noticed by now."

"Aye, she's pretty intense," I agreed.

Faith was just about to answer me when the bedroom door flew open and Chloe stormed back. "I hate him," she cried out and plumped down on the couch, her arms crossed like a pouting child.

"So do you like American football?" Spencer asked me, ignoring his daughter's obvious distress. Either he was used to it, or he didn't know how to address her anger.

"Ehm…" I forced myself to look away from Chloe. "Nah, I can't say that I do. I'm not a huge sports fan."

Out of the corner of my eye, I saw Faith place her hand on Chloe's arm and stroke it caringly. "Are you okay?" she asked softly.

"No," Chloe hissed out and looked like she was about to cry.

"Come." Faith took her hand and they retreated to the kitchen, where I heard them talk quietly.

"Not a football fan, huh? Please tell me that at least you like whiskey?" Spencer said.

"Och, now ye're talking. Of course I like whiskey. I wouldn't be a true Scot if I didn't."

"Wonderful." Spencer got up and went to a fine cabinet where he sorted through bottles. "I've told Chloe that Jack Daniel's is good enough for her old dad, but she insists on buying all sorts of fancy brands." He gave me an earnest glance over his shoulder. "It's the money," he said and pulled out a fine bottle. "It changes people. We certainly didn't raise her to waste money on luxury items, but once she got a taste for it..." He opened the bottle and shrugged before serving me a glass. "Oh, well, can't complain that your kid is successful, can you?"

"Nah, and good whiskey is never a waste of money," I said and clinked his glass.

Sipping my whiskey, my attention was caught by Faith's voice growing in volume from the open kitchen.

"No, it's not about *loyalty*, Chloe. He pulled a gun on you, for Christ's sake. Don't you see that Niko's bad for you and that you owe him *nothing*?" she argued.

"Who are you to talk?" Chloe argued back with her hands on her hips. "Don't talk to me about loyalty when you're loyal to a dead guy. At least mine can make love to me."

Faith gasped out loud and looked like she had been physically struck by Chloe's words.

"I'm sorry," Chloe said quickly and tried to touch Faith.

"Don't." Faith pulled back and held up her palm as a stop sign. Her face was pale and her eyes teary.

"Don't fight, girls," Marianne pleaded. "It's Thanksgiving, and we have a guest." She turned to me, wringing her hands. "Sorry about that."

"I have brothers," I said, "And believe me, we fight all the time."

Marianne gave me a strained smile. "I know, right? Some even say it wouldn't be a real Thanksgiving without a little family dispute."

I nodded sympathetically. "This is nothing. My brothers and I, we prank each other in the meanest ways."

Marianne frowned. "That doesn't sound too nice."

"Nah, they are both pure wankers, but it's become a sport of sorts, ye know, to nag and jest."

"I see," Marianne said, all eyes on Faith, who was picking up her purse with a glance in my direction.

"Logan, I'm leaving. You can stay or come with me."

I instantly got up from the couch.

"Don't go, Faith," Chloe begged and followed Faith, tugging at her dress. "I'm truly sorry. I didn't mean it like that."

"Yes, you did mean it. You think I'm a whacko for holding on to Allan's memory."

"It's not what he would have wanted."

"How would you know?" Faith hissed.

"I feel it."

"Ha," Faith scoffed harshly. "And what are you, a medium now?"

"No, but maybe you should see one," Chloe retorted.

"Maybe I will," Faith said stubbornly. "And maybe she'll tell me to warn you against Niko, before he shoots you for real."

"Girls." Spencer held up a hand.

"No, Dad, I'm sick and tired of hearing about Chloe's psycho boyfriend." Faith turned back to Chloe, pointing a finger at her accusingly. "What happened to you? You used to be fun and confident. Now you're just sassy and whiny. It's pathetic," she yelled with unshed tears in her eyes.

I got the feeling that this had accumulated over time and was finally spilling out.

"I'm pathetic?" Chloe blinked. "Take a good look in the mirror, Faith. Everyone knows people who study psychology are really trying to fix themselves. Don't think you can fool me." Chloe pointed to me. "I bet Logan is one of your pet projects, isn't he?"

"What?" Faith narrowed her eyes. "I don't know what you're talking about."

"Look at him. He's as broken as you, and I bet you think you can fix him and feel really good about yourself."

"I'm not trying to fix him," Faith screamed.

"Of course you are! You want to help the whole damn world before you help yourself."

"I don't need help," Faith defended herself.

"You do," Chloe screamed back at her. "I love you but you're so screwed up you don't even realize it."

Faith was huffing with anger. "Oh, yeah? Well, at least I'm not the one doing drugs and locking myself in a closet because I'm scared of my boyfriend when he's high."

Chloe paled and looked at her parents. "It's not true – it wasn't drugs, just a bit of pot."

"Whatever!" Faith turned to me. "Let's go, I've had enough family time for today."

CHAPTER 12

Crying

Logan

I couldn't drive with all the alcohol I'd drunk, so we took a taxi home.

"Are ye okay?" I asked, knowing full well it was a stupid question to ask a crying woman. Clearly she was heartbroken

I thought about offering her a hug, but I didn't want to impose myself on her.

"I'm sorry," she sniffled.

"For what?"

"I'm sorry you had to witness us fighting. She's such a pest."

"Yer sister?" I said and squirmed uncomfortably in my seat.

"Yeah, she's so mean to me."

"Uh-huh." I thought it better to just agree with her, although, I had a feeling that Chloe actually worried about Faith, and was in her own misguided way trying to help.

"At least now you understand why I don't want to live in her apartment," she said.

"Aye."

She was quietly looking out the window. "I just want to go to bed,' she muttered to herself.

"I understand," I said softly and wondered what Mary would say in a situation like this. Mary always seemed to know what to say, at least to me.

We sat in the back seat of the dark taxi, looking out on the cold and wet streets, both of us deep in thought.

When we arrived at my apartment, I paid the driver and followed her upstairs.

Faith went straight to her own room and closed the door behind her, effectively shutting me out.

I sighed, wondering if Chloe had been right. Was I a "pet project" to Faith?

Something told me Chloe wasn't completely off target, and it would certainly explain Faith's bizarre behavior when she ran after me that night.

Did she see my scars and recognize me as a fellow wounded soul?

Was she drawn to me because of her need to fix me?

With a hand on the back of my neck, I rolled my head from side to side, trying to rid myself of the tension that would surely grow into a headache.

Women! Why did they have to be so complicated?

Mary, who was so easy to talk to but insisted on hiding behind the phone instead of meeting me in person.

Faith, who could pick any man she wanted, but was stuck in the past.

Chloe, who had men worshipping the ground she walked on and still chose to stay with a scumbag boyfriend.

There wasn't much I could do to help either one of them, I decided, and retreated to my office. At least in this domain I was in control.

I logged on to my computer, and answered the most urgent emails before I opened one of my favorite porn sites and typed "cheerleader" in the search bar. For a few minutes I scrolled through all the pictures of beautiful women in tiny uniforms.

Nothing!

It did nothing for me.

I didn't even press play to see the videos.

With a groan I rested my head in my hands. *Damn it,* my sexual fascination wasn't with cheerleaders. It was with Faith.

No matter how many times Mary had told me I wasn't a pervert for having these thoughts, I still felt like a creep when I unzipped and started fantasizing about Faith in her blue dress. On my internal movie screen she was asking me to make love to her, stripping out of her dress seductively, telling me how much she wanted to feel me inside her.

I came in record speed and sat for a few minutes contemplating why I hadn't fantasized about Chloe. After all, she'd been unbelievably hot in her outfit. Still, it was Faith I thought about.

$\langle \infty \rangle$

Faith

I stared at my phone.

Seven text messages from Chloe. All apologizing and asking me to call her back.

Her words kept looping through my mind.

She had called me out in front of Logan. Humiliated me by not only flirting shamelessly with him when I had specifically told her to go easy on him, but also by pointing out that I wanted to fix him.

Did he believe her? And if so, did he hate me now? Did he feel used?

I thought about calling him as Mary to ask him how he felt. But Mary was always happy and bubbly, and there was no way I could pull off playing joyous in my condition.

Chloe's hurtful words about Allan made me cry.

"You think I'm a whacko for holding on to Allan's memory," I had accused her.

"It's not what he would have wanted," she had told me. And maybe she was right.

"Allan," I whispered. "Tell me what to do. I miss you so much."

There was no answer.

There never was an answer.

By default, my fingers played with the necklace around my neck. It was the last gift Allan gave me and had been my anchor since his death.

"I wish you could talk to me," I whispered. "Just a small sign that you still love me."

But of course, nothing happened.

I was alone in my room.

Alone in my bed.

Allan couldn't make love to me. Chloe had been right about that part.

For hours, I tossed and turned, feeling sorry for myself.

It wasn't true that everyone who studied psychology was motivated by inner pain. I had chosen psychology before Allan died. Sure, a few of my classmates would fit Chloe's description, but far from all.

My frazzled thoughts kept me awake and I was thirsty. *I should brush my teeth*, I reminded myself. But the bathroom felt a mile away, and I wanted to stay under my warm covers where I was snug and warm. Besides, I always slept naked and if I left my room I would have to put on clothes again.

After another twenty minutes of overthinking everything, I couldn't ignore my need to relieve my bladder any longer.

Where is my long t-shirt? I searched my closet, but it wasn't there, and with my bladder pressing and me squeezing my pelvic muscles hard, I grabbed the best thing I could find: a long cardigan and a pair of panties.

It was ten past midnight and the apartment was dead silent. Logan had to be sleeping, since there was no light coming from the living room area or from under his bedroom door.

Still thirsty after my visit to the bathroom, I grabbed my phone to use as a flashlight, and tiptoed to the kitchen.

I cursed under my breath when the fridge shot out ice-cubes instead of water. *Shoot* – I needed to press the button to change it to water, but in the confusion ice cubes fell noisily to the floor and in my eagerness to press the right button, my phone flew out of my hand. *Geez, can I be any louder?*

I held my breath for a second, standing quietly in the darkness. The apartment was still quiet. *Phew...*

The screen on my phone was unbroken, and with the flashlight still on, I left it on the floor as a light source and focused on picking up the many ice cubes spread around the kitchen.

I was working quietly, placing the ice cubes in the sink and checking to see if there were more lying around, when I took a step back and accidently kicked at my phone.

My whole body stiffened as the light disappeared and I heard a skittering sound.

Scolding myself for being such a clumsy ox, I kneeled down, placed my face to the floor, and saw my phone all the way by the wall under the fridge.

"Shit!"

There was no way I could get my hand under the fridge, and even if I could, I wouldn't be able to reach that far. I had to find something long and thin, and started searching through the whole kitchen.

In my desperation I came up with an idea of using straws.

With my cheek pressed to the floor and my tongue sticking out in concentration I used two long tubes made of ten straws each.

"Come on," I muttered and managed to reach the phone and move it from side to side with the straws. This would be a game of patience and determination.

"What the hell?" The deep voice made me freeze to the spot.

Double shit!

Aware that I was on my knees with my ass in the air and that my cardigan didn't cover much, I closed my eyes and cursed inwardly. Logan couldn't hold this against me, could he? It's not like I'd purposely waltzed around him half naked.

Straightening up and sitting back on my heels, I looked up at him. "I'm sorry."

If Logan hadn't turned on the light already, I bet my flushed face would have lit up the entire room like Rudolph's red nose.

"What are ye doing down there?" he asked with wide eyes. He was wearing gray boxer briefs, revealing what I had suspected all along. Logan wasn't as buff as the football players I saw at the games. He looked more like a runner who was in good shape, with defined muscles and a flat stomach.

"Just cleaning," I croaked out, embarrassed.

"Cleaning? At this time?"

"No, of course not. Isn't it obvious that I'm trying to get something out from underneath the fridge?"

"Get what out?"

"My phone."

"Ohh." He was finally getting the picture. "Did ye do this on purpose?" he asked.

"Of course not," I cried out. "You think I push my phone under the fridge every night just hoping for you to walk in on me while I'm in the most compromising position possible?"

He shrugged. "Nah, probably not."

"Good, then go back to bed while I get it out."

"What are ye using?" he asked and moved closer.

"Straws," I said and showed him my homemade tools.

"Do ye mind if I take a look?"

I swung my hand to the fridge, "Be my guest."

Logan hesitantly squatted down next to me and lowered his face to the floor, bringing with him a pleasant scent of masculine perfume.

"I like yer idea with the straws," he said, and in my excitement that he was on board with my idea and had his eyes fixed on the phone, I resumed my task of getting the phone out.

"But I dinnae think that's going to work," he followed up dryly.

"It has to work; I need my phone."

"I have an idea that might work better," he said and moved away.

I stubbornly continued pushing at the phone with my tubes of straws, hoping to get it out before he returned.

"Let me try," he said a minute later and unfolded a wooden measuring stick that slid under the fridge without a problem.

"More to the left... no, you pushed it too far... this way," I ordered and received a grunt from him.

"I'm trying, but it's a bit hard to focus when I keep remembering how ye pushed yer naked ass in my face."

I scoffed, "It wasn't in your face, and I'm not naked. I'm wearing panties."

"More like a thong," he muttered.

"What?"

"Nothing." Logan kept fiddling with the measuring stick and was making progress.

"Yes... yes, that's it," I cheered on.

It took him a few more seconds and then my phone was out.

"Thank God," I said and leaned back on my haunches, shutting off the flashlight app on my phone. "Thank you so much for helping me ou–" I stopped talking when I saw Logan stare wide-eyed down at my breasts.

Shoot – my hands flew up to pull the cardigan together.

"I'm sorry," I said, remembering again how he had specifically asked me not to walk around half naked.

Logan swallowed hard enough to make his Adam's Apple bob in his throat. "No, I'm sorry, I shouldn't have... It's just that..." He nodded toward my chest, unable to complete a sentence.

I got up on my feet, ignoring the tent in his boxers. "Don't worry about it."

"Good night, Faith," he said behind me when I hurried to my room. *Oh my god, oh my god, oh my god,* I reproached myself. *How awkward was that?*

Tired but restless, I tossed and turned, haunted by my worries. The most current one was that Logan would kick me out for having broken his rule of walking around half naked.

I tried meditation, calm breathing exercises, and positive visualizations, but at 3:22 a.m. I was still awake.

That's when I got out my vibrator. Maybe an orgasm could help my body relax and fall asleep.

I thought about my handsome Highlander fantasy, but something was different. This time he didn't have dark hair and brown eyes. He was tall and strong as always, but he had blond hair, clear blue eyes, and scars that made him look rough and devilish sexy.

My eyes shot open and I sat up, panting a little. He was Logan. I didn't want him to be Logan.

I tried again, pinning my eyes closed and focusing on the Highlander of my dreams: the one I had seen on all the book covers, with long dark hair blowing in the wind.

Yes, it was working and my mind played out the fantasy I had shared with Logan. I could hear his magnificent accent and, bam, the Highlander was Logan again.

Annoyed and frustrated, I decided to listen to the advice I had given him. It was okay to fantasize about your roommate and it really didn't mean a thing. In fact, it was perfectly normal to fantasize about a fit and attractive man who lived in the same apartment with me.

There was nothing wrong with that... it didn't mean I actually *wanted* to have sex with him.

Absolutely not!

Content with my reasoning, I put the vibrator back in position and allowed the fantasy to play out with Logan as the primitive and rough Highlander who took me for his own.

It worked like a charm. My orgasm left me relaxed and I finally dozed off. My last conscious thought was that tomorrow I would do what I should have done a long time ago.

CHAPTER 13
Long Overdue

Faith

I remembered Violet's house from the day her brother, Christian, brought me to her birthday party. It wasn't hard to find.

As if she had expected me, Violet opened the door before I knocked.

"Faith," she said with a happy grin. "How nice to see you again."

She hadn't changed much and still had fine features and those incredibly warm brown eyes that I remembered. Only her dark hair was slightly shorter.

We hugged and she gestured me into her kitchen.

"Good thing that you came, Faith."

"What do you mean?"

"Your ex has been driving me crazy since last night. He's a stubborn type."

I gaped at her.

She confirmed the question I hadn't articulated. "Allan told me you were coming."

I bit my lip hard and my hands started shaking. "Allan is here?"

"Right there." Violet pointed behind me. "He has a message for you."

"He does?" My voice trembled.

"Yes." Violet took a seat at the table and I followed her example.

"Would you like some tea?" she asked.

"No…" I shook my head. I couldn't think of tea when Allan had a message for me.

Violet poured herself a cup and chatted away. "I've been hearing all about how he was stupid enough to drink and drive and how much he regrets it. He was going to see you that night, but you know that, right?"

I nodded, unable to find my voice.

"It's okay, Faith." Violet took both my hands in hers and looked deeply into my eyes. "But you need to listen carefully, okay?"

"Okay."

"Allan is asking you to let go."

"Let go?" I frowned.

"Yes. Let go of him," she said, squeezing my hands lightly and brushing her thumbs over my knuckles.

I pulled my hands back. "He would never say that."

Violet tilted her head sympathetically. "It's been seven years, sweetie, you need to move on."

"I know," I said dismissively. "But it's natural to grieve."

Violet nodded. "Yes, it is. But it's not healthy to get stuck in that grief."

"I can't love another," I argued.

"Of course you can. And you will... I'm sensing there is someone."

"No!" I exclaimed, horrified by her claim. "You're wrong. There's no one."

Violet sat back and observed me closely. "Then how come I see a bond between you and another man? Surely you must know this."

"There's no bond," I said dismissively. "And I sure as hell don't *love* another."

Violet wrinkled her forehead. "Hmm. I'm not going to argue with you, but Allan wants you to know that he approves of you moving on with this man."

"I have no idea what you're talking about."

She tilted her head. "Are you sure?"

"Yes, I think you're picking up on my roommate but we're not in a relationship."

"He's interested in you."

"Only sexually," I said quickly. "He told me so."

"And you?" she breathed out. "Are you attracted to him?"

I felt shame for having fantasized about Logan last night. *Does Allan know?*

"I asked you a question," Violet said quietly when I didn't answer her.

"No, I'm not attracted to him. Not that way, anyway... he's nothing like Allan."

"What do you mean?"

"Allan was outgoing, charming, and full of confidence. Logan is a hermit who suffers from anxiety, and his face is disfigured." God, I felt awful for saying that last part. His scars had never bothered me. I just didn't see him as a potential partner. I didn't see *anyone* that way.

"Faith," Violet said solemnly. "Why did you come today?"

My eyes welled up. "I was hoping to speak to Allan."

"Okay. And what would you like to say to him?"

"That I love him."

She reached over and took my hands again. "Oh, honey, he knows that, and he loves you too."

My voice broke. "He does?"

"Of course he does. He didn't want to leave you. You know that."

"Yes." I sniffled. "I know."

"Faith, Allan says that you need to remember *everything* and not just the good parts. He wasn't perfect, and it saddens him to see you build a wall around yourself."

"I haven't built a wall around myself. I'm very social."

"He's talking about love."

My shoulders sank.

"Sweetie, he's not coming back and you need to accept that."

"I know he's not coming back," I cried.

"So what are you waiting for?"

I couldn't answer that question.

"Allan wants you to be happy. Do you understand?"

I looked away.

"What do you want for Allan?" she asked quietly.

"I want him to be at peace," I whispered.

"But how can he be at peace when you're unhappy?"

Her words moved me. "What's it like?" I whispered. "On the other side?"

She looked past my shoulder and after a while she answered. "Allan says that it's beautiful and that you'll see for yourself when you pass over."

"Did he suffer when he died?" I asked.

Violet shook her head. "He says there was no pain. It happened so fast. But he regrets leaving you."

"Me too."

"He wants you to try."

"Try?"

"Try to be open to love."

I had to press the words pass my throat. "Okay, I'll try."

"Good."

"Violet?" I asked and looked down to hide the tears forming in my eyes.

"Yes?"

"Is Allan stuck here? Is that why you can talk to him? Did he miss his chance to go into the light because of my grief?"

"No, Faith." Violet shook her head softly. "Allan has passed on, but he watches over you from time to time."

"But how is that possible if he's in heaven? I don't understand."

121

"I don't think we're meant to understand. The afterlife is so different from what we know. For one, physical laws don't apply like here on earth and time isn't linear like we know it. It makes little sense to us before we cross over."

We continued talking for another half hour and I insisted on paying her for her services although she told me I didn't have to.

"So what part of what you heard today are you taking with you?" Violet asked when we hugged goodbye.

"That Allan loves me and wants me to move on and be happy with someone else," I said slowly.

She smiled. "That's right. Are you going to follow his advice?"

"I might go on a date or two. We'll see."

She smiled and stroked my arm. "Good, Faith, and remember, I'm always here if you need a friend."

"Thank you." From the first time I met Violet and felt the strong empathy that radiated from her, I knew she was special. She was quirky, but never sassy or pretentious.

"Right back at ya," I said and gave her a last hug before I left.

$\langle \infty \rangle$

I was cheering that Sunday night.

Century Link was filled to the brim with eager fans, and we won against Tampa Bay after a nail-bitingly close game.

We cheered our asses off. The fans were already fanatic, so the noise in the arena was deafening.

"You know Tyson is looking over here a lot, right?" my friend Marlene said with a wink.

My head flew to Tyson, the guy who had transferred from New Orleans in the beginning of last season.

"He's had the hots for you ever since he moved up here – you should give him a chance."

Tyson shot me a smile from the bench. He was a beautiful specimen of a Latino male with dark eyes and shoulder-long black hair. Although he was a giant in size he had the charming smile of a college kid.

"I can't, it's prohibited. I already told him no," I argued.

Marlene laughed. "Is that your excuse? Just keep it quiet like the rest of us."

"You dated a player?"

She held up two fingers and grinned. "Don't act surprised, I know they make us sign the agreement, but really, it's inevitable and management knows it."

She was right, there had been rumors of couples among the players and the cheerleaders, but officially there was a no-dating policy. According to my contract, I couldn't even date the mascot.

"He's too young anyway," I muttered.

"Girl, you've got the worst excuses. You're about the same age."

"I heard he was engaged," I said and took my position for the next cheer.

"Yeah, but they broke it off six months ago. She didn't want to move up here."

"Still," I said.

"Ohh, come on, Faith. That boy is delicious and you know it. Hell, his Creole accent alone would make most women drop their panties." Marlene raised her hands with her pompoms "Come on, Seahawks," she shouted.

When Tyson shot me another charming smile ten minutes later, I smiled back. And when he found me after the game and discreetly asked me out, I looked up at the giant and narrowed my eyes.

"How many times have you asked me?"

He grinned. "You can't blame a guy for being persistent. I'm a fighter, and we never give up."

Follow the fighter with the accent.

Violet's advice popped up again. Maybe Tyson was the person Violet had spoken about at the party. Marlene was right, Tyson had the most amazing Creole accent, and I supposed he was sort of a modern-day fighter. Football was a rough sport, after all.

I tilted my head. "You know I'm not allowed to say yes."

"I know," he said and looked over his shoulder. "But no one has to know about it. We could be secret rebels," he coaxed.

I shook my head with a grin. "I'm no man's secret."

"Hey, that's not fair chère. I would take you out and flash you on my arm for the whole world to see, if I could. You know I would." He looked around us, making sure we were alone and then he stepped closer, touching my shoulders. "Faith, you're the most beautiful girl on the squad, and I really want to be with you."

"You don't know me."

"No, but that's what I'm saying. I want to get to know you."

"Why?"

He grinned. "Because I'm attracted to you. I t'ought I made that clear."

"I'll think about it."

"At least give me your number," he pleaded and when I gave in, he left with my phone number and a huge smile on his face. "I'm calling you tonight and persuading you to hang out with me, you know that, right?"

"Don't get your hopes up." I called after him and watched him walk away with his helmet tucked under his arm, and his tight blue pants revealing a firm behind.

"Hey, Faith," Tyson turned and looked back at me.

"What?" I asked.

"I'm a really cool guy, you really should give me a chance."

I smiled. *Maybe I should. After all, Allan wanted to me to move on.*

CHAPTER 14

In Love

Logan

When my phone rang I picked up quickly.

"Hello."

"Hey, handsome, it's me, Mary."

A smiled spread on my face and I leaned back in my office chair. "Mary, why haven't ye called me?" I said and instantly regretted blaming her.

She didn't seem to take offence, but chuckled. "It's only been a few days, darlin'."

"It's been five long days. We spoke last Wednesday, and today is Monday."

"Did ya miss me?"

"Aye, I did."

"Why? I thought you were much too busy with work, and your roommate, to talk to me," she teased.

"I'm never too busy to talk to ye," I flirted back. "How was yer Thanksgiving?"

"Fine, I went home to Georgia and celebrated with my family. How 'bout you?"

"I had my first American Thanksgiving. Faith invited me to join her and her family."

"Oh, that's nice, and how did it go?" Mary sounded serious.

"Her parents are really nice and the food was good," I started and trailed off.

"But?" she asked.

"It's just that Faith and her sister got into a massive fight and we left abruptly. I didnae like to see her so upset."

"You have brothers; don't you guys ever fight?"

"Of course, it's not that." Spinning my pencil on the desk in front of me, I said, "It's just that she cried, Mary, and I didnae know how to help her."

"What do you mean?"

"I felt powerless and didnae know what to say or do."

"Did you hug her?"

"Nah"

"Why didn't you try to console her?"

I sighed. "I should have, but sometimes I freeze up around her. I was afraid she wouldnae like it if I gave her a hug."

"Next time a woman cries, Logan, offer her a hug. The worst that can happen is that she says 'No thank you.'"

"That's easy for ye to say. But me and Faith… it's complicated."

"Why?"

"She makes me do and say stupid things. I get so fucking nervous around her. I think I offended her the other day."

"Okaaay…" she said, drawn out. "What makes you think that?"

I sighed, "Och, Mary, she's the most beautiful woman. I'm so screwed."

"Why?"

"On Thanksgiving night, I had gone to sleep and then I woke up and found her in the kitchen. You willnae believe the sight that met me."

Mary was quiet.

"The lass was on her knees, her head down and her ass in the air. I thought I was dreaming."

"But you weren't."

"Nah, she was trying to get her phone out from underneath the fridge.

"Poor woman." Mary said. "That must have been humiliatin' to her."

"I dinnae know if she did it on purpose. I'm so confused, Mary. Do ye think she was trying to test me somehow?"

"No, Logan, I don't think so. It sounds like an accident."

"She's been avoiding me since then. That's why I think I offended her, because I told her it was hard to focus with her flashing her bare ass in my face."

"She's prob'ly just embarrassed."

"Hmm." I grunted. "The cheerleader fantasies were bad enough, but now..." I gave a deep sigh.

"They're just fantasies," Mary reminded me.

"I know, but still, I'm not sure living with Faith is healthy for me. I'm thinking about telling her to find a new place."

"No!" Mary said adamant. "Don't do that."

"Why not?"

"Because... because it's good for you to have a female around. Don't you think?"

"Nah. I was already struggling with the image of her in her uniform, but now that I've seen her almost naked, I can't stop thinking about it. I wish I could un-see it."

"Why?"

"Because I feel like a bloody schoolboy, way out of my league.

"With Faith?"

"Aye, it's bad, Mary. She's pure physical perfection."

"You said she fought with her sister?" Mary asked me.

"Aye, she has a twin sister and they don't agree on much."

"What did they fight about?"

"This and that. Her sister thinks Faith is trying to fix me."

"Really?"

"Uh-huh." I put my feet up on my desk and leaned back in my seat. "I think she's right."

128

"You think Faith is tryin' to fix you?"

"Aye, it makes perfect sense. Remember I told you how Faith ran after me that night at the bar?"

"Yeah."

"It made no sense then – I mean, who does that? But with what her sister said, I'm thinking that she was drawn to me because of my scars." I paused. "She saw me as a wounded soul and wanted to help, ye see?"

"And has she? Helped you, I mean."

"Nah, I dinnae think so."

"Really? You wouldn't say that she's helped you at all?"

"She does a fine job with the house chores."

"That's it?"

"Aye. Why do you sound like that?"

"I don't know what you mean. All I know is that as your friend I'm telling you not to give up. You need to get over your anxiety around women. And I think Faith is helping you do that."

"Maybe, but I dinnae see her very often."

"But, Logan, you seem much more relaxed around me. I thought she was part of the reason."

"Nah, I think that's all you, Mary." My voice lowered. "Can I be honest with you, lass?"

"Of course. You know you can."

"I think about you a lot. Like *a lot*, Mary."

"Aww, that's sweet," she said and chuckled.

"No, I mean it. I wonder what ye look like and how it would be to be close to ye. I want to lie on a bed and talk to ye like this, play with yer hair and stroke yer arm."

"I told you," Mary said quietly. "I'm chubby and nothin' special."

"Ye're special to me," I said.

"But you always talk about Faith's perfection. I can't live up to that."

129

"I'm sorry, lass. But I thought ye knew that I'm not looking for physical perfection. Faith is like her sister. They're like celebrities. Ye know, something from a magazine... unreal and untouchable."

"Do you fantasize about her sister too?" There was something in Mary's voice that warned me she wouldn't like to hear it.

"Nah," I said honestly. "I'll admit that I'm physically attracted to Faith because I'll never lie to ye, but her sister is different."

"Why?"

"She's a bit intimidating, to be honest."

"Intimidatin' how?"

"Och, I dunno. You can tell she's used to getting her will and she speaks like a bloody Sassenach. It's stupid."

"A Sassenach?"

"An English person. She speaks like the English queen, but I dinnae ken that she's ever been to England."

"So you like Faith better?"

"Uh-huh, but I like you the best," I said and smiled. "Please give me yer number?" I asked and added an extra "Please."

Mary laughed a little. "Logan, my handsome Scot, I love talkin' to you, but I don't want to lose what we have. If you saw me, our friendship would be over."

"What do ye take me for?" I asked offended. "What aren't ye telling me?"

"I told you, I'm not your type," Mary said with a small chuckle.

"Send me a picture and let me judge for myself," I said firmly. "Listen, Mary, I've known ye for five weeks and we've spoken for hours and hours. I more than like ye. Dinnae ye get that?" My heart was beating fast.

"I like you too, Logan," Mary said in her charming Southern accent. "Why do you think I call you?"

"Then meet with me. Let us take it a step further."

"I can't."

I frowned. "It's because of my scars, is it not?" I asked.

"No, why would you think that?"

"Because I keep telling ye that I don't care how ye look and yet ye refuse me. Are ye married?"

"No, Logan, that's not it."

"Are ye in a different country? Why will ye not meet me?"

"I'm here in Seattle like you."

"Then meet with me," I pleaded.

"Please stop askin' me. I don't like to refuse you."

I wanted to scream in frustration.

"Logan,"

"Aye, what is it?"

"Let's not argue. Why don't we play instead?"

I rubbed my face. "What do ye wanna play?"

"Where are you?" she asked.

"In my office, at home."

"Okay, why don't you imagine Faith knockin' on your door, asking if she can come in."

"I don't know, Mary." I closed my eyes. "I'm not sure I'm in the mood for…"

"Can I come in, Logan?" Mary asked.

I sighed.

"Can I?" she asked.

"Aye, come in," I said.

"I brought you some cookies. Thought you might want to try my bakin'."

"Thank ye."

"Does your neck hurt? Why are you rollin' your shoulders like that" Here, let me give you a quick neck rub." Mary said amorously. "It's easier if you take off your shirt. Do you have some lotion I can use?"

"Uh-huh."

"Wow, Logan, you're really tense. Relax. Do you like it when I touch you here?"

131

"Aye." I had my eyes closed and envisioned the scene in my head. "That feels good."

"You do so much for me, Logan, I'm happy to give you a massage – close your eyes and lean your head back against me."

"All right."

"Do you feel how your head is resting against my cleavage and my hands are slidin' under your shirt, playing with your chest hair?"

"Aye." I opened my pants and started stroking myself.

"How about ye, Faith, do ye need a massage too?" I asked.

"Actually? I do have an ol' injury that still bothers me a bit, but I can't ask you to massage me there."

"Why not? I'm good at it. Where is your injury?"

"My inner thigh," Mary said slowly.

"Okay, then maybe ye could sit back on my desk and let me help ye?"

"You don't mind?"

"Nah, not at all. Come, sit right here in front of me."

"Like this?"

"Yes, exactly. Do you mind if I lift your skirt?"

"No, I'm sorry, I didn't have time to change out of my uniform."

"That's okay, I like yer uniform. Can ye point to your injury?"

"It's there, on my right inner thigh."

"Here,"

"Higher. It's here."

"How did ye get this injury?"

"I did a split without warmin' up. Oh, that feels good," Mary moaned a bit. "Yes, use your hands."

I smiled. "I am using my hands. Do ye feel how I'm letting my hands slide up along the seam of yer white panties?"

Mary gave a confirming moan. "But that's too high, Logan."

"No, it's not. You want this."

"Noo," she said weakly.

"Aye. Spread yer legs wider and let me pleasure ye."

"But we shouldn't. You're my roommate, Logan," Mary whispered.

"It's just sex, Faith, we both need it," I whispered back. "Feel how I'm pushing ye down on my desk and removing your panties."

"Yes."

"Do ye like my tongue licking your clit, and my fingers moving in and out of ye?"

"Yes, I do," Mary moaned.

"What do ye want, Faith?" I asked, imagining the real Faith on my desk, ready to be fucked.

"I want you inside me," she breathed.

"Good." I grunted and kept my eyes closed, imagining sliding inside her. "God, it feels good to be inside ye."

"Harder," she whispered.

"Yes…. Tell me if it's too rough for ye."

"It feels so good." My hand worked up and down my shaft and my breathing was ragged.

"Mary… it's so good," I breathed.

Mary's breathing was heavy too. "Faith – remember I'm Faith, Logan."

"Yes, Faith," I repeated, but something was shifting. I saw a chubby dark-haired woman with Faith's sweet smile in front of me. This was how Mary looked in my mind. A warm and sensual woman. I wanted to make love to this woman. Mary.

"Fuck, yes… Come for me, Mary," I moaned and couldn't hold back any longer. Only a few more strokes and I could feel my sack tightening, my balls ready to fire.

"I'm coming, Mary."

"Yes, come, Logan, oh, yes."

When I was done panting and opened my eyes, I cursed that I had spilled my seed on my shirt.

"What's wrong?" Mary asked out of breath.

"Och, I came on my shirt."

"So?"

"Faith does the laundry. She's gonna think me an adolescent schoolboy for spilling on my clothes."

"Why did you call me Mary? I thought we agreed I was playin' Faith."

"I dunno what happened, but something changed."

"What changed?"

"I started seeing ye in front of me. Not her."

"But you don't know what I look like."

"Nah, but I saw a sexy chubby woman with dark hair and a beautiful smile in front of me. That's how I see ye."

Mary was quiet.

"You would rather have sex with me than Faith?"

"Aye, it's the truth. There's something more with ye. Something I can never have with her."

"You don't know that."

"Aye, I know. The connection we have is special, Mary. Don't ye think?"

"Yes."

I rubbed my forehead and took a deep breath. "I think I'm starting to see ye as my..."

"What?" she exclaimed.

"As more than my friend – is that bad?" I asked, afraid she would find me too much.

"Logan, you don't even know me."

"But I do know ye. And I have feelings for ye."

Mary spoke in a low incredulous tone, "I don't know what to say."

I swallowed hard. "Say that ye have feelings for me too."

"Logan, I..."

I waited for her to continue with a lump in my throat.

"It's complicated. I mean I like you, a lot…"

"But just not that way?" I asked quietly, already feeling my emotional shutters close down.

"Logan… I'm not goin' to deny that I love talkin' to you. You're special to me, but I want you to find a real girlfriend. That's what I want for you."

If Mary could have seen my face, she would have seen a hard expression form – the same expression I had seen on my father's face whenever emotions threatened to make him look weak.

"Okay, whatever ye say, Mary."

CHAPTER 15
Desperation

Logan

My skull was splitting in two from the pressure of feelings I didn't know how to cope with.

Rationally, I felt humiliated for having told Mary how I felt about her only to be rejected. Hell, allowing myself to feel that way in the first place was stupid.

Getting close to women only meant pain. I should have learned that by now.

Sad and grumpy to my core, I worked through Tuesday and even though Faith was home that night, I kept to myself.

Sure, reclusiveness was lonely, but at least I was safe from rejection.

On Wednesday afternoon, a man suddenly walked into my office. His black suit made him stand out in an office where the "uniform" was typically jeans, t-shirts, and sneakers.

"Are you Logan McKay?" he asked rather formally.

"I am, and who might you be?"

He moved closer and lowered his voice. "I represent someone who requests a private meeting with you."

"Who?"

"If you'll come with me, everything will be explained."

With a slow motion, I leaned back in my chair and tilted my head. "That sounds like a line from a bad movie. Just spit it out, man."

The man rose up to his full height, which was substantial, and gave me a scowl. "All I can tell you is that my employer is waiting for you five minutes from here."

I stood up too. With my six foot one, he was taller than me, but I wasn't prepared to let someone boss me around in my own office. "Listen, ye can tell yer boss that if he wants to meet with me, he's free to contact me for an appointment, but if it's about a job, I'm not interested."

"It's not about a job."

"Then what is it about?"

"I honestly don't know," the man said with a small shrug. "My job is simply to fetch you."

"Fetch me?" I scoffed. "Forget it. I'm not going anywhere with ye until ye tell me whom I'm meeting with."

He gave this some thought and then he pulled out a phone. "Let me see if my employer has further instructions."

"By all means." I swung out a hand as if to say "Do your thing," And then I sat back down again.

"Mr. McKay refuses to go until he knows your identity." The suit spoke into the phone, and ten seconds later he handed it to me. "Here you go, sir."

I was a bit annoyed with this intrusion, but mostly curious to know why someone would make such a secret out of meeting with me.

"Hello," I said and held the phone to my ear.

"Logan, it's me, Cleo. I need you to come meet me."

I frowned. "Why can't ye just come here?"

"Because I can't. Stop being so difficult and get your butt down here. We need to talk." She hung up.

With an annoyed puff of air, I got up and followed the suit down the elevator and out of the building.

Only a block away he stopped outside a small laundromat and spoke a few words with a black guy who looked like another security guard.

"She's waiting inside," he said and held the door open for me.

With a raised eyebrow I stepped inside to see the world's most glamourous Hollywood star sitting on a table used to fold clothes, her head down and her phone in her hand.

I cleared my throat, which made her look up.

"Finally. Took you long enough." She placed the phone on the table and jumped down to walk to me.

"Why are we meeting here?" I asked and scanned the empty washing machines and dryers.

"Because of the paparazzi of course." She pointed to the tinted windows that provided a shield from nosy pedestrians. "They can't see us here."

I scrunched up my face.

"I desperately needed to talk to you, but if we met in a public place they would spin it to make Niko jealous. They do it all the time to provoke him, you know."

"Who are *they*?"

She rolled her eyes. "The media. They know Niko has anger issues, and they always try to make it look like I'm seeing men behind his back to get a reaction from him. It's cruel, really."

"All right, but what do ye want from me?"

"You need to talk to Faith for me."

I took a step back. "I dinnae want to meddle in her affairs."

"You have to. She's been avoiding me and won't pick up her phone."

"Give her time," I suggested.

"I have. It's been a week."

"So? A week isnae that long."

"It is for Faith. She never holds a grudge for that long." Cleo was starting to tear up. "She's really angry with me and I don't think you understand. She's my twin, Logan."

"But what do ye want me to do about it?" I asked, confused.

"Talk to her. She likes you."

"We're not that close, and I don't thi–"

Cleo cut me off. "You live with my sister, surely you can talk to her for me," she pleaded with teary eyes.

Uncomfortable, I shifted my weight from one foot to the other. Was I supposed to offer her a hug?

"Please," she said and moved closer.

"Even if I talk to her, what makes ye think she'll listen to me?" I asked and when her tears continued, I stroked her arm a little. "Please dinnae cry."

"She might not listen. She's so *angry* with me." Cleo cried. "But you have to try... promise that you'll try."

"What do ye want me to say to her?" I asked.

"I want you to tell her to stop ignoring me."

I shook my head slightly. "I'll tell her that, but I really dinnae think it'll make much difference."

"Thank you, Logan." Cleo gave me a fierce hug; her lovely perfume and soft hair engulfed my senses. "You're a good guy," she said, pressing a kiss to my cheek.

I stood stiffly for a second before I patted her clumsily on her back, and muttered, "Thank you."

"It's best if you don't tell Faith that we met," she warned me with her face turned up toward mine.

"All right," I answered, still tense from her closeness.

"You know," she said and tilted her head. "You have beautiful eyes, Logan, I bet you were gorgeous before the accident." Her fingers slid down the good side of my face. "It's ironic in a way..." she said and paused.

I didn't answer her but stood stiff as a statue, all my anxiety flaring to life with her touching me and assessing me.

"Faith always had a thing for smart guys like you, I really think you would have been her type." She sighed. "Such a shame, really."

Before I knew it, she rose up on her toes and planted a loud kiss on my lips. It startled me and in reaction, I pushed her away.

"What's wrong?" she asked perplexedly. "It was only a little kiss."

I frowned and dried off my lips with the back of my hand. I didn't need or want her pity.

"I'll tell Faith to stop ignoring ye, but in the future I'll have ye keep me out of yer affairs. I don't have time for this."

"Thank you, Logan," Chloe called out as I left the shop.

I didn't look back or answer her.

$$\langle \infty \rangle$$

Faith

As I biked home from work, my head was full of questions.

Have I unintentionally hurt Logan by talking to him for hours as "Mary"?

How can he fall in love with a voice only? Aren't men supposed to be visual?

Why do I feel disappointed that he prefers sex with Mary instead of me? It's ridiculous. It's like being jealous of your alter ego. How bizarre.

Isn't it a good thing that he's able to open up and love again?

If only I can help him channel that love to someone else, but who?

And what's up with him being so dismissive of me, saying that I'm not girlfriend material? I would be the best damn girlfriend in the world. I'm fun, and down to earth, and loving. Surely, he would be lucky to have me as a girlfriend.

Then there's Tyson. What am I going to do about Tyson? I like his long dark hair, and his confidence. He's like an older version of Allan, really, and he's not as broken as Logan. Should I hang out with Tyson? And if I did...

I heard the screeching brakes of the car only a split second before it hit me from the rear.

CHAPTER 16
Injured

Logan

It was the sound of a man's voice that made me raise my head from my computer.

"Logan, are you here?" Faith called from the entryway.

I got up and moved to see what the commotion was about. What I saw made me frown.

"Hey, man, are you Logan?" A huge Hispanic guy was carrying Faith in his arms.

"Who are you?" I asked.

"This is Tyson, he's a friend of mine and kindly offered to help me home from the hospital."

"Hospital?" My eyes scanned her, finding small cuts and bruises on her hands and face, but the biggest thing was the boot thingy on her foot. "What happened?"

"An idiot ran me down on my bike. I sprained my ankle badly and two of my ribs were pressed." She looked devastated.

"Where's your room?" Tyson asked.

"Oh, I'm sorry, am I heavy?" Faith asked. "You can set me down, it's fine."

Tyson grinned and tightened his grip on Faith. "Not a chance. I could hold you all day, babe."

"It's that way," I muttered and pointed to Faith's room.

Not only was Tyson half a head taller than me – and I was in no way a small man – but he also filled the doorway with his wide shoulders as he carried Faith to her room.

I followed and stood in her doorway watching him place her on her bed.

"Thank you, Tyson, I'm good now," she said.

"No problem. Do you need me to help you undress or anyt'ing?" Tyson winked at her.

"No, I can manage, but thank you again. I appreciate it."

"Okay, beautiful," he said with the charm laid on thick. "I'll call you tomorrow."

"Sure." Faith smiled at him.

As Tyson passed me, he smacked a hand on my shoulder. "Nice to meet you, Logan," he said and leaned in to whisper, "Take good care of my girl for me, will ya?"

His girl? My eyes flew to Faith, but she was bent over her ankle and didn't seem to have heard him.

"Are you in pain?" I asked her.

"No, they gave me some pain relief at the hospital. I'm just pissed at the driver. The idiot was texting; he completely destroyed my bike."

My brows furrowed. "Screw yer bike, what about yer ankle?"

Faith sighed. "The doctor said there's a grade two sprain, and that means four to six weeks of healing." Her voice grew thick with emotion. "There's no more dancing for me this season. I'm fucked. I *need* the money, Logan."

"Won't the driver's insurance compensate you somehow?"

"I don't know." She placed her head in her hands for a second and then looked up at me. "It all sucks."

"Aye, it does." I watched her slender body on her bed. She looked young and fragile with her mascara slightly smeared. I wanted to help, but wasn't sure how.

"Are ye hungry, lass?"

"No, just thirsty and sad."

"I'll be right back."

143

She thanked me when I returned with a large glass of water.

"Ye're welcome."

While she drank I took a deep intake of air, suppressing my curiosity about Tyson; it was none of my business.

Faith wiped her mouth with the back of her hand. "What is it, Logan? Is something wrong?"

"Nah, I just dinnae know ye had a boyfriend."

"Oh, you mean Tyson. He just happened to call me when I was done at the hospital and when I told him what happened he offered to give me a ride home."

"So he's a friend?"

"Yeah." She yawned. "Something like that."

"It's late. Ye should try to get some sleep, and hopefully by tomorrow it'll all look better," I suggested.

"You're right. I'm super tired anyway, and the doctor did warn that the pills would make me drowsy." Her words came out in another loud yawn.

"Do you need my help?" I offered, but she shook her head.

"All right. Good night, Faith. Call if you need me," I said and closed her door.

Ten minutes later, I heard her call my name and hurried to see what had her yelling like that.

"What is it?" I asked her and wrinkled my brow when I saw her on the floor – her face red, her hair tousled, and a shirt hanging skewed around her neck.

"I can't do it."

In a long stride, I was at her side and knelt down. "Let me help ye."

"Everything hurts. I can't lift my arms, just breathing hurts, and it's like my lungs are too small."

"It's your pressed ribs?" I said sympathetically.

Tears welled up in her eyes. "I don't need this shit. I don't have time for it" she cried.

"I know, Faith. Just tell me what ye need."

She looked down in defeat. "Can you help me get this shirt off?"

Gently I lifted it off her. "What about yer tank top, do ye want it off too?" I felt my heart pump faster and my neck flame up from her closeness and the prospect of undressing her further.

Faith took a deep breath. "No, I'll just sleep in it. But I need to brush my teeth," she said softly and looked up at me. "Will you help me to the bathroom?"

"Of course," I said softly and helped her up.

"I'm so sorry, Logan, I don't like to be an inconvenience," she mumbled and leaned against me. "You know, my friend Tina has crutches from the time she had a knee injury and I'm planning on borrowing them."

"The hospital didn't offer you crutches?"

"They did. But my co-payment is pretty high, and I'm not sure if the driver's insurance is paying or if it's on me, so I declined in order to keep the costs down."

"All right, then I'll be your crutches tonight," I said firmly.

"Thank you," she whispered and dried a tear away.

Seeing her so vulnerable pulled at my heartstrings. It had to be a real blow for Faith, who was the poster girl of strong and independent.

I waited for her outside the bathroom and when she was ready to go back, I supported her again. I thought about carrying her like Tyson had, but I figured it would only make her feel more helpless.

"The medicine," she muttered when I got her back to her bed. "The doctor told me to take two pills before going to bed."

"Where are they?"

"In my backpack." She pointed to the floor where Tyson had placed it. "The front pocket."

She had already crawled under her covers when I handed her the pills and the glass of water from her side table. "I wish I could sleep and not wake up until everything is fine again," she said.

My brows creased. "I dinnae blame you. I've been there myself."

Faith placed two pills on her tongue and washed them down with a large sip of water. I was just about to leave when she caught my hand and made me turn to her again.

"Won't you stay for a little while?" she asked and patted the bed beside her.

I blinked in confusion. I had helped her to the bathroom, she had taken her medicine – and didn't she just say that she wanted to sleep? *Why does she want me to stay?*

"All right," I sat down a bit stiffly.

"Thank you, Logan." Her head was on the pillow and she looked tired. "When you said that you've been here, do you mean after the accident?"

I nodded.

"Were you different before the accident?"

"I was."

"Were you funny?" She gave me a tired smile.

"I'm still funny," I said but realized she'd never seen that side of me.

She was polite enough to not disagree. Instead she took my hand. "Logan?"

"Aye."

A tear streamed down her nose. "Today has been a really shitty day for me."

I squeezed her hand and gave her a look of sympathy.

"I know you don't like physical touch much." She used her blanket to dry the tears from her face. "But would you hold me until I fall asleep?"

"Aye, if you want me to, I will."

"I want you to." She moved over on the queen-sized bed and lifted the covers.

"How do you want me to hold ye?" I asked nervously.

"Could we spoon?"

I wanted to say no. If I spooned with her there was about a hundred percent chance that I would get hard, and that would be extremely awkward for both of us.

"Please," she said and like an idiot I nodded and lay down behind her.

"I'm sorry, I can't." She rolled toward me. "It hurts when I'm on my left side." For a second we were face to face and it almost took my breath away how beautiful she was in her fragile state.

"Ehm, okay," I swallowed hard. "Then what would you like?"

"When I was with Allan," she whispered. "I used to cuddle up and place my head on his naked chest."

Her eyes were boring into mine. "I know you're not him, and we're not..."

I waited for her to continue.

"But would you mind if I used your chest as my pillow?" she asked and bit her lip.

When I didn't answer quick enough, she added, "Just until I fall asleep, that is."

"You want me to take off my shirt?" I asked quietly.

"Yes, please," she whispered.

With my heart in my throat I took off my shirt and lay back down, lifting my arm to make room for Faith.

Like a small child seeking comfort and protection, she cuddled up against me, her arm over my stomach, her head on my shoulder.

"What is that?" I asked and dug under the pillow to pull out the hard object.

"Ohh, I'm sorry, it's just a book I'm reading. You can just put it on the nightstand."

Turning the book in the air I read the title. "*The Laird and His Enemy's Daughter.*" That made me chuckle.

"What's so funny," she asked.

"Don't tell me you read Highlander novels too?"

"So what if I do?"

"Do all American women read this nonsense? I have a friend who reads this stuff too."

"Historical fiction is a huge genre, and I learn a lot from those books."

"Like what?"

"Like historical things... you know, the wars between England and Scotland, the rules and laws of that era, and the culture too. I could tell you a lot about your ancestors and the way they lived." She yawned again.

"And I suppose they are all flawless people with fairytale lives?" I asked.

"No, that would be boring. They have to go through challenges and defeat enemies in order to survive."

"Right." I looked at the cover, where a couple looked lovingly at each other. "But at least they're beautiful."

"That's how they're described."

"Doesn't that bother you?"

"What? That they're beautiful?"

"Aye, it's not very realistic, is it? We can't all be gorgeous."

Faith turned to look at me. "I don't think they are. But we're seeing them through the eyes of a person falling in love with them. Freckles, soft curves, and a crooked tooth can be described as charming. It all depends on the perspective we hear it from."

"Good point."

"Like in this book, the laird has an eternal scowl and at first the young women find him terrifying, but later she begins to see his scowl and scars as something that makes him look roguishly handsome."

I snorted and she yawned for the tenth time.

After reading the back cover, I placed the book on the nightstand with a shake of my head.

Faith relaxed against me and had her eyes closed. I wanted to breathe normally and act like this was nothing special, but it wasn't easy.

"Thank you," she muttered drowsily.

I didn't answer her, nor did I move a muscle. But on the inside of my skull, my brain was running around in circles, analyzing the heat from her body, the fragrance of her perfume, the softness of her skin against my skin, and her slow breathing telling me that she had already fallen asleep. At least she had no idea I was battling my body's response to her feminine presence. Thank God, she hadn't insisted on spooning.

I stayed with her, listening to her steady breathing, and lifted my right hand to brush a strand of hair from her face. She was close enough for me to kiss her.

I thought about my erotic fantasies of loving her in her sleep. In real life the idea of violating her in her drugged state was repulsive.

Placing a protective kiss on the top of her hair, I caressed her shoulder with lazy strokes, feeling deeply honored by her unconditional trust in me.

Faith made a breathy sound that sounded like "Allan."

No doubt, she was cuddling with the love of her life in her dreams. I was merely a prop.

Placing a hand above my eyes, I forced myself not to care.

I'll just use Faith as a prop too, I thought and imagined a cute chubby brunette pressing herself against me.

"Mary," I whispered and kissed her hair again, letting my mind imagine the impossible: a loyal woman loving me fiercely and passionately.

Of course, Mary hadn't called back since I told her I had feelings for her. The list of possible reasons why she didn't want to meet with me was long and painful to go over.

Before I fell asleep that night, I made myself a promise. I would find out Mary's identity one way or another.

CHAPTER 17

Roses

Faith

The sound of my phone ringing woke me up. Reaching for the phone on my side table made me wince in pain and then I remembered my strained ankle, pressed ribs, and broken bike. *Shit!*

As I fumbled with the phone, it slid out of my hand and fell to the floor. Before I got it up to my ear, it had stopped ringing.

Great! Five unanswered calls from Chloe.

I would have to call her back today. Her behavior last week was still bothering me, but we were twins after all.

With a deep exhalation, I rested my head on my pillow again, needing a minute to get my head together.

That smell.

I pressed my nose deeper into the pillow, inhaling the masculine fragrance of Logan. God, it smelled good and brought up feelings of comfort and safety. Falling asleep in his arms yesterday had felt wonderful.

The smile that spread on my lips just from thinking about it quickly faded when confusion hit me.

Am I falling in love with Logan?

Surely not! If I were to have a boyfriend again, shouldn't it be someone confident and outgoing like myself? With all his quirks and insecurities, Logan wasn't my type at all.

Clearly, my feelings were merely a sign that I'd become too invested – a beginner's mistake that was common in psychology.

"Keep your head straight, Faith," I whispered and turned my head to see a note on the side table.

Faith,
I had to leave for an important meeting in the office, but I'll be home no later than three. Text me if you need anything.

Logan

PS: You'll find two of my golf clubs beside your bed. I'm hoping they'll make it easier for you to move around. Please be careful though!

I looked down to find two golf drivers on the floor. *How thoughtful of him.*

After making a round of calls to spread the sad news about my condition to my two bosses and my parents, I called Tina, who promised to stop by with her old crutches.

My body was sore and my movements slow, but with determination I managed to wash myself, brush my teeth, get dressed, and make myself breakfast before I took a seat on the couch to spend the day studying.

I was still firmly planted on the couch when Logan came back around three o'clock, carrying with him a bag of groceries.

"I see ye got the crutches," he said with a small smile.

"Yes, Tina stopped by."

"And how are ye feeling today?"

"Like I got hit by a car," I said dryly, and looked down at my vibrating phone. "It's Chloe – she keeps calling me."

"Maybe ye should answer her then."

My gaze lifted to follow Logan's movements as he unpacked the groceries in the kitchen. With the open floor plan, I could see him well enough from the couch in the living room and with my brows creased, I turned the volume on the TV down a bit.

"Why do you care?" I asked.

"She's yer sister.'

"And?"

"And everyone makes mistakes," he said and moved closer to look at the weather report that was showing on KIRO 7, the local news station.

I kept quiet for a while, pondering his words. "You don't know half of the shitty things she's done to me over the years," I said quietly. "Why do I always have to be the bigger one?"

Logan spun around to face me. "The bigger one?" he said with deep frown lines. "I thought the bigger one meant taking the first step. How many times has she called ye?"

"You wouldn't understand."

"What wouldnae I understand?" he asked and came to sit on a chair next to me.

I fiddled with the strings on my hoodie and pursed my lips downward. "With Chloe it's always drama and always about *her*. And the last two years with Niko has changed her for the worse." My hands brushed back my hair from my face, gathering the blond locks in a knot. Without a hairband my hair fell down the minute I let go, but there was something calming about letting my fingers play with it. "To be honest, I hardly recognize my sister anymore. Trust me, Niko might be worshipped by millions of raving fans, but the man is a psychopath. Chloe's relationship with him is so toxic and unhealthy that just hearing about it makes me sick. I know this sounds horrible, Logan, but lately I can only stand to be around my twin in small doses."

"If he's so toxic, dinnae you think she needs ye more than ever?" Logan asked calmly.

"I'm not sure," I said quietly. "Our relationship is dysfunctional as well. You saw it for yourself... the fighting between us."

Sadness marred his face when he leaned back in his armchair and looked out the window. "I never fought with Patricia," he said softly.

"Your sister?"

"Aye."

"But she was eight years younger than you, maybe that's why."

"Aye, maybe. But you know what?"

"What?"

"I would give anything to talk to her again. Even if it meant fighting with her, because if I could do that, she wouldnae be dead, would she?"

I cleared my throat. Emotions caught in my chest. "Okay, good point. I'll call Chloe."

"Good," Logan got up from the chair. "Let me make ye a cuppa. My mum says tea always helps."

"You talk very fondly of your mom; I'd like to meet her one day."

"Aye, my mum is a good woman," Logan said while filling the kettle with water. When the doorbell rang he looked back at me. "Are you expecting someone?"

"No, Tina already stopped by."

The doorbell rang again. "I'll get it," Logan said and left the kitchen.

A minute later he returned with Tyson.

"Hey, my chère." Tyson wore a charming smile as he handed me a large bouquet of flowers.

"Thank you," I said and looked to see Logan's reaction. He had specifically told me not to invite people over when I first moved in, but technically I hadn't invited Tyson.

Logan looked calm and disinterested, and for some reason that bothered me. Disappointment made my chest feel even tighter than it already did with my pressed ribs. Apparently Logan had spoken the truth when he told "Mary" that he didn't see me as girlfriend material.

He's certainly showing no sign of being uncomfortable with Tyson bringing me flowers, I thought before I chastised myself. *Why does it even matter what Logan thinks? Tyson is here and he's gorgeous, sexy, outgoing, and confident as hell. Wasn't that what I wanted in a man?*

My eyes found Logan's as I searched for the smallest sign that he cared, but he merely gave me a small nod and said, "I'll leave you two some privacy."

"Thanks, dude." Tyson smiled and plunked down beside me on the couch. "How are you holding up?"

"Better," I assured him. "Thanks for helping me home yesterday."

"My pleasure. You know, yesterday I was actually calling to invite you over for a date, but I'm glad I got to be the knight in shining armor and carry you to your bed."

I chuckled a bit forced. "You make it sound so medieval."

"Hey, it's not every day a man gets to be noble." He grinned.

"Or humble," I added.

Unaffected by my sarcasm, Tyson leaned closer. "How about I take you on a date right here on your couch? We could order some takeout, and watch a movie together."

I raised a brow. "You mean Netflix and chill?"

He grinned back at me with glee in his eyes, sliding his finger suggestively down my shoulder. "I'll be a gentleman, don't worry," he said playfully. "We can do Netflix today, and chill next time. I'm very good at chilling." The way he wiggled his eyebrows made me think of a horny high school kid.

"I'm afraid, I'm not allowed to have visitors," I told him.

"Seriously? Why not – did the Scot tell you that?"

"Yes."

"But yesterday you said he wasn't your boyfriend."

"He's not. But it's his apartment and since he lets me live here for free, I follow the few rules he has."

"You live here for free?" His suspicious tone made me roll my eyes.

"Before you get any funny ideas, I should clarify: I do all the cooking, cleaning, and laundry instead of paying rent."

"So you're like... his housekeeper?"

"Uh-huh."

Tyson whistled low. "The Scot is a clever man. Wanna come live with me? I could get you one of those skanky little maid costumes and you could pamper me," he joked.

I lifted my foot. "Sorry, I don't think the costume would match my glamourous boot here."

"That's okay, I'd be too busy looking at your gorgeous body to notice."

I knew Tyson meant it as a compliment, but I still tried to change the subject and asked, "So are you ready for the game on Sunday?"

"I will be, if only the coach would give me more time on the field."

"Maybe this Sunday, he will," I said optimistically. But he didn't seem to be listening.

Squirming in his seat and brushing his thighs several times, he was suddenly throwing off nervous energy, and when he avoided my direct stare, I frowned.

"Tyson, what is it?"

He broke into a nervous grin. "Nothing, it's nothing."

"Liar. Something's up with you."

He looked away, scratching his collarbone. "Actually, there was something I wanted to ask you."

I waited for the question.

"Your sister is Cleo, right?"

"Yeah."

He met my eyes for a nanosecond. "Well, I'm kind of a huge fan, so I wondered..."

Silently, I clenched my hands, trying not to blame Tyson for all the guys who had used me to get to Chloe in the past.

"I would really like to meet her. Maybe you could invite her to a game and we could all hang out afterwards."

"She doesn't like football," I said dismissively.

"Then maybe we could just go out for dinner sometime."

I tilted my head. "I don't think you understand the concept of going out for dinner with a celebrity like my sister. I avoid it as much as possible because of the fans and paparazzi."

"I wouldn't mind," Tyson said eagerly. "But it doesn't have to be a public meeting. Maybe you could just bring her to my place or something."

"Yeah, maybe," I said but already knew that it wouldn't happen. I couldn't date one of my sister's fans. No way.

A painful memory surfaced: me kissing with a cute guy only to freeze up when he called me "Cleo."

"I'm tired," I lied. "I think I need to take a nap."

"Oh, okay So you don't want to watch a movie with me?" Tyson asked.

"No, not today."

"How about I call you tomorrow?" he asked and leaned in to kiss me. I turned my head, making his kiss land on my jaw instead of my mouth.

"It's okay. I'll call you when I feel better," I said with a smile that didn't reach my eyes.

When the front door closed behind Tyson, I sank down on the couch, buried my head under the blanket, and cried my eyes out.

My ankle was injured, I had no money – and poor prospects of making any when I couldn't cheerlead or get to Blue Ribbon on a broken bike.

And to top it all off, my love life sucked too. For years I'd avoided men because of my love for Allan. And now that I was coming out of my shell, it turned out nobody really wanted me anyway.

Tyson never liked me; he wanted my sister.

And Logan thought I had no humor and wasn't girlfriend material. He wanted Mary.

I sobbed from the humiliation and unfairness of it all until a hand on my shoulder made me stiffen.

"Faith, what is it?" Logan asked.

"Nothing, I'm fine." I sniffled and tried to dampen my sobs.

"Ye're not fine." He pried the blanket down to see me, his eyes full of concern. "Did he hurt you?"

"No."

"Are you in pain? Do ye need me to get ye some pills?"

"No."

"Then what is it, Faith? Tell me."

Through teary eyes and with a running nose, I took a deep breath and spilled it all in a fast ramble. "This psychic woman I know told me to follow the fighter with the accent. But Tyson only wants me for my sister and you don't like me either."

Logan leaned closer and creased his brows together.

"Sorry, come again? I only heard something about a psychic woman."

In a voice distorted from my crying, I repeated the whole thing.

"Sorry, you have to speak slower." He fetched me a paper towel to blow my noise and dry my tears away.

"Violet told me to follow the fighter with the accent," I said in a more controlled voice.

"And who is Violet?"

"The psychic," I answered.

"And?" He gestured for me to continue.

"And Tyson has a strong accent and he's kind of a modern fighter, but he just told me he's a major fan of my sister," I rambled again.

From the way Logan's eyes were narrowed I could tell he was trying to make sense of it all.

"All right, first of all, Faith, ye cannae be listening to psychics. I dinnae mean to say they're all fake, but what she told ye makes no sense. Think about it, lass. Everyone on this planet has an accent. It's not specific enough, is it?"

"I don't have an accent," I argued, but that only made him laugh.

"Aye, you do. Ye've a strong North American accent."

"That doesn't count."

"And why not? Did this Violet tell ye that it had to be a specific accent?"

"No."

"Exactly. So you see. Her description fits everyone."

I sat back realizing he was right.

After a bit of silence, I rested my head in my hands and looked up with glazed eyes. "I used to think it was you."

His eyes widened. "Me?"

"Yes."

"Because of my accent?"

"Yes, and your scars. You looked like a badass fighter."

"Is that why ye ran after me that night?"

I shrugged my shoulders. "I was curious about you."

"But ye couldn't possibly think…" He stopped talking and I didn't pressure him to continue.

"Faith…" Taking a deep breath as if to summon his courage, he moved to sit next to me. "If I ask ye a question, will ye answer me honestly?" He looked intensely into my eyes.

I nodded and tilted my head, waiting for whatever question was making him so visibly nervous.

"Did ye ever feel sexually attracted to me?"

I could tell it took everything in him to ask me that question and I thought about my answer.

"You have to understand that I'm still mourning Allan."

"I understand," he said.

"I'm…" I cleared my throat, pushing the words out. "I'm so confused."

"Don't be. It's a yes or no question."

"Is it?" Sudden anger rose in me, thinking about Tyson's words about my body. Logan had said similar things. None of these men wanted me for my personality, that much was clear.

"Answer me this, Logan; am I the kind of girl you want as your girlfriend? No, better yet; am I the kind of girl you would want to marry one day?"

Pain slid over his face and he pressed his lips into a firm line, but said nothing. He didn't have to. His expression said it all.

"I thought so," I said with resignation. "I'm the hot cheerleader every man wants to bang, but doesn't want to marry, aren't I?"

"Is that what you think?" he asked harshly.

Angry tears were falling in fat drops from my eyes again. "You're no different. I see you looking at me," I accused.

160

"You want me to apologize for that?" Logan asked with his eyes narrowed. "I take it that's a 'no' to your being interested in me?"

"*Interested* in you?" I cried out. "That's not what you asked me before. You asked me if I was sexually attracted to you, implying that sex was all there could ever be between us."

He blinked in confusion. "But, Faith…" he started as if to tell me how ridiculous the thought of us together was. Yes, I knew he found me a chatterbox without humor and that he was in love with the bubbly "Mary."

But sleeping close to him yesterday had awoken longings in me that I'd suppressed for years.

I want that closeness again with someone.

No, not just someone.

Hiding my face in my hands I gave in to my tears again, reluctantly admitting to myself that despite my current anger with him, I *was* falling in love with Logan, and probably had been for a long time. The hours of conversations in the disguise of wanting to help him, the cooking his favorite meals, the neatly folded laundry on his bed with little notes of optimism… it had made me happy. *He* made me happy. The sound of his key in the door telling me he was home from work made me happy.

Logan was sweet, considerate, generous, shy, and complicated. But I was complicated too.

If I were to move on from Allan, I wanted it to be with Logan.

I heaved in a sob of sadness, and held my hand to my sore ribs.

"'But Faith' *what*?" I repeated his words with frustration.

Logan's head fell down and his hands ran through his hair. He couldn't even look at me.

"I'm right, aren't I? You only think of me as someone you would have sex with."

He kept his head down.

"Your silence says it all," I muttered harshly and pushed myself up, my chest hurting from the knot of emotions as well as my injured rib cage.

"Faith, please…" Logan looked up at me with his blue eyes swirling with emotions. "You're right. I never saw you as a potential girlfriend, but I think it's because…"

I cut him off. "Because you're in love with someone else."

He swallowed hard and nodded. "Yes, I am, but that's not the only…"

All I wanted was to go back to my room and be alone. I didn't want any bad excuses and held up a hand to silence him. "Stop. I don't want to hear it."

With the last shred of my dignity, I grabbed my crutches and thumped to my room, slamming the door behind me.

$\{\infty\}$

Logan

The sound of Faith's door slamming woke me from my stunned state.

Did Faith just tell me she had feelings for me?

What the hell just happened?

I went back, analyzing every word said between us and, no, she hadn't said anything to imply that she had feelings for me. She had never admitted to being attracted to me either, just curious. *What does curious mean?*

Getting a beer from the fridge, I concluded that the whole thing had been about Tyson, and that I'd simply been dragged into it because I was the only male in the room.

So why did it feel like it was about me and her?

Because I'm a fucking fool who wants to believe it.

162

Faith was vulnerable and hurting right now – her conflict with her sister, her accident causing her financial worries. It wasn't hard to forgive her emotional outburst. I just wished she would have given me a chance to explain that guys like Tyson weren't worthy of her.

Hell, I didn't know a single man who was worthy of a woman like Faith. I certainly wasn't.

I plunked down on the couch, turned up the volume of the TV, and froze to my very core when I read the text in the red 'breaking news" line running across the screen.

CHAPTER 18
Niko

Logan

"Faith," I shouted as loud as I could. "Faith, ye've got to see this."

Just to be sure she heard me, I ran to her room and opened her door.

"Come see this, quickly," I shouted.

Her eyes were still full of tears from our emotional talk but she got up from her bed.

Focused on hurrying, I wanted to pick her up and carry her to the living room, but when she understood my intentions she held up a hand and hissed, "Don't you dare."

"But it's about your sister... on the TV."

Worry spread on her face and she moved as quickly to the living room as her crutches would allow.

"Turn it up," she ordered and sat down on the couch.

I did, and we both stared in horror at the text still rolling over the screen.

Breaking news: Pop star phenomenon, Niko, on the run after shooting girlfriend, Hollywood star actress Cleo.

"No!" Faith gasped out loud and moved to the edge of her seat. "No." She turned to look up at me. "She's not dead. I would know if she was. I'm her twin." The look in her eyes was pleading, as if she wanted me to confirm that it was a universal truth that a twin could feel the death of their other half. I didn't think it was.

"I don't know," I said quietly.

"Where's my phone? I need to call Chloe right now."

Her phone wasn't on the table, but with her directions I found it next to her bed and brought it to her.

"Pick up, Chloe, pick up," Faith kept murmuring, but there was no answer.

"You should call your parents," I told her and tried to hear what the anchorman on the news was saying.

"I'm just being told we have our reporter, Alex Johnson, with us from the crime scene. Alex, what have you learned so far?"

A black man with a grave expression stood in front of Chloe's apartment building. Police were moving in the background and a crowd of people stood behind a police barrier.

"Well, Felix, the Seattle police aren't saying much at this point but the shooting took place in the building right behind me, and what we know is that the police reacted to a 911 call that came in about thirty-seven minutes ago from a woman who identified herself as the twenty-six-year-old Cleo."

"And has it been confirmed that it was in fact Cleo who was shot?" the anchorman asked.

"Cleo's identity has not been confirmed officially. According to the Twitter statement from the police department we know that a twenty-six-year-old female has been shot and taken to the hospital following a scene of domestic violence," Alex Johnson explained. "But I'm here with a neighbor, Vanessa, who saw the ambulance leave."

The camera swung to an Asian woman in her early thirties. "Vanessa, can you tell us what you witnessed."

"I was just coming home from work and was walking up the stairs when I heard three shots. At first I thought it might be a type of firecracker, but then a man came storming down the staircase and almost knocked me over."

"And was this man Niko?"

"I'm not sure. He was wearing a cap and I didn't get a good look at him, but it could have been."

"Did you see Cleo?"

"Only when they carried her out. You see, it only took a few seconds before the police arrived and ordered me outside. I think they must have been on their way before he shot her."

"And when they carried her out, did you see her condition?"

"She didn't have a sheet over her head or anything," Vanessa said gravely, "but she looked dead to me. I mean, there was no movement at all and there was a lot of blood right here." The woman held her hand to her chest.

A howl came from Faith, and I instinctively bent down and took her in my arms while the interview continued on the screen.

"She's in good hands. The doctors will save her," I whispered.

"I want to go to her," Faith sniffled into my shoulder.

"But I don't know where they took her."

We didn't have to wait long for that piece of information as the anchor said, "Let's take a look at what is happening in front of the hospital where the press and a few fans are already gathering to show their love and support for Cleo."

A female reporter said, "Yes, I'm here at Swedish Hospital First Hill, where world renowned actress 'Cleo' is assumed to be fighting for her life."

With a stern expression I stood up, and reached out my hand to Faith. "Let's go."

Horrible thoughts filled my mind on the way to the hospital. Faith reached her parents, who were out with friends when she delivered the horrible news. Her mother on the phone asked all the questions we all wanted answers to and when her fear erupted in sobbing, Spencer took the phone. I could hear him try to understand what Faith was saying, but she too was crying hard and her voice was shaking too hard to make sense.

I took the phone and told him I was with Faith and that we were on our way to the hospital. Spencer told me they would leave for Seattle right away.

"Drive safely," I said knowing in my heart that the four-hour drive from Spokane to Seattle would feel like five days to them.

"Keep me updated, will you?" Spencer asked solemnly.

"Of course," I said and ended the call.

When we walked up to the hospital, a line of press was forming and Faith was recognized right away. She tensed up and walked as fast as she could on her crutches while cameras flashed and journalists were calling out questions to her. I wanted to pull her under my arm and shield her, but those damn crutches were in the way.

As Cleo's twin, Faith had no problem getting through the police barrier and I followed right on her heels, hoping we would find Cleo well and fine inside.

Of course, that didn't happen.

What we found was a grim-faced doctor who told us Cleo was on the operation table, with a gunshot to her chest.

I cried with Faith.

Not only had I lost my own sister, but I could relate to the self-blame that Faith was experiencing.

Cleo had called her over and over, and Faith had ignored her. Why had I let her think there was all the time in the world to reconcile, when I of all people knew that wasn't always the case?

I should have pushed harder like Chloe asked me to.

My warning had come too late, and now Cleo's life was in the hands of the surgeon.

Faith was leaning against me as she listened to the voice messages with Chloe pleading Faith to call. You would have to be a cold prick not to tear up.

About forty minutes after we arrived, two police detectives came to ask Faith questions and confirm that Niko was still on the run. They asked about possible motives and Faith spewed out her hatred for the man, calling him a disturbed psychopath consumed with jealousy and possessiveness.

They noted down her words and promised to update her if anything changed.

We stayed in the private room we had been given, looking up at the TV that kept repeating the story about Cleo and Niko. Fans were being interviewed, friends that claimed to be in the inner circle, and a psychologist who specialized in victims of domestic violence spoke about how to get help before it escalates to a tragedy.

I offered to get Faith food or candy, but she had no appetite and just sat pale and quiet waiting for the operation to be over.

Minutes felt like hours, but eventually a doctor entered the room and we both eagerly got up.

"I bring good news," the freckled woman said with a small smile and reached out to shake our hands. "I'm Doctor Amaya and I performed the surgery on your sister. We removed the bullet and I'm very satisfied with the result."

"She's going to live?" Faith asked and fiddled with her hands.

When Doctor Amaya nodded it made her curly orange hair bob around her. With her freckles, red hair, pale blue eyes, and rangy build she reminded me of an adult version of Pippi Longstocking. "Yes, your sister was lucky," she said

"Lucky?" I burst out incredulously.

"No, I'm sorry." The young doctor shook her head. "Wrong choice of words. Of course getting shot is never lucky..." She took on a more serious expression. "I just meant that for a gunshot wound to the chest, this bullet did a minimum of damage." Her eyes flickered from me to Faith before she continued. "The bullet entered close to her heart and there is damage to her tissue, of course, but had the bullet taken a slightly different angle, the outcome would have been fatal." She stopped talking when she saw Faith's wide eyes. "In any case, ehm..." Doctor Amaya cleared her throat. "Your sister will need time to heal."

Faith dried away her tears and sniffled loudly. "Can we see her?"

"Yes, the nurse will take you to her in a few minutes."

"Thank you," Faith shook the woman's hand with both hers. "Thank you so much."

"My pleasure." She nodded to me before she left.

Faith and I hugged then – long and hard – and when she lifted her face to look at me with red-rimmed eyes full of relief, I felt like I was free-falling high in the air. It was completely inappropriate, but I wanted to kiss her so bad.

"I'm so glad you're here," she whispered. "Thank you."

"Ye're welcome," I said slowly and tightened my grip around her. With the way she kept my eyes locked, the position of our faces so close, and our arms around each other, it would have been perfect for kissing; but I was scared shitless that I was misinterpreting the situation, and restrained myself from leaning in.

"Logan?"

"Aye."

Faith sighed and gave me a small smile.

I smiled back, feeling the relief that crackled between us. Chloe was going to survive. We could breathe again.

169

"Just so you know: the answer is 'yes,'" she said.

"Yes?" I asked and wrinkled my eyebrows. "What do ye mean?"

"You asked me a question earlier today and I never answered you, but the answer is yes, I did think of you that way."

I narrowed my eyes. "What did ye say?" I asked in disbelief just when a knock on the door made us both look over to see a nurse in the doorway.

"Would you like to see Chloe?"

"Yes." The intimate moment was broken and we followed the nurse to a room with a couch, two chairs, and a hospital bed where Chloe lay unconscious. She was bruised and had dark marks on her neck. The bastard had strangled her.

Faith pressed a kiss to Chloe's forehead and brushed her hair behind her ears, exposing her large black eye and her swollen chin.

Seeing Chloe so beaten offended me as a man. What kind of pathetic little coward would hurt a woman like this?

"I told you he was bad news, didn't I?" Faith muttered low to Chloe and kissed her again.

"She should wake up soon," the nurse informed us. "It can take anywhere from fifteen minutes to a few hours, but please press the button to call us when she wakes up."

We sat silently on each side of Chloe's bed. My mind was reeling over what had just happened between Faith and me.

There was no way I could press the subject of Faith's possible attraction to me; it would be insensitive to ask her in the current situation. But the mere thought that Faith had thought of me sexually excited me beyond belief.

Don't get carried away. It doesn't mean she wants anything to happen between us, I reminded myself, but I sat straighter and lifted my head up knowing that she had thought about me sexually.

❰ ∞ ❱

Faith

Chloe woke up after almost an hour and was confused and disoriented. Her eyes were bloodshot from the strangling and her voice was hoarse. I tried to explain what I knew, but it wasn't until the detectives came to question her that I was able to make sense of it myself.

The two detectives asked Logan to step outside while I stayed and held Chloe's hand.

"Can you tell us what happened?" the thin-haired police officer asked from his seat next to Chloe.

"Niko just showed up and acted irrationally. He was accusing me of being unfaithful and said that he had proof," she explained.

"Did he say what kind of proof?"

"No, he was waving his gun around, and it scared me."

"When did you call 911?"

"After he tried to strangle me." Her hands automatically went to her throat where her skin had darkened from his brutal force. "I locked myself in the bathroom and called for help."

"And then what happened?"

"Then he knocked the door down."

"Is that when he shot you?"

"I think so. I don't remember being shot."

The officer took notes and looked up. "What do you remember, Miss Olsson?"

"I remember Niko shouting at me and throwing things around. He wanted me to admit to being unfaithful but I wouldn't, and then he hit me again and again. As I said, I don't remember being shot."

"Maybe you were already unconscious at the time," a tall slender police offer speculated.

"I don't know," Chloe answered low, as if it hurt to talk.

"Do you have any idea where Niko would likely run to?"

"Canada maybe. He has family in Vancouver."

"Anywhere else you can think of?"

"His dad lives in Pennsylvania."

"If you think of anywhere else, please let us know. Until then we'll be placing a guard outside your door."

"Do you think Chloe is still in danger?" I asked the two men.

"Hopefully not, but we can't take any chances. Until we have Niko in our custody we'll be posting a guard."

"How long will you be staying here?" The slender man asked.

"I don't know," Chloe croaked.

"And where will you go when you leave?"

"Not sure. To my home in Los Angeles, I suppose."

The two men exchanged a glance of worry. "Hopefully Niko will be behind bars by then, but if not, we would suggest you lay low until we have him. You survived being shot this time. You might not be so lucky next time."

When the police left, I crawled up in Chloe's bed and held her in my arms. My pressed ribs hurt like hell and she didn't notice the boot on my foot, but it didn't matter and I didn't tell her about my accident. It seemed insignificant compared to what she had been through. All that mattered was that she was my sister and I loved her.

Whispering reassuring things to her, I promised her everything would be fine. And when Logan popped his head in again, she was sleeping from the exhaustion and medications.

"Logan," I whispered and waved him closer.

"Is she okay?" he whispered back and came to stand next to me with concern written on his face.

"I'm staying here tonight," I told him.

"Would you like me to stay too?" he asked and looked to the couch. It made me smile. Thank god that men like Niko weren't the norm. Good men like Logan would use their strength to protect their women – not beat them.

He had been close to kissing me in the other room. I figured it was his love for Mary that held him back, but Mary was me, and I would explain that to him as soon as we were alone again. Logan might be confused about having feelings for two women, but I only had feelings for him. We would find a way to make it work.

I tugged at his shirt, and slowly he bent down enough for me to reach behind his neck and pull him close enough for our foreheads to almost touch.

It surprised him and he stiffened, but I didn't let go. Instead I nuzzled his hair.

"I know you want to know," I whispered.

"Know what?" he whispered back.

"What I meant when I said that I thought about you."

"Aye, but..." He looked at Chloe.

"It's okay, she's sleeping heavily."

He had a small frown on his face as he placed his hand next to mine on the bed.

"I had a sex dream about you," I whispered.

"A sex dream?"

"Yes."

His Adam's apple bobbed in his throat. "Are ye jesting with me?"

"No."

"What does that mean... a sex dream? Were ye sleeping or were ye awake?"

I bit my inner cheek. "Both," I admitted.

"Seriously?" he said and I almost felt bad for him with the way his face flashed red. The deliberate movement he made when he moved his hand closer to mine made butterflies flutter in my stomach. He was insecure, but brave enough to ask my permission through the touch of my hand. A small touch of my pinky finger grew into our fingers weaving together, and then he raised our joined hands and kissed the back of mine.

I smiled softly.

"Faith," he said and looked down at my lips. It was a loaded question that made me lean forward in answer.

He wasn't breathing when he kissed me. He was like a burned child reluctantly getting close to the flame with the expectation of getting burned again.

"It's okay, Logan," I muttered into his mouth.

The first reluctant kiss changed into something different. He was getting braver now and his hands were cupping my face.

"Faith," he whispered breathlessly, his fingers playing with my hair. "I've been wanting to do this for so long," he said and pulled back to look into my eyes. "Are ye sure about this?"

"No. Are you?" I asked still holding my breath.

He kissed me again but when Chloe stirred in her sleep next to me, he pulled back.

"It's okay, we'll continue tomorrow," I said with an optimistic feeling in my gut. Chloe was finally done with Niko, and Logan and I would figure out a way to move past our grief and anxiety, together.

With a squeeze of my hand and a last kiss to my forehead, Logan left the room.

I lay still next to Chloe reflecting on the crazy day this had been, and knew that I would keep my sister safe from harm any way I could.

Unfortunately, it wasn't just men with guns that were threatening her.

Soon our parents would arrive, and then her agent, who was flying in from Los Angeles. Family and friends would all need updates, and then there were her millions of fans to consider. Chloe was already volatile at best. She was a magnet for drama and if I were to keep her safe, it would have to be from herself.

How would I make her see that she needed a break from the media circus? No doubt her agent would suggest she milk the situation and get maximum media exposure. But inside that glamourous Hollywood star was my twin. The girl I had played Barbie with, dressed up with, shared secrets with. The girl who cried her eyes out when Dad accidently hit the neighbor's cat with his car. The girl who was afraid to sleep alone and begged me to hold her hand until she fell asleep. To others Chloe was strong and confident, but I saw through it all and knew it was a façade. She was just a scared little girl who wanted everyone to like her. Even her crazy boyfriend.

What she needed most of all was to love herself.

I placed a kiss on the top of her hair and gave a sigh. "What am I going to do with you?" I asked and said a silent prayer.

Dear God, protect Chloe, from others and herself. Teach her to see clearly and make better choices. Fill her with love – pure and strong enough to carry her through the turbulent life she has chosen. Amen!

Little did I know that I should have said that prayer for myself.

CHAPTER 19

Motive

Logan

I didn't sleep much that night. My head was in the clouds, thinking impossible thoughts about me and Faith, together. I hadn't heard from Mary since she told me to forget about her and find myself a real girlfriend.

My feelings for Mary hadn't changed, but if she didn't want to see me, I couldn't force her. And with Faith showing an unexpected interest in me, I would be a fool not to take the chance.

My TV kept me updated about the hunt for Niko, and Faith texted me a few times, letting me know she missed me.

She missed *me*!

I had to pinch myself several times that day, and could hardly control my anxiety when she told me she was coming home for a quick shower and a change of clothes.

We would be alone.

Her staying for a short time or long didn't matter, as long as she didn't regret our kiss from yesterday.

Faith looked tired when she arrived home. Her father had given her a ride.

"I told him you offered to pick me up, but I think he wanted a break from the situation," Faith explained to me.

"And what is the situation?" I asked, moving a bit closer.

"That I feel icky and want a shower." She took my hands. "Jane, Chloe's agent, is running the show now. I

176

hate that woman, but Chloe does as she says and apparently *this will all benefit Chloe.*" Faith said the last words in an exaggerated tone.

"Benefit her how?" I asked, stupefied.

"Sympathy. It's good publicity and works well for ratings. She already has tens of millions of fans wishing her well on Twitter."

"And you, how do ye feel?" I asked.

Faith lifted her arms to hug me and I didn't hesitate to wrap my arms around her.

"I'm worried," she said and leaned her head on my shoulder. "Worried that he'll be back to harm her, and if not Niko, then some other boyfriend just like him. It's not like it was a stranger who did this to her. It was her boyfriend. She let him into her life and didn't kick him out after the first ten times he mistreated her. That's what worries me: that it could happen again."

"And us? How do ye feel about us?" I asked with my heart hammering in my chest.

Her smile said it all, but her words made me want to pick her up and kiss her. "I feel pretty good about us. I think you're the opposite of Niko. You're kind and trustworthy. I feel really safe with you, Logan."

"Normally, safe and kind aren't very sexy words to say to a man," I said, "But with what just happened to Chloe, I'll take it as a compliment."

"You should. There's nothing sexier than a man who treats his woman right." She pulled away, used the wall as support, and headed toward the bathroom while saying over her shoulder, "I really need a shower and my toothbrush now."

I bit back my offer to scrub her back in the shower. This new thing between us still felt too unreal and fragile, like carrying a beautiful rainbow-colored soap bubble, just waiting for it to burst in your face.

"Shout if ye need help," I said and went into the living room, where the TV was on.

When Faith joined me twenty minutes later, she sank into my lap and folded her arms around my neck. I fought the anxiety that made my body stiffen slightly, and gave her a smile.

"Can you give me a ride back to the hospital?"

"Of course," I said, my eyes staring at her lips. We had only kissed once and it had been on her initiative.

Just kiss her already, the old Logan inside me shouted, embarrassed by the frightened man who had the most beautiful, amazing woman on his lap and didn't make a move.

Man up and kiss her already!

Faith's lovely smell of shampoo engulfed me and drove me mad, and so did her soft fingers when she caressed my cheek.

What the hell are ye waiting for?

With a heart racing a mile a second, I took the leap and pulled her in for a kiss. In my eagerness we bumped teeth, but she didn't pull away.

"I'm sorry," I muttered, but she just laughed.

She tasted fresh and minty and our tongues were dancing around each other.

I was in heaven – lost in our first French kiss.

With my eyes closed and my hands moving down her arms, I pushed through my fear of rejection and gently cupped her right breast. Her little moan of pleasure egged me on and made me suck her lower lip and release it with a loud "plop" sound.

"I can't believe we're doing this," she whispered into my mouth.

"Me neither." I whispered hoarsely while placing kisses along her jawline. "I like the way ye kiss."

"Oh yeah?"

"Aye," I said, muffled because I was nibbling at her earlobe.

"You're a pretty good kisser yourself." Her tone was playful, and she rotated her hips.

"Dinnae do that." I held her hips to keep them from moving on top of me, afraid I would embarrass myself.

"Cleo."

The name broke through our bubble and we both turned our heads to the TV.

"The police are still looking for Nikolas Carpenter, also known as Niko, after he shot his longtime girlfriend, actress Cleo. The big question everyone has been asking after the tragic incident yesterday is 'Why did he do it?' and 'How could things end so tragically between two lovers who have shared so many magical moments together?'"

Pictures of Cleo and Niko on the red carpet smiling for the cameras rolled over the screen, and one that I hadn't seen before of him carrying her on the beach. They looked so happy together – the poster image of rich and successful.

"So far the motive has been speculated on as jealousy, but with a new witness stepping forward we might get a clearer picture. Just an hour ago the Hollywood insider channel 'Glam' brought the big scoop, showing pictures that allegedly led to the drama."

A picture of a white guy in a baseball cap came up. "Michael Teller, a private investigator, has stepped forward sharing how he personally handed pictures to Niko a few hours before Cleo was shot. Michael Teller is quoted to have said, 'I believe her infidelity caused Niko to act irrationally.'

"So far there has been no response from Cleo's spokespeople, but what you're seeing on the screen right now are the pictures that Michael Teller says he gave to Niko just hours before the attempted murder." My eyes grew to double size when I saw myself in a grainy picture with Chloe, hugging her tight.

Faith froze in my lap as more pictures from the laundromat came on the screen. In one of them Chloe was looking up at me as if we were about to kiss. In the next her lips connected to mine. From the angle of the photos it had to be from a security camera in the ceiling.

"It's not what it looks like," I hurried to say.

Faith's jaws pressed together and her lips turned into fine lines.

"Let me explain," I said but she was already moving away from me.

"It isn't what it looks like," I repeated. "She wanted to talk to me about ye. Because you didnae call her back."

Faith shot me a glance of fury, but didn't answer.

"Seriously, I would never... I dinnae like your sister that way, you know I dinnae."

"Do I?" she hissed. "Looks to me like you and Tyson are both the same. But at least *he* was open about being more interested in Chloe than me."

"Stop, Faith, ye got it wrong." I got in front of her, but the way she hissed, "Let me go," made me back off.

"Why won't ye listen to me?" I shouted after her, when she stubbornly fumbled for her crutches.

"I trusted you, Logan. I thought you were different, but I should have known better." Her hand flew to her mouth as if she just realized something. "Oh, God, you even told me you were in love with someone else... I thought it was..." Her eyes darted around the room and she moved her hand from her mouth to her belly and looked like she had swallowed an insect. "You're in love with Chloe. How could I not see that?"

"No, Faith, stop it. I'm *not* in love with Chloe. You're wrong."

On TV they kept pushing the rumors and speculations on who Cleo's new love interest was.

"According to the witness, Michael Teller, he's stepping forward to warn the unnamed man in the photo, whom he believes might be in danger from Niko. He says, quote: 'Niko knows the identity of this man and if he was capable of shooting Cleo, who knows what he'll do to her lover?'"

Faith and I both stiffened and stared at each other for a second. "Did you hear that?" she asked.

"Aye, but why dicnae this Michael guy come to me instead of the press?"

Faith snorted. "Because he had a story to sell. That's why."

"But I didnae do anything," I exclaimed and threw my hands in the air. "Honestly, I was working when a guy came and asked me to go with him. And then I was shown to this tiny laundromat where Chloe waited for me."

"And?" Faith asked with one hand on her hip.

"And she was upset and started begging me to help her. I told Chloe that I didnae want to meddle in your affairs, and that made her cry." I took a deep breath. "A friend of mine recently told me that when a woman cries, I should offer a hug, so I did."

"I can see that." She looked back to the screen where the pictures were being shown again.

"It was just a hug, Faith. Nothing more."

She pointed to the screen. "Then why does it look like you're kissing her."

"I didnae, I swear it," I almost shouted. "She kissed me!"

"She did *what*?"

"It was a quick goodbye kiss and I was stiff as a board. There was nothing romantic about it. I honestly didnae like it."

"Well, the whole world is going to think you did, and Niko could be coming for you."

181

I squatted down and covered my eyes with my hands. "SHITE!"

My fine rainbow-colored bubble of soap had turned into a big black bowling bowl coming to hit me hard. I needed to move, *fast*.

"What should I do?"

"The only thing you can do. Hide!" she said. "Go back to Scotland or check into a hotel... or something. You don't know Niko, but I do. The man is a lunatic and if he finds you, you're dead."

"That's *crazy*. I havenae done anything wrong," I said in an angry growl.

"Neither did Chloe, but he still put a bullet in her chest." Faith jumped when her phone rang.

"Gosh, that scared me," she said and held a hand to her heart. "We should probably make sure the door is locked."

I went to secure the door while she answered her phone.

"Hi, Mom. Yes, we saw it. Can I talk to Chloe?"

When I returned to the living room, Faith moved back and forth using the chairs for support. I figured it was the closest thing to pacing the floor she could do with her injured ankle. Even from four feet away I could hear Chloe crying and explaining on the other end of the phone. Her words escaped me, but I prayed to God she was telling the truth.

"Okay. It's a hell of a mess you got us in this time, but I understand that you meant well," Faith said and brushed her hair back. "No, Chloe, I don't hate you." Her eyes went to me. "Uh-huh. Yes, of course he's scared. I don't think he has time to hate you right now. He's more concerned about being shot, I think."

Her comment made me move away from the window. *What if Niko hired a hitman, like a sniper?* I closed my eyes and took a deep breath through my nose. How had my life come to this? Being a hermit suddenly felt like the better alternative.

"And how is that going to help? Uh-huh. Sure, but do you think it'll work?" Faith's forehead was wrinkled and she was picking at her lip. "Okay, I understand. No, I agree – it's worth a try. Yes, I'll talk to you later," Faith said into the phone and hung up.

"Did she tell you what happened?" I asked eagerly.

"Yes, your stories are clean copies. The question is; do I believe the pictures or you two?"

"Please, Faith, you know I would never..."

"No, I don't know." She paused and shook her head in resignation. "I don't know what to believe."

"But, Faith," I said and stepped toward her.

She held up a hand. "Stop. I can't think about you and me now. We have to focus on protecting you from Niko, and Chloe had an idea."

"What?"

"We're going to pull the old twin trick and say that I am the woman in those photos. We've done it before, and hopefully it'll calm Niko down."

"Okay..." I said slowly. "And how do we do that?"

She held up her phone and waved me closer. "We're going to make this picture look like we're deeply in love."

I put my arms around her, placing a kiss on her cheek.

"No," she said as she looked at the picture. "It doesn't look real. Let's try again."

This time I cupped her face and kissed her as if my life depended on it. I was scared shitless. Scared that I had blown my chance with Faith. Scared that I was being hunted by a crazy person. And scared that this would be the last time we ever kissed. I poured so many feelings into that kiss that it left me a bit dizzy.

"Better?" I asked.

She blinked and was out of breath from the intense kiss. "What?"

"Is the picture better?"

"Oh, yes, right, let's see," she said and showed me.

The picture wasn't perfect with half of my head out of the frame, but the part that mattered was clear. There was passion in that picture.

"Okay, Instagram, here you go," she muttered and wrote a few words.

"Can I see?" I asked and reached for her phone.

There it was, the picture of Faith and me kissing like there was no tomorrow and her caption saying: *Let me clear this up. Logan is MY man!*

I whipped my head up with hope in my eyes. "Do ye mean that?"

"No. This isn't about you and me. This is about keeping you and Chloe safe from a crazy person."

"So, I'm not yer man?" My voice was dripping with disappointment.

"Please don't do this. I need some time to get my head together." She pulled out a chair and sat down. "Chloe is going to retweet the picture to millions of people. Then the press will share it, and everyone will think Chloe is innocent in all this."

"But she *is* innocent," I argued. "There's no affair."

"So you say." She pointed to the TV. "But the way that security guy spoke about her made her sound like a nymphomaniac who meets up with men in dark corners while her dear boyfriend stays home with the kids."

"Kids?"

"Oh, for God's sake, Logan, I'm speaking metaphorically."

"Okay. I'm sorry. This is just a bit much to take in."

"Well, you better get used to it quickly, because tomorrow you're going to have a horde of people wanting to hear your side of the story."

That made me rub my forehead in acute stress. "Geez, maybe I *should* go back to Scotland and hide for a while," I pondered out loud.

"Yes, maybe you should."

"Will you come with me?"

She looked away.

Bending down, I cupped her face and placed my nose against hers. "Come with me."

"I can't," she whispered.

"Then ask me to stay, Faith." My eyes were moist but I didn't care. I wanted to be her man and to take care of her.

She kept her eyes down, but didn't move her face away.

"Faith. I don't want to leave without ye. We can barricade the door and hide in bed all day. Eventually they'll lose interest and go away. Right?"

When she lifted her gaze, tears hung on her lashes. "Maybe we could, but I'm not leaving my sister to fend for herself. She was almost murdered last night. I'm not going to let that happen again."

"I get that." I sighed. "But this thing is all a misunderstanding. Don't let it come between us."

"I'm sorry, Logan." She pulled back and looked at me with resignation. "Go home to Scotland and ride this out. Maybe you're right and it'll only take a few days. Either way, I have to get my sister the help she needs."

"And what about ye? Who looks after ye?"

"I don't need to be looked after," she said with pretend bravery.

"Come on. Don't hide behind that superwoman façade, Faith. I was there, remember?"

"You were where?"

"In your bedroom, when you needed help. Remember how you asked me to stay until you fell asleep. Of course you need support too – let me be there for you."

185

Her eyes closed and I guessed she was battling the well of emotion inside her.

"We're good together," I argued, but the second she opened her eyes and looked at me, I knew I had lost her.

"I can't," she said. "I just can't."

An hour later I had packed my things and booked a ticket for the first flight home. The news stations were already sharing the love declaration that Faith had planted. It was going according to plan – just not my plan.

CHAPTER 20
Collecting a Favor

Faith

How long do you fight someone else's battle?

I had fought as hard as I could to make Chloe see that she needed help. When we were alone, she would tell me I was right, but as soon as her agent or others were close, she put on her Hollywood face and that fake accent of hers, pretending to be everything she wasn't.

Niko still hadn't been found and the constant security around my sister was suffocating. Ever since she had been released from the hospital almost six weeks ago, she and I had been at her LA home. All the locks had been replaced, the security system was on, and security guards were posted outside the gates. Chloe had even explained to me about the safe room behind the panel in her bedroom.

Our parents had stayed the first week, but they both had jobs to get back to, and now Mom called every night instead. Most nights she ended up talking to me, since Chloe was entertaining the constant traffic of her friends that stopped by to hear first-hand how she got shot.

Her bruises were mostly gone, but the scar on her chest served as a constant reminder of her close call with death. So did the bullet that the doctors had removed, which she now kept in a little jar. Chloe made sure every guest got a small theatrical performance about the horrible day she was shot.

"Do you have to make it so dramatic?" I asked one evening after the last guest had finally left.

"What do you mean?"

187

"It's almost as if you're enjoying the attention. It's not like having a crazy boyfriend who shoots you is something to be proud of."

"Who said I was proud?"

"Well, maybe not proud, but you're certainly enjoying the drama of it all," I accused.

"I'm not. Can't you tell how devastated I am?"

"Yes, once in a while, when it's just the two of us, but most of the time you gossip excitedly with your friends."

She looked offended. "I don't gossip!"

I rolled my eyes. "Are you serious? You gossip all the time. Don't think I didn't hear you talk about that poor woman whose husband is unfaithful to her."

"So what?"

"So maybe you should tell her instead of telling others."

Chloe tilted her head. "Not everyone wants to hear it."

"Of course they do. Remember when Niko cheated on you again and again. How much did it hurt to find out that everyone knew except you?"

"Are you saying that you would want to know if your boyfriend cheated on you?" she asked.

"Duh." I make a gesture to underline how obvious it was.

"But I always thought you preferred not to know."

"Why?"

"Because you told me."

"When did I tell you that?"

"I don't remember. When we were teenagers, I think."

I shook my head. "I have no idea what you're talking about, but if I ever have a boyfriend – and you catch him cheating – I hope you'll tell me."

Her face fell.

"What?" I asked uneasily. "Something *did* happen between you and Logan," I whispered in disbelief.

She shook her head. "No, Logan never made a pass at me, but..."

"But what?"

"You're not going to like it," she said and looked away.

"Tell me, Chloe, what is it?"

"Allan cheated on you."

"You slept with Allan?" It came out as a shriek.

"God, no. What do you take me for? He tried – remember, I told you."

"You're lying!" I exclaimed, my body tensing up.

She shook her head again, sadness radiating from her. "See, this is why I didn't tell you. You always saw Allan as perfect, but he wasn't. He cheated on you. Several times."

"No," I yelled and picked up a pillow, holding it to my chest as a shield against the horrible truth I saw in her eyes.

"Remember Carmen, the pretty girl, who played Ophelia in the spring production?"

"Yes."

"Allan slept with her."

"No," I whispered in denial.

"Carmen admitted it to me a few weeks after it happened. But she wasn't the only one."

"How many?" I cried out.

"I don't know for sure. A handful maybe."

"A handful," I closed my eyes and asked the question I didn't want the answer to. "Carmen and who else?"

"Therese and Lisa."

"*My* Therese and Lisa?" I was shocked to the core.

She nodded with sympathy written on her face.

"Why didn't you tell me?"

189

"I didn't want to hurt you, but I confronted him about it. I told him to stop or I would tell you."

"When?"

She looked down. "Every time I found out."

"And how many times was that?"

"Six or seven, I'm not sure."

I found it hard to breathe and kept shaking my head in resistance to her words. "You never told me." I pushed the words out despite the iron band around my neck and chest.

"No."

"Why?"

Chloe was crying too. "He loved you. I know he did, and I believed him when he said it was the last time."

"You *believed* him?"

"Yes."

"Like you believed Niko?"

"Uh-huh." She sniffled.

I was rocking back and forth now, my nose flaring from the air I was trying to suck into my deprived lungs. "What's *wrong* with you?" My voice was accusatory; she didn't answer. "If I had known, I would have kicked him out so fast his head would still be spinning in his grave."

"Faith," Chloe gasped. "Don't talk badly about the dead."

"Why the hell not? I didn't get to be furious at him when he was alive, and if what you're telling me is true, I've wasted years glorifying the memory of a cheating bastard who wasn't worth a minute of my time." I resolutely took off the necklace I'd been carrying for seven years to remind me of Allan.

"But he loved you. I know he did."

"How can you defend him after what you just told me?"

She didn't look like a Hollywood star in that moment. She looked like a lost little girl. "Love is complicated.

Don't judge someone for cheating. I've done it myself... sometimes it just happens."

"No," I shouted. "It doesn't just happen. It's a choice. It's always a choice and I chose to be faithful, trusting he would too."

"But..."

"Do you even know what integrity means, Chloe?" I said in a disgusted voice. "How can you find it when you don't know what it looks like? You know what I think?"

She shook her head.

"I think you need some serious help. You need to get some therapy and get away from all of this." I spread my hands out, gesturing to the fancy chandeliers and beautiful art on the walls. "Remember when I did you a favor and you said I could ask you for anything?"

"What favor?"

"I went on a date with your friend, Christian, because you asked me to."

"Yeah, but it's hardly a chore to go on a date with Christian; he's smoking hot."

"But I wasn't interested and I told you so. You said that if I ever needed a favor, I could ask you *anything*."

Chloe held my gaze and wrung her hands. "What exactly are you asking me?"

"I'm asking you to get some help, and I don't mean in some posh spa center." I paused while a plan took form in my head. "There's a woman I've heard of and I want you to go to her."

"What woman?"

"An old Native American medicine woman who has worked miracles with people in the past."

Chloe looked suspicious. "What kind of people?"

"Lost souls like you."

"I'm not lost. I'm highly successful." She pointed to the display of her many awards, the most prestigious one being her Oscar statuette. "Do you realize that I have more than sixteen million fans following me on Twitter?" she defended herself.

"I don't care if you have a billion followers," I retorted. "We both know your life isn't all you're posting it to be."

"Like your life is any better." Chloe's voice was shaking.

"At least I have integrity and that's what I want for you. I want you to love yourself and be selective of the people you let into your life."

"And you think some old pipe-smoking Indian woman can teach me that?" she snorted.

"Yes. If you let her."

"Maybe when they find Niko. Until then, I'll have to stay safe."

I shook my head. "No, this is the perfect time. You've put your work on hold to heal. No one will ever expect you to be with Onava. And I bet that if we don't tell her who you are, she won't even know. This lady lives in the forest without a TV. I bet she hasn't ever seen one of your movies." I got up on my knees and spoke with excitement. "It'll be like summer camp, without the circus atmosphere of paparazzi and security. Just imagine how nice it would be to have time to reconnect with who you are and spend time in nature."

Chloe was listening.

"Remember how you used to love being in the forest?"

"I did love it," she said softly. "I could bring a book."

"Yes, and leave your make-up behind."

"I would probably bring my mascara and some lip gloss, though," she said thoughtfully.

"And some comfy socks and sweat pants," I added.

"Is she nice?"

"Onava? Yes, she's amazing. People come from all over the world to learn from her. But she only works with people she considers special."

Chloe arched a brow and I knew I was hitting her vanity. "Do you think she would work with me?"

"Possibly."

Chloe thought about it for a while. "How long do I need to stay?"

"I'm not sure. But it's not a prison, so if you don't like it, you can leave." I assured her. "But please give it a few weeks."

She nodded slowly. "I was thinking about taking the jet somewhere exotic anyway. A vacation might do me good, you know?"

"Exactly." I nodded enthusiastically. "So you'll do it?"

Chloe tilted her head from side to side as if weighing for and against. "I might. But of course, this would be as a favor to you."

"Thank you." I opened my arms and gave her a warm hug. "Thank you so much."

Five minutes later, I began researching to find Onava, the Native American. What I hadn't told Chloe was that this woman was a spiritual teacher with a great amount of followers. I had read several of her books and loved her teachings. One article about her had said that she lived in a remote forest, but it had also mentioned her seminars across the nation, so she wasn't a complete hermit.

From what I knew, Onava's view of the world resonated with me. She was wise, grounded, and the opposite of materialistic. Chloe could learn a lot from her, if only I could convince Onava to give Chloe some intensive therapy sessions.

Hours later, after calling four people who couldn't help me, I finally found a man who knew Onava personally. He gave me her cell phone number.

"You're a hard woman to track down," I said when I managed to get through to her.

"Oh, you're lucky you caught me in town. There's no reception where I live."

"No, I mean finding your phone number was hard."

She chuckled. "But you found me."

"I did, and I'm hoping you can help my sister."

She was quiet.

"She lives a glamourous lifestyle and is currently in a bad place. I truly think it would be healthy for her to get away from everything and spend some time with you."

"You honor me."

"I've heard so many great things about you," I said.

"And your sister. Does she want to meet me?"

"Yes. She's willing to stay with you for a few weeks to work intensively on her issues." I left it at that.

"*Stay* with me?" She paused. "My accommodations are very primitive."

"So, it'll be like camp. She used to love being at camp."

"Tell me a little about your sister."

"She's my twin."

"Ahh… I see."

"What… what do you see?"

"You're talking about that actress who got shot."

I raised my brows, stunned. "How do you know she was shot?"

"My dear, the whole world knows what happened to her. When you mentioned glamour, said she was in a dark place, and that you were her twin, the actress was the first person to come to mind. Remind me of her name please."

"Her name is Chloe."

"Hmm, that's not what they call her on the news."

"No, her public name is Cleo. But I thought you didn't have a TV. The article said you didn't."

Onava laughed. "I don't. But I have a computer, and occasionally I read the news."

"But still, it's a pretty lucky guess."

"Or intuition." She chuckled.

"So will you work with her?" I asked and crossed my fingers.

She was quiet for a few seconds. "I sense your love for your sister and I agree that she would benefit from time away from Hollywood, but I'm not a therapist. I'm just an old woman with a lot of opinions and life experience that I share from."

"I think time with you will be really good for her."

"Okay, then she can come."

"Really?"

"Yes."

"What is the price and when do you have availability?"

"The price. Hmm... let me think." She was humming before she finally said. "Tell your sister that I'll work with her for two weeks if she donates ten percent of what she made this year to a wild life foundation."

"Ten percent?"

"Yes, with her contribution we could do a lot of good and she can deduct it on her tax return anyway."

"So you don't want any of the money yourself?"

"Three hundred dollars should cover food and lodging for two weeks."

"Three hundred. Okay, I got it."

"Good, I expect her here on Wednesday."

"Wednesday? But that's only three days before Christmas."

"So? I thought you said she needed help?"

"She does, but Christmas is a big thing."

"Getting well is a big thing too. Wouldn't you say?"

"But what about your own Christmas?"

"It's nice of you to care, but I don't celebrate Christmas, so I'll be fine."

"All right," I said slowly.

"Chloe will never find my address, but you can tell her to meet me in Port Gamble at noon."

"Where?"

"It's a small town called Port Gamble. The town is minuscule but they have a cafe and I go there to get books and groceries."

"Should she meet you at the bookstore?"

"Yeah. Give her my cell number and then we'll figure it out."

"And what should I tell her to bring?"

"Warm clothing and hiking boots. Tell her to leave the glamour at home; it will only be me and her, and I don't care much for glitter."

"I will. And thank you."

She broke into a low chuckle again. "Don't thank me yet. Thank me when your sister returns to you, healthier and stronger."

"I will."

I hung up and went to tell Chloe the good news. To my surprise she didn't throw a fit about missing out on Christmas and she only pouted a little about the ten percent.

"There's something about this forest thing that feels right," she said and patted the couch for me to join her. "I was thinking about something while you were gone."

I slumped back in the couch next to her and raised my foot up on the table. My ankle was almost back to normal.

"You were saying?" I said in a good mood.

"You know how reporters have tried to get an exclusive interview with you and Logan?"

"Yeah."

196

"I know you've refused them all out of respect for me, but I can't stop you if you need the money."

"Have you lost your mind? You're my sister. I'm not going to make money on your misery," I said.

She gave me a sly smile. "Maybe you should."

"What are you talking about? Logan is still working from Scotland, hiding from Niko. I'm not going to expose him."

"Then don't. But you could easily make a hundred thousand if you do an exclusive interview. My agent can set it up."

My eyebrows shot up. "A hundred thousand dollars?"

"Absolutely. And if we do the interview together, it'll be even more."

"You want to do an interview?" I asked, my eyes narrowed.

"Why not? You're not making any money because of your injury and you're missing classes because you're keeping me company; it's only fair there should be some type of gain for you."

"Still."

"Well, since you won't take money from me, this is my way of helping you make your own money. Besides, Jane has been pressuring me to give an interview.

"One hundred thousand dollars?" I said and whistled low.

"Uh-huh. Probably more."

"That would pay the rest of my college fees and my student loan too."

"I know." Chloe smiled at me.

"Are you sure?"

"Yes. But you should probably clear it with Logan. You know he'll be a topic and he needs to be prepared in case anyone asks him questions. We need to be sure he's on board with the story."

"I could call him, I suppose."

"Good, then call him." Chloe picked up my phone from the table and handed it to me.

"I didn't mean right now. It's four in the morning in Scotland," I objected.

"Who cares? We both know he sleeps with his phone next to him; we all do."

"Yeah, but I don't want to wake him."

"Why not? He'll be thrilled to hear your voice no matter the time of day."

I shook my head. "Only you would think like that, Chloe."

She rolled off the couch with a lazy moan. "While you call Logan, I'll call Jane and ask her to set up the interview and negotiate a good price for both of us."

"All right." I sat up straighter and blew hair out of my face. Nervous energy crackled through me like a vibration from head to toe.

In the past five weeks only a few text messages had passed between Logan and me. He had asked for us to talk; I had answered that I needed more time.

Somehow it had been easier to just bury my feelings for him and forget what happened between us. My head just wasn't in a place where I had anything to offer him.

But now, the prospect of hearing Logan's voice again both excited and scared me.

Chloe had told me a hundred times that nothing had happened between them, but with what she had told me earlier today about Allan – my confidence in men was at an all-time low.

"Just call him up and make it short. You can do that," I muttered to myself. "You're not asking for his permission, you're just warning him, so he's prepared," I added.

And then I called up Logan, like I had so many times as Mary. This time, however, I would be me.

CHAPTER 21
Scotland by Night

Logan

My cell phone woke me up.

"Hello." My voice was raspy from sleep.

"Logan?"

"Aye," I said with my eyes still closed and cleared my throat.

"Did I wake you?"

Lord, I would recognize that velvet voice anywhere. "Mary," I said in a breathy sigh and smiled. "It's good to hear yer voice."

"Ehm… this is Faith."

My eyes jerked open. "Faith?"

"Yes. I'm sorry to disappoint you."

Fuck, was that hurt in her voice? "No… ehm, you're not disappointing me," I babbled and pushed up to sit against the headboard. "I'm glad ye called… how are ye?"

"Who's Mary?" she asked.

"She's, ehm…" I trailed off and bit my lip. Why did I always mess up with Faith? Maybe she was calling me to get back on track and I'd derailed the whole thing in my first sentence. "Mary is a woman I've never met," I explained.

Faith stayed quiet, waiting for me to continue.

"She's, ehm… someone I've talked to on the phone. A lot."

"Logan?"

"Aye?"

"When you said you were in love with someone, did you mean her?" she asked.

I formed a fist wishing I could just lie, but I was raised better. "Yes," I whispered, "but I haven't spoken to her in a long time."

"Are you still in love with her?"

"No... I don't know. Look, it's complicated."

"Right," Faith said. "But if you could choose between her and me – who would you choose?"

"Faith..." I frowned.

"It's a simple question."

"I've never met Mary. I don't know what she looks like."

"Then how can you be in love with her?"

"It's her personality." *Stop talking, you fool!*

"What about her personality? What makes her so special?"

"Listen, I dinnae want to discuss Mary with ye. Tell me how ye are."

"I'm still in LA with Chloe."

"And how is she?"

"Better. And you? How are you coping?"

"Och, dinnae bother yersel."

"Your accent is more pronounced now."

"Sorry, it's because I'm back home."

"Ohh, okay. Is the press still hunting you?"

"Nah, everyone here knows I'm hiding and they're keeping my visit a secret. I'm fine."

She sighed loudly. "That's good to hear."

"Faith."

"Yes."

"I miss ye."

Her silence spoke volumes.

"The reason I'm calling you," she said slowly, "is to warn you."

"Of what?"

"Chloe and I will be doing an exclusive interview. It's a way for me to get enough money to pay for college."

"All riiight," I said, drawn out.

"And I'm sure the journalist will ask about you and our relationship; you know, with your role in all of this."

"Uh-huh"

"I just felt I should warn you in case someone shows you the article."

"It's an article?"

"Yes, I think so. I don't know exactly."

"And what will ye tell them?"

"That we live together, that we met in a bar... you know, that sort of thing."

"And you want me to confirm that story, in case someone asks me?"

"Yes, please."

I nodded slowly. "Ye do realize that ye're asking me to lie to my own family?"

"It's just until everything settles down again and Niko is caught. Won't they be happy that you've found someone?"

"Undoubtedly... and wondering what the hell I'm doing in Scotland letting my drop dead gorgeous girlfriend fend for herself in the US."

Faith was quiet.

"Listen, I can tell them all day, every day, but they'll see right through me. It's not the Scottish way of things, Faith. They'll expect me to stay close and protect ye, especially with Niko on the loose."

"So, if we were truly together, what would you do?"

"I would take ye away from the danger. Have ye come here, or at least stay close to ye."

"You're a good man, Logan," she said quietly. "Maybe I can visit you in Scotland some time. I always wanted to see the old castles and go horseback riding in the beauties of nature."

201

I swallowed a laugh. "You and yer bloody Highlander novels, can ye even ride a horse?"

She laughed. "No. But it looks amazing in the movies."

"Aye, but trust me, ye get a sore arse after a while."

"I would still like to try it."

"Then pack yer bags and come spend Christmas with us."

"Christmas?"

"Aye, think of it as a *cultural experience,*" I teased, thinking of all the times she had told me the same thing.

"But won't it be awkward, I mean, with what happened between us? I don't want you to expect..."

I cut her off. "I'm gonna stop ye right there. I dinnae expect anything. Ye can come here as my friend if ye wish, but I should warn ye. I'm at my dad's house and my brothers are coming to spend Christmas. They're a bit rough around the edges."

"What do you mean?"

"Och, it's just that we tend to swear a lot and make crude jokes, but dinnae fash yerself," I said again, "ye'll be perfectly safe here. Contrary to what yer novels say, we Scots dinnae force ourselves on young lasses."

"Your ancestors did."

"So ye say, but we are modern men and can take a hint. At least I can, and if Andrew or Derek tries anything, I'll kick their arses for ye."

She laughed. "How heroic of you. So you would be okay with me coming as your friend?"

"Of course."

Because she was silent, I added, "Faith, I give ye my word. I willnae touch ye."

"You know what? I think I'll do it then. As long as you promise not to expect anything other than friendship."

"I promise."

"Wow, I can't believe I'm going to see Scotland for real."

I smiled and tried to hold back my eagerness when I asked, "Do ye need money for the ticket?"

"No, I think the interview should take care of that – or maybe I'll make an exception and borrow Chloe's private plane."

"She has a private plane?"

"Of course. What else would she spend her money on?" she said sarcastically. "It's not like there are humanistic or environmental issues that are more important than skipping the lines at the airport."

"Of course not." I grinned. "When can ye be here?"

"I'm not sure. Probably Thursday, but I'll email you my arrival time as soon as I know."

"I can't wait," I said honestly before we hung up.

The thought of Faith among my friends and family terrified me a little. She wouldn't understand half of what they said.

Still, I would be there to help her and make sure she had a good time.

But my brothers – damn, I already knew the two would be drooling all over her.

CHAPTER 22
Mistaken Identity

Faith

Wednesday morning, Chloe and I were clever and made it look like I left the mansion while she stayed behind.

She wore my clothes, I wore hers, and her acting skills paid off. She imitated my walk to perfection while I had a harder time with her British accent.

Still, Jane, her agent, didn't catch on to us and I had to swallow my laugh when the woman confided in me that she thought that Faith had overstayed her invitation.

"I get that you're twins and all, but truly you're as different as two people can be," she announced to me.

"What makes you say that?"

"Forgive me, but it's hard to understand someone with as much class and grace as yourself can have a sister that vulgar."

"Vulgar?" My eyes widened.

"Well, yes, it's rare to see her with nail polish – she doesn't care about fashion, does she? I bet she doesn't even wax." Jane wrinkled her nose and gathered her papers from the counter. "In Faith's case, beauty is truly wasted."

"You're just an old plastic hag," I muttered.

"Excuse me?"

I turned and gave her a fake smile. "I just pondered if you might need a plastic bag." I pointed to her papers. "You know, for all your things."

It was impossible to tell if she was shocked, upset, or surprised, as her Botox-infused face stayed completely impassive.

"Thank you, dear, but I'm fine. You know I wouldn't be caught dead with a plastic bag."

Unless I suffocate you with one.

"So you're really serious about taking a vacation?" she asked.

"Yes."

"I wish you would tell me where you're going."

"Somewhere remote and tropical. That's all you need to know."

She shook her head disapprovingly. "All right, enjoy your Christmas vacation, and promise you'll read through all the scrips I gave you. I want you to pick your next project; I wrote my notes on all of them. A lot of people are asking to meet with you."

"Don't make any plans, Jane. Until Niko is caught, I'm not comfortable going out."

"Oh, I know, sweetheart. I still don't understand how he could do that to you." She patted my hand and I refrained from moving away. "You two were always so good together."

My eyebrows lifted. "Are you serious?"

"You know I adore Niko. He's been good for your career."

I wanted to throttle the money-hungry bitch. "He shot me, Jane," I said, staying in my role as Cleo.

She blinked at me. "I understand that, dear. It was horrible of him, but I'm sure he didn't mean to harm you and that he's suffering too."

So this was the kind of verbal poison and manipulation that Jane used to make Chloe docile. No wonder Chloe had become such a doormat. This woman practically controlled Chloe's life; five minutes with her alone had told me all I needed to know. This snake didn't have Chloe's best interests at heart, just her own.

"You need to go now," I said harshly and crossed my arms.

"Yes, I'll leave and you should pack for your vacation. Don't worry about anything on the home front, I have it covered," she said, completely ignoring my hostile attitude.

The moment the door closed behind her, the air felt lighter. *Jesus, Chloe needs a detox from toxic people in general. Not just Niko.*

Hopefully her time in the woods would make her see that she needed to make changes in her life.

Big changes!

I talked to my mom on the phone. She was nervous and kept worrying about Niko tracking down Chloe.

"Don't worry, it's going to work," I assured her.

"It had better."

Chloe had come up with an elaborate plan that would make the world believe she was spending Christmas in a tropical paradise with her parents. Tomorrow I would play the role of Cleo leaving on her private jet to go pick up her parents in Spokane and fly off to a secluded resort in the Philippines.

But my parents were the only ones actually staying at the resort, since I would go to Scotland instead.

"Did you order a taxi to the airport as we talked about?"

"Yes. We're leaving tomorrow morning."

"Good, you'll have a wonderful time. Send me some happy tropical pictures. Will you?"

"Are you sure you don't want to come with us?"

"Yes, I'm going to experience Scotland."

"It'll be rainy and wet. Why not come with us and get a nice tan?"

"It's okay, Mom. We'll celebrate Christmas together next year; I promise."

That night I ate a bucket of ice cream and watched sci-fi movies on Chloe's humongous flat-screen.

The mansion felt awfully big and I missed my room at Logan's place. In the five weeks I had stayed here with Chloe, we had slept in her large bed, curled up together, talking about life and dreaming of better days to come. It had been just like when we were little girls and Chloe hadn't been able to sleep by herself. I was convinced her fear of being alone was part of her problem.

But tonight, I was the one finding it hard to sleep, and yet I must have dozed off eventually. Otherwise I would have heard him sneak up on me.

I woke up with the instant realization that something was wrong. Unable to move from the body pressing down on me, I pushed and shoved with my hands.

"Shh... babe, it's me. Don't worry, I won't harm you. I'll never harm you."

Niko.

I panicked and bucked to get him off me, but he only pushed me down by force. "I came to apologize, babe. I thought it was you in those pictures and it made me crazy with jealousy. You know I can't stand the thought of another man touching you."

My eyes adjusted to the dimmed light and I grew still. Clearly he was too big and strong for me to push off.

"Shh..." he repeated and stroked my chin.

With his unshaven, disheveled, and worn-out look, he didn't resemble the fashionable pop star that teenage girls across the nation worshipped. I held my breath, disgusted by the foul stench of cigarettes that reeked from him.

"I tracked him down, babe. I'm so sorry that I doubted you. The moment I saw him in real life, I knew something was wrong."

"You found Logan?" I asked with a trembling voice.

"God, he's an ugly son of a bitch. I know you would never touch someone that hideous. What is your sister thinking?"

I swallowed hard.

"They said on the news that I shot you, but I would never lay a hand on you. You know that, right, babe? You know how much I love you." His eyes were teary as he held my face in place and kissed me.

I lay stiff as a corpse, but my mind was running in circles, trying to find a way out of this situation.

Where the hell are the security guards?

How did he get past them?

If I tell him I'm Faith, will he let me go or hurt me?

Probably hurt me – he hates me as much as I hate him.

If he could manage to get inside this fortress, then surely he can track down Chloe too.

I have to protect her. No matter what happens, I'll protect her from this crazy person.

I had underestimated Niko's determination and possessiveness. He was dangerously sick.

"Let me make it up to you," he pleaded but got no response from me.

"I always make it up to you, don't I, babe?" he whispered in a raspy voice and pulled my shirt up, his hands splaying over my abdomen. "I knew they were lying. There's no bullet hole. Why would you let them tell those lies? I would never shoot you," he rambled.

I was scared to even breathe, which made my chest tremble with shallow breaths of air. My eyes were wide open and tears were running silently down onto the mattress. The man was delusional and in denial of what he had done to Chloe.

"Shh, don't cry," he whispered. "It's okay, babe, just breathe. I've got you. I'm going to make you feel really good. Just like I always do, you'll see." His hand was squeezing my breasts and he pressed a kiss to my lips, making me turn my head in disgust.

"Don't touch me," I pleaded in a thick voice.

"Shh, it's okay. Don't be scared. It's me, your charmer... remember how you always call me your charmer?"

I kept my head to the side, my mouth pressed shut and my nostrils flaring to breathe in air.

"No?" The tone of his voice changed. His brown eyes turned black. 'Oh I see, you're in *that* mood, babe. You wanna play our little game, don't you?" He yanked at my hair and placed a hand under my chin to force my head back to look at him and his sardonic grin. "I like that game."

I tried to push him away with my hands, but he quickly pinned them to the mattress. "Tsk, tsk, are you going to fight me now? I wouldn't do that if I were you."

"Let me go," I rasped out.

He lowered his whole body on top of mine, pressing all the air out of my lungs and using his heavy body to show me one thing. He was in control.

His mouth was by my ear and he whispered in a gruff voice. "I know it turns you on, babe. You can pretend all you want that you don't want me to press your knees apart and take what's mine, but we both know you're longing for me. You love my cock, don't you?"

I wanted to scream "no" but I was suffocating from his weight on top of me.

"Are you going to be a good little girl and do as Daddy tells you to?"

Daddy? What the hell?

"Nod your head 'yes,' and I'll ease off of you," he whispered. It was like answering the question, "Do you want to live or die," so I nodded.

"Good girl," he said and eased off of me, sitting back on his heels.

Coughing violently, I held my hands to my sore neck, and desperately sucked in air to my deprived lungs.

I was too weak to fight him when he pulled at my pants but the sound of material ripping made me scream. With my sore throat it wasn't loud and he quickly bent down, covered my mouth, and furiously hissed, "I told you to be a good girl, didn't I?" Drops of his spit landed on my face. "You don't want security to come and disturb us, do you?"

His hand constricting my throat told me what he wanted me to say. "No," I forced out.

"Good, because remember, we're just playing, right?" He caressed my face before he sat back on his heels again.

With terror I watched him rip off my panties and unzip his own pants. The sight of his cock springing out made me almost pass out. It was hard and a long string of pre-cum dripped from it.

Fuck! I was panicking inside as he lowered himself against me and slid his cock over my pelvis. I couldn't let this happen, but if I enraged him by fighting, I would end up in a hospital bed like Chloe or possibly in a morgue.

Still, I couldn't let him take me. Chloe would never forgive me if I didn't tell him I wasn't her. She wouldn't want me to get raped for her, and she was hours away. I could warn her and she could get police protection. Yes, I had to tell him.

"I'm Faith," I burst out. "Not Chloe. I'm Faith."

"What?" Niko pulled back, narrowed his eyes, and scanned me. "No, you're not."

"I am. That's why there's no bullet hole."

"Where's Cleo?"

"Gone."

"Gone where?"

"In therapy."

His initial shock of mistaken identity turned to rage. "Where is she?" he snarled and grabbed around my neck with both hands again.

"I don't know. She wouldn't tell me."

The cold expression in his eyes frightened me. "Faith," he spat out. "The bitch who thought I wasn't good enough for her sister."

I closed my eyes when his cock ran up my thigh. "Do you realize how many times I've thought about fucking you into submission, *Faith*?" He snarled my name. "Then you would understand why your sister is crazy for me.

"In fact this might have been your *faith* all along. To be my little cock slave. You know you always wanted me. They all do. I've seen you look at my crotch, and we both know you were always jealous of Cleo. That's why you kept trying to get between us. You wanted me for yourself, didn't you?"

"You're delusional." I hissed.

"Look down, Faith," he ordered. "I want you to see when I penetrate your uptight little pussy."

I stubbornly turned my head away but he smacked my face and yanked my head around.

"Open your eyes."

I squeezed my eyes tighter.

"Open your fucking eyes and watch when I fuck you."

"No."

Smack! The sound of his fist hitting my collarbone was loud and I opened my eyes, with a fury so deep that I wanted them to burn a hole in his soulless skull.

"You are a pathetic coward," I shouted and spit in his face.

He's going to kill me. His eyes told me that much and the roar of fury underlined it.

"You dare spit on me?" He twisted my right nipple and I bucked in pain.

211

"If you won't look, then at least you'll *feel* me fucking you. Let me give you a little taste of how it's gonna be." He growled and licked my face.

"Open your mouth," he ordered and when I didn't he pushed hard on my jaw until I gave in. His assault on my mouth felt like an imitation of rape. His tongue thrust in and out like a jigsaw cutting through wood. His foul taste of cigarettes made me think of licking an ashtray and it made my stomach convulse.

The pressure was all over my body – his legs holding mine down, his cock against my inner thigh, his torso on top of mine, his hands pinning my wrists down, and his disgusting tongue raping my mouth.

I didn't plan it, but the bucket of ice cream in my stomach came at him like a projectile and filled his mouth with my vomit.

Niko jerked back, sputtering and coughing, and then he started vomiting himself.

It was my chance, and I took it.

Naked, terrified, and with a chest covered in half digested ice cream, I slid down from the bed and crawled to the safe room just a few feet away. My hands trembled and my eyes were blinded by tears, but I was in survival mode and remembered how to activate the secret panel. When I was inside and the panel slid shut behind me, I pushed the red button on the wall that Chloe had instructed me to use.

Thonk. The sound of the metallic locking mechanism told me I had sealed the door. An electrical control panel next to the button flashed red saying, "Stay calm, help is coming!"

"Thank God," I cried out, curled up in a ball, and sobbed.

CHAPTER 23

Arrival

Logan

"So where is she?" my brother Andrew asked.

I hung my coat and tried not to murder him with my eyes.

"I told you, didn't I?" Derek joked. "No lass that bonnie would be with our Logan."

I didn't laugh, but trampled up the stairs to my room.

"Och, I was only jesting," Derek called after me.

"Get tae fuck," I snarled and heard Andrew laugh.

She hadn't been there. I had waited for three fucking hours and she hadn't come.

I felt like the stupidest bloke in the world.

It was late and only my brothers had stayed up to greet Faith, probably because they were still skeptical that the article had been true.

I picked up the colorful magazine and threw it across my room.

Amazing chemistry and the most panty-dropping Scottish accent, my arse.

In the article, Faith had called me "a real man" and talked about being attracted to me the first time we met. She had talked about feeling safe with me, and yet here I was, alone.

That cursed article had given me *hope*. If she meant half the things she had said about me in that article, there was a chance for us. There had to be.

But it was all part of the show and as meaningless as that fucking article that taunted me from across the room, with the front page showing Faith and Chloe, fingers intertwined, chin to chin, the headline saying, "Twins to the end."

I wish I could say her beauty was a matter of photoshopping but that would be a lie. Faith was fucking flawless.

A glimpse in the mirror told me why she hadn't come. *How did I think she could love someone as ugly as me? How did I manage to fool myself for even a second?*

I fumbled through my closet. *It's here somewhere.*

My fingers reached the cold steel and I pulled it out. My old knife that I had used for hunting with my father. This knife had skinned rabbits and taken lives before.

Taking a large gulp of my bottle of Scotch, I raised the knife in front of me.

I'm done being taunted by women!

⟨ ∞ ⟩

"Hey, wanker, ye better get yer arse out of bed."

Still fully dressed, I lay sprawled on my bed, chest down, and my head hammering. Without opening my eyes, I threw my pillow in the direction of the door, hoping to hit Andrew in the head.

"Fuck ye doing? Ye almost hit yer girlfriend."

With my head still turning away from the door, I flipped him my middle finger. "Yer talking pish," I mumbled and wished he would just go away.

"Logan," a female voice said softly.

I stiffened.

"Logan," she repeated.

I pushed up on my elbows and turned to look.

Faith was standing in my doorway, holding my pillow. Andrew was right behind her with a goofy grin on his face.

"I dinnae ken why ye would come all the way to Scotland for me wee brother, lass, but if he willnae be kind to ye, maybe ye should stay in ma room instead."

Faith blinked a few times; clearly she hadn't understood Andrew's strong accent.

"Leave us," I told him and rolled out of bed.

"Where were ye?" I asked her and rubbed my face. "I thought ye got cold feet."

Her eyes darted around the room taking in the scene. "I can see that." She walked over slowly to pick up the magazine cover where only Cleo's picture was left. "What happened to *my* picture?" she asked with a grimace.

"I cut it out." I pointed, embarrassed, to her picture on the wall where a knife was penetrating her mouth. "Wanted to cut out all yer lies too."

She had deep frown lines on her face. "A lot of things happened before I left. I got delayed."

"Would have been nice to know."

"I left you a voice mail," she defended herself.

"And how did ye find me?"

"Your brother answered your phone when I called. He came to get me."

I scratched my chin. "How long have I been sleeping?"

"It's a quarter past one."

"In the afternoon? Jesus," I mumbled and rubbed my face.

"May I sit?" Faith asked.

I didn't look at her but pointed to the chair by the desk.

She came to sit next to me instead.

"Logan." Her voice was brittle and weak and stirred concern in me.

"What is it?" Had my treatment of her picture upset her that much?

"They found Niko."

I lifted my gaze to meet her wet eyes and drew a deep breath of relief. "Finally."

She nodded.

"Where was the bastard?"

"I don't know where he'd been hiding, but he came to Chloe's house and was arrested."

"*After* she left?" I asked.

"Uh-huh."

"Och, thank God, she wasn't there. Did ye see them arrest him?"

Faith shook her head. "No, I was hiding."

Something in her voice made me narrow my eyes and watch her closer. Her body was rigid and her hands folded in fists.

"Tell me," I said gravely. "What happened?"

She couldn't look at me. Her shoulders bobbed up and down as tears overwhelmed her.

"Faith." I pulled her into my arms and held her tight for the longest time while she sobbed. In my heart I knew something horrible had happened to her, and that I couldn't fix it.

When she finally calmed down enough to talk she asked for a tissue to dry her nose. I fetched it and gave her a minute to gather herself while I brushed my teeth.

When I returned, I closed the door to my room and sat back beside her.

"Tell me what happened?" I asked again, and she started to tell. It took every bit of self-discipline not to tear my room apart from the fury that was running through my body.

"It was so repulsive that I threw up in his mouth."

"Ye did what?" My eyebrows flew up.

"It wasn't a little either. It just came cascading out of me, and all the vomit made him let go."

"And then what?"

"I hid in the safe room and activated the alarm."

216

I hugged her tight. "Good job, Faith."

We sat like that for a minute before she spoke against my chest. "You know, I haven't told anyone except you and the police."

I lifted her chin to look at her. "Not even yer family?"

"No. I can't tell them."

"Why not?"

"What good will it do, Logan? Chloe is already hurting and trying to get better. My parents have worried constantly for weeks. This would break their hearts."

"Ye were raped, Faith. They need to know."

"I wasn't fully raped."

I didn't comment on that. What that swine had done to her was bad enough.

"I'll tell them after Christmas." She sighed. "It'll come out during the trial anyway. Maybe the news will report it. They always find out, don't they?"

"But yer family must already know that Niko was arrested at the house."

"Oh, they do. It was all over the news, and I sent a text to my parents and one to let Onava know so she can tell Chloe. I just didn't tell them what he did to me."

"Were ye taken to the hospital?"

"Yes."

"And?"

"The worst part is my neck." She untied her scarf, and I had to close my eyes when I saw the black marks on her neck.

"What kind of man does something like that?" I felt nauseated.

"I thought about not coming," she said softly. "But my parents are on a tropical Island. My sister is in a cabin in the forest, and my best friend in Seattle wasn't home."

"I'm glad you came," I said.

She gave me a sad smile. "You wanna hear something crazy?"

217

"Uh-huh."

"When I lay naked and frightened in the safe room..."

I nodded for her to go on.

"I thought of you, Logan. How I wished you were there to hold me and tell me everything would be okay."

"Me?"

"Yes."

I didn't know what to say or what to make of it, so I didn't say anything.

"I wanted to go home to you in Seattle," she continued. "But as I said, you weren't there."

I tilted my head when I realized she had meant me when she referred to her best friend. It didn't make much sense to me, but I wasn't going to argue.

"I'm here for ye. Whatever ye need. Just tell me."

Faith used the back of her hand to dry away her tears. "Do you mean that?"

"Of course."

"I think what I need most, right now, is your friendship and your strong arms to hide in."

I hugged her again and stroked her back.

"Now that Niko is behind bars, we don't need to pretend anymore with your family. You can tell them the truth," she said and pulled back.

"Aye." I nodded, dreading to tell Andrew and Derek. They had been right. Faith wasn't my girlfriend and never had been. "But ye know... The minute I tell my brothers, they're going to be coming on to ye like humping hounds."

She creased her brows slightly. "Can't you tell them to back off?"

"Aye, I can, but I doubt they'll listen much, if they know ye're single."

"All right," she said slowly. "And if we keep up the charade, could I sleep with you in your bed?"

I nodded. "If ye want."

218

"And would you hold me like you did that night in my room?"

"Aye, I would."

"Promise you won't try anything." Her eyes were big and pleading. "I think I would freak out."

"I promise. I won't touch ye," I said and squeezed her hand. "Ye're safe with me, Faith."

She leaned her head on my shoulder. "Thank you, Logan."

I kissed the top of her hair. "No, thank ye, for confiding in me and for coming here."

We sat for a few minutes before I stirred a bit. "Are ye hungry?"

"Not really."

"But I am, and I reckon my family is dying from curiosity. Should we go down and get the introductions over with?"

"I already met Andrew," she reminded me.

"I know; did he try anything?"

"No, he was really nice and courteous."

"Impossible," I chuckled. "I dinnae believe ye."

"But he was. All gentleman-like."

"Ha. That wanker. He was trying to impress ye."

"Is he older than you?"

"Aye, but only by a year."

"You look very much alike, I think."

"Aye, he's handsome – I was too."

Faith nudged her shoulder against mine. "I would choose you any day over him."

Fuck. She had no idea how happy her words made me. I loved my brothers, but the eternal competition between us and my anxiety around women had made me fear that she would be interested in one of them.

"And Derek?" I asked.

"I haven't met him yet, but I'll let you know what I think tonight when we cuddle up together."

I was lucky that she got up from the bed in that moment and asked for the bathroom.

"Second door on the right," I said and pointed toward the hallway.

When she left, I closed my eyes and pressed on my crotch. *Down, boy*, I commanded, but her words that we would be cuddling tonight had alerted parts of my body that mistook those words for something else.

My brothers would think me the luckiest bastard on the planet, and I smirked at the thought that they would be green with envy in their beds tonight.

It was all good, except I was handpicked by Faith to restore her trust in men, and I couldn't fail. I had to control my desire for her.

The thought of Niko raping her made my erection fall limp. How I wished he would meet someone in prison who would rape him with an iron stick long enough to reach his brain. At least then he would die with something between his ears.

CHAPTER 24
The Real Highlander

Faith

Logan's family was wonderful. They spoke with a thick brogue that made it hard for me to understand them.

I was beginning to appreciate that Logan had been right when he said he was trying to speak American, because hearing him speak with his family made it clear that they had a completely different language among them.

Luckily his stepmother, Anna, was English, and kind enough to translate when we sat down for a late lunch.

"This house is actually the old vicarage. My husband's grandparents were the last ones to live in the old castle," Anna said and pointed out the windows. "It's a short walk up the hill that way."

Logan's father had a full beard and kind eyes. "Logan tells us ye fancy Scottish history, Faith, is that true?"

"Yes," I blushed a little. "I like to read about the Highlands."

Andrew and Derek exchanged glances and grinned. "Is that why ye swooned when ye met Logan? Ye thought he was a romantic Highlander warrior?"

I looked to Logan, not sure what Andrew had just said.

Derek laughed and pounded his fist down the table. "Och, ya bas, Logan. The poor lass thought ye were the best of our lot. Bloody lucky for ye that I wasnae around to give ye a bit of competition."

"Lucky for her ye mean," Logan retorted

"How about yer twin?" Andrew said and leaned closer. "Mayhap she fancies herself a Highlander too?"

I looked to Logan. "Is he asking about Chloe? I thought I heard him say twin."

"Och," Andrew threw his hands up. "Are ye daft, lass? Dinnae look at Logan every time I say something."

I understood that and creased my brow. "I apologize, Andrew, but perhaps you could try speaking English," I said politely. "I find it hard to understand you."

Andrew, who was almost a copy of Logan but with longer hair and a rounder face, gaped at me. "A am speaking English," he said with a thick brogue, and his offended expression made everyone around the table laugh.

"Don't worry, Faith," Anna said friendly. "I had a hard time understanding them in the beginning too. You'll learn in time, and when they want you to understand them badly enough, they'll speak with less of an accent."

"Dinnae listen to the Sassenach," Andrew jested.

"Ah, I know that word. It means English," I said triumphantly.

They raised their glasses and clinked mine with nods.

"Faith, why don't you tell us about the first time you met Logan? I'm curious to hear it from your side," Anna said smilingly.

"Aye, tell us," Derek said and wiggled his brows. "How bleutered were ye?"

Logan gave me a patient smile. "Bloothered means plastered, or drunk if you will."

"I wasn't drunk at all. Actually I hardly touch alcohol."

"What? Are ye a religious nutter?" Derek asked and narrowed his eyes suspiciously.

"No, I can drink. I just don't like to," I explained. "Anyway, I was drinking coffee in a bar and then I saw Logan sitting alone, looking rough and sexy. I was just about to go talk to him, but then came this beautiful woman and approached him."

Logan sat quietly with a smile tugging at his lips.

"I was really disappointed," I continued, "But then he rejected her and left the bar. I knew I had to take the chance, so I ran after him."

"Ye ran after him?" Derek was gaping. "Bollocks, clearly I'm living in the wrong country," he added with a sigh.

"And then what happened?" Anna asked excitedly.

"Well, it was raining and he seemed a little surprised."

"A wee bit surprised... that's an understatement," Andrew slammed Logan on the shoulder.

"Shhh," Anna hushed Logan's brothers.

"I convinced him to invite me home, and then when I got him to loosen up a bit, we really hit it off."

"But tell us again, how is it that you moved in with Logan so quickly?" Anna asked and poured herself another glass of wine.

"Well, I was in a bit of a predicament with my living situation and when he mentioned he didn't like to do house chores, I suggested I could do it, if he let me stay for free."

"But when did you two fall in love?"

I looked to Logan, but he was looking down at the table.

"I'm not sure exactly, it wasn't like a certain moment in time. It just snuck up on me. Suddenly the sound of his key in the door made me smile, and I caught myself sniffing his shirt while doing laundry."

Logan eyes found mine, questioning.

"I guess I never told you that," I said with a small smile.

"Ohh, that's so sweet." Anna sighed and looked at her husband. "Remember when we fell in love?"

"Still am," he said and kissed her.

We talked for another hour, the jet lag catching up with me and my yawns growing longer.

"Are ye tired?" Logan asked.

"Yes. I'm sorry, I didn't sleep much these last few days."

"Hey." He stroked my cheek and gave me a sympathetic smile. "Meeting Derek and Andrew will drain most women; ye dinnae need to explain."

"Aye, but only if ye bed us." Derek and Andrew laughed.

Logan shook his head with a chuckle and took my hand. "Come on, I'll take ye upstairs."

"Call if ye need a *real* Highlander," one of the brothers called behind us."

That made Logan stiffen a bit and although it was meant as a joke, I still turned to look at them.

"I just realized that I *do* know the moment I knew I loved Logan.

"Ohh?" Anna said and smiled.

"It was the first time we made love. You know that feeling when it feels like a perfect fit and you're home?"

"I do," Anna said softly and shot a smile at her husband.

"It wasn't just that Logan is a superior lover. It's more the fact that he makes me feel completely safe and protected."

Logan squeezed my hand and I knew I was overdoing it. "Anyway, we'll see you later."

"Enjoy your nap," Anna called to me.

There were no more comments from his brothers, and I felt good about myself for putting them in their place.

Logan was quiet when we lay down on the bed.

"Are you okay?" I asked.

"Aye. Go to sleep, Faith."

I yawned. "All right, but shouldn't you thank me for showing your brothers they were wrong about you?"

"Let's not talk about it."

I was sensing some strange vibes from Logan. "What's wrong?" I asked. "I made you look good."

"Yes, but it's lies, Faith. I don't like deceit."

"I won't tell them."

"It doesn't matter. I know it's not true. It's just empty words."

"But I meant some of it," I said softly to defend myself.

"Then I'm honored. Dinnae think about it, just rest now."

The last thing I saw before I closed my eyes was my picture on the wall with a knife in my mouth.

"I wanted to cut out your lies," he had told me.

How am I going to tell him that I'm Mary?

He's going to be so mad when he learns that I created that whole character to talk to him.

My own words to my sister came back to me. "I want you to know integrity." God, was I a hypocrite. Who the hell was I to talk about integrity when I was the biggest liar around?

I had never caught Logan in a lie. He had told the truth, even when it was inconvenient to him. I knew because I had grilled him about Mary and he had been painfully truthful when it didn't serve him.

I nuzzled up against him, placing my head on his shoulder. "Will you wake me in an hour?" I asked and yawned again. "I just need a nap."

"I will," he promised and kissed the top of my hair. "Don't worry about a thing."

CHAPTER 25
The Real Mary

Logan

"What did you find out?" I asked and squeezed the phone a bit harder.

Faith was still sleeping in my room, but I had stepped out when the private investigator I had hired in Seattle called me.

"I talked to the owner – Nigel – and as expected he refused to give out information on his staff," Jake informed me in his characteristic gruff voice. "But I've worked with his type before, and they play tough and honorable until you offer them the right bribe."

"How much?"

"A thousand."

I snorted. "A thousand dollars. Really?"

"Yup, I'm putting that on your bill."

"By all means – just tell me ye know who she is."

Jake huffed out air. "Here's the situation. Blue Ribbon Escort Service currently has three female phone operators. One is his wife. She's a co-owner and a heavy smoker with a dark voice."

"That's not Mary."

"Then there's two others, and one only just started so we can rule her out."

"All right, so what did you find out about the last one?"

"She's a student at the local college, has worked for him for six months, and is a Latina. He says she's got a pronounced accent."

"What kind of accent?"

"I assume Spanish, since she's Latina."

"That's not her. Mary has a Southern accent."

"Right, but that only leaves one woman and she doesn't work there at the moment."

"Did she work there two months ago?"

"Yes."

"Then she could be the one. What do we know about her?" I said eagerly.

"Local student. Has worked there for about a year and is expected back after Christmas. She's got an injury. A car crash or something."

My heart started beating faster.

"This last one is in her mid-twenties, and Nigel was very protective of her identity. Apparently she's got a famous family member and doesn't want anyone to know she works for him."

"Faith," I muttered low.

"Yes, her name is Faith Olsson. Do you know her?"

"Aye. I know her."

"Then you've got your answer right there. She must be your Mary – don't you think?"

I closed my eyes. "Aye. She must be."

We finished our talk and I went downstairs, put on my coat, and went for a walk.

Why didn't I see it?

That's why she was at Trolls and Dolls that day. That's why she ran after me.

The Highlander novel in her room should have been a clue – or the many times "Mary" defended Faith.

Oh, no. The many conversations about my erotic fantasies came back to me. Faith knew everything. Everything I had told Mary, I had really told Faith.

I walked aimlessly, thinking back to the role-playing we had shared. Why hadn't she stopped me from embarrassing myself so profoundly?

227

Astonishment and shock were followed by disbelief. This wasn't happening. This couldn't be happening.

A surge of anger became my companion on my walk.

How can she make a fool out of me like that?

What have I done to deserve such deceitful lies?

Is she ever going to tell me?

Short, chubby, and brown hair – yeah, right.

I walked for hours ruminating upon the situation and considering my options. It was tempting to go back and confront Faith, but I was too angry and with everything that had happened to her, she was too fragile. After what Niko did to her, the last thing Faith needed was a large male shouting at her.

Instead I shouted from the hilltop. I screamed out my anger and frustration just like my therapist had told me to do when the emotional pressure became too much.

And it helped.

Feeling calmer, I squatted down and picked up a long twig from the frozen ground, breaking it into tiny bits.

I really only had one option.

I'll go back and pretend I don't know.

With a heavy sigh I rose up to my full height, my breath forming a cloud of condensation in the cold air, my hands tucked deep in my pockets as I started walking back to my father's house thinking, *But I do know, and I no longer trust her.*

$\{\infty\}$

I didn't realize I'd been gone for close to three hours until I stepped inside the house and saw dinner on the table.

"Where the hell have ye been, son?" My father asked me with a frown. "We've been worried sick about ye."

I entered the dining room and noticed Faith squeezed in between my brothers on the bench.

228

All five at the table were looking up at me.

"Next time ye fancy gaun fur a wee swallae doon the pub, could ye tell us?" Andrew said.

Faith looked to Anna, who interpreted. "He said, next time you want to go to the pub, you should tell us."

"I didnae go to the pub," I grumped.

"You must be freezing," Anna said and got up to pour me a cup of soup. "I'm afraid we already ate, but dinner is still on the table."

"Aye, it's cold outside," I said and took a seat, deliberately not looking at Faith.

"Awfy cauld," my father chimed in. "Where were ye?"

"Just walking."

Derek smacked his tongue. "Och, dae ye think me a twat? Walking my arse."

"I was," I insisted with a firm tone that told him to back off.

"Hey, dinnae flap," he said and raised both hands as white flags before turning to Faith. "So, ye're goin with us to the dancin' tonight?"

"Derek," Anna interjected. "Faith already told you no."

"It's nice of you to invite me to go clubbing, but I'm too tired. Maybe another time," Faith said softly and added, "What's a twally?"

"Bollocks, A wanted to show ye off to me mates," Derek complained at the same time as Anna leaned in and whispered to Faith: "Twally is an idiot, and he says he wanted to show you off to his friends."

I kept my head down and ate my soup feeling Faith's eyes burn my scalp.

"What is wrong with ye?" Andrew said. "How come ye dinna geez Faith a winch when ye came in?"

"A French kiss," I heard Anna translate to Faith.

"Cummon," Andrew continued.

"No," I muttered, but kept my head down.

229

"How no?" he asked. "Are ye feart?"

"No, I'm not afraid, I just don't need to constantly show my affection in public, Andrew," I said harshly.

"What's wrong, son? You seem tense," My father asked and I could tell he was minimizing the accent because of Faith.

I raised my head and looked at him. "I'm sorry, I just received a call from Seattle with some disturbing news."

"Work, is it?" Derek asked.

I didn't respond but went back to eating.

"Och, the hardships of ma minted brother."

"Minted?" Faith asked.

"Rich," my father translated, and turned back to me. "Is it true Faith beat ye in arm wrestling?"

I tensed as my brothers laughed.

Slowly I put my spoon down and sat back in my chair crossing my arms. For the first time since I got back I looked at Faith with a raised brow saying, "You told them?"

She gave a nervous smile. "Just your father and Anna."

"Yer talking oot yer arse," Andrew burst out, grinning widely.

"No, Faith isn't lying," I said and added in my head. *Right now.* "It's true, she did win over me in arm wrestling."

Both my brothers looked skeptical. "Nah, lass, I cannae believe it." Andrew said shaking his head.

And my father added, "Logan has always been the strongest of them all."

"I'll wrestle ye," Derek said with mischief and pushed his plate away. "Cummon, Faith, show me how strong ye are."

Faith handed her plate to Anna and made room between her and Derek. "All right, but don't be upset if I beat you," she said, but that only made him laugh harder.

It took him less than a minute to beat her three times, and then Andrew wanted to try.

Faith's cheeks were red as a boiled lobster and the veins on her neck popped out as she gave it all she had. For a moment I actually thought she was going to win, but Andrew used his weight and raised his hands in victory.

"See," Derek said to Faith. "Logan *let* ye win."

"No, he didn't. He tried hard to win."

"Uh-huh."

"Logan, tell them, we had a fair game," she pleaded.

"Ha, the only thing Logan had was spondoolyitis," Andrew exclaimed and spoke directly to Faith. "In English that would be a medical condition for talking shite."

"Ye sleekit bastard," Derek said with a grin to me. "Ye let her win, didnae ye?"

The truth hit me hard. I had walked for almost three hours blaming Faith for lying to me, when the truth was that I had deceived her too. I could have won in arm wrestling, but I let her believe she won.

"What was the prize for winning?" Anna asked Faith.

"If I won, Logan would let me move in with him, and if he won..." She paused and looked at me. "I forgot. What was it you wanted if you won?" she asked.

"If I won, I got my apartment to myself. If ye won, ye got to move in," I murmured and that had my brothers smacking their thighs with laughter.

"Faith, you sweet hen," Andrew said. "Dinnae ye ken it a strange bet for Logan?"

"Did you just call me a hen?" she asked with an arched brow.

"It's a term of endearment here in Scotland," Anna hurried to say, "but I have to agree with the men. Logan already had the apartment to himself before you moved in, so it does sound like you were the only one with something to gain."

"Yes, but..." Faith's hands were in the air as if she was about to make a point, but then she lowered them to rest on her lap. "Ohh, right... I see."

Her eyes lifted and found mine. "You wanted me to move in?"

I didn't answer.

"Aye, Logan wanted ye to move in," Derek confirmed.

"Then why didn't you just say so?" Faith asked me.

I ignored her and turned to Andrew and Derek, placing my elbow on the table. "Which one of ye ugly buggers want to go first?"

CHAPTER 26
Rocking Bedframes

Faith

They drank whiskey that night. A lot of whiskey. I waited for Andrew and Derek to leave for town, but apparently they were in no hurry and found a deck of cards and started playing instead.

It was hard to understand what they said and the slurred drunken talk certainly didn't make it easier. I talked to Anna, who was sweet, but I was still relieved when, finally, Logan declared that he was ready for bed.

"Och, ye lucky bastard," Andrew said and winked at Logan. "Are ye sure ye dinnae want me to warm her tonight? Ye can have her back in the morn."

Logan ignored his brother and turned to me. "Are ye coming?"

I nodded and asked Derek to move so I could get up from the bench.

Derek grinned. "We expect to hear rocking bedframes all night long."

"I'm too drunk for that," Logan mumbled and was booed by his brothers.

"Are you all right?" I asked Logan when we were alone.

"Aye" was his short answer.

"What happened? Why did you leave and what bad news did you get from Seattle?" I asked like a machine gun firing questions at him. All night my mind had been reeling and worrying, because whatever had happened, it had impacted him greatly. He had been cold toward me from the moment he came back.

"It disnae matter," he said and undressed in front of me, right down to his boxer briefs. "Guid night an' sweet dreams!" He was already crawling under the duvet and turning off the light.

"Hey," I protested. "I'm not ready. Can you keep the lights on until I've brushed my teeth?"

"Uh-huh," he grunted on his side and turned the light back on.

"Are you angry with me?" I asked, but he was either too drunk or too uninterested to answer me.

Feeling sad, I walked to the bathroom in the hallway and got ready for bed. When I entered the bedroom again, I could tell from his heavy breathing that Logan was asleep.

Disappointment filled me and my thoughts went to my sister, hoping that she was having a better time than me.

The bed was a twin bed and with him lying on his side by the wall, there was plenty of room for me.

"You can turn off the light now," I said and waited but there was no reaction. I had to lean over him to reach the switch and in the process he rolled onto his back.

I stretched again, determined to reach the switch this time, and that was when Logan opened his eyes a little.

"What are ye doing?" he asked and I didn't blame him because my sports bra and its contents were right above his mouth.

"Turning off the light," I said and finally got it. Darkness spread and I had to feel my way to get the pillow and the duvet just right.

"I willnae touch ye," Logan slurred and turned his back on me again.

"No you won't, but we got to make it look like you are," I said. "Remember, rocking bedframes."

I could hear Logan turn around to face me "What?"

"We need to make them think we have sex."

234

"Nah we dinnae. I'm too tired."

"They will tease you tomorrow," I warned him.

He yawned in response and thirty seconds later he was snoring lightly.

I snuggled up against his warm body and hoped that tomorrow he would tell me what troubled him.

But I didn't have to wait that long because before I fell asleep, I heard him mutter a name. "Mary."

I closed my eyes and felt my bad conscience gnaw at me. I needed to tell him and soon, but how?

$\{ \infty \}$

Logan

I woke up with Faith sprawled on top of me. I was uncomfortably warm and pushed her gently off me.

The clock on my wall showed it was almost seven in the morning. Slowly, yesterday came back to me.

Faith is Mary.

The silliest part of this was the regret that I would never meet the chubby brunette with the Southern accent whom I had fantasized about.

Mary had been real to me, and I had a hard time connecting her to Faith.

It was irrational and pathetic, but it felt like a loss. A break-up of sorts. There was no Mary. There never had been a Mary.

Faith stirred next to me and opened her eyes with a long stretch of her arms. "Good morning. You want to rock the bedframe now?" she asked.

"Nah."

"Why not?"

"I swore I wouldn't touch ye, remember?"

"No, I meant we should make it sound like we have sex. Not actually have it."

I frowned. "Why? Ye're not in my bed to impress my brothers."

"But I don't like it when they mock you."

I shrugged. "I mock them too, it's what we do."

"Yes, but..."

"What?" I asked and propped myself up on my elbow. Faith fiddled with the duvet.

"What, Faith?" I repeated.

She didn't look at me when she said. "I don't want them to think I'm boring in bed."

"Excuse me?"

"Well, if there's no noise from us they'll assume we don't have sex or that we have quiet, boring sex."

I shook my head. "How can ye even think about sex after what happened to ye? I would think the mere thought of sex would be disturbing to you?"

Faith looked thoughtful and for minutes she lay quietly looking up at the ceiling. "I hate Niko for doing that to me."

"Me too," I said sympathetically.

"I'm angry at Allan too."

"Allan?" I asked and raised my head to look at her. Why are ye angry at him?"

"My sister told me something..." Faith swallowed hard and took a deep intake of air. "She told me he cheated on me."

"Och, lass," I said and stroked her shoulder.

"It wasn't just once either. Apparently he slept with several of my friends."

"And you never knew?" I asked.

"No. But everyone else probably did." She blinked away tears. "Can you believe I've mourned him for seven years?"

I didn't answer because she seemed to be pondering out loud with her eyes glazed.

"I think Chloe and I have the worst taste in men."

"Uh-huh."

"Or maybe we bring out the worst in men?" she speculated.

"Hey..."

Faith turned her head and focused in on me. "What?"

"Not all men are like that, and if ye find the right man he willnae cheat on ye."

"And are you that man, Logan? That right man?" she asked.

My anger and indignation from yesterday made me look down. I still hadn't forgiven her deceit.

"I dinnae know," I said honestly and looked back up to see her eyes tearing up.

Faith tried to roll out of bed but I grabbed her and pulled her back. "Dinnae cry. Let's talk about this," I said without knowing how to address all the conflicting emotions inside me. All I could boil it down to was, "It's complicated."

"Because you're in love with someone else?" she asked accusingly.

"Nah," I exclaimed. "I dinnae know how I feel about anything anymore. And dinnae forget that ye came here as my friend and nothing more. Ye made me promise not to touch ye. So why are you messing with my head and asking me to be the right man for you?"

"I'm not asking you to *be* the right man for me," she said defensively. "I asked if you *were* the right man. There's a difference."

"You want me to declare my love for ye? Is that it?" I couldn't hide the anger I felt, because we both knew I already had declared I was in love with her. I had told her as Mary and she had left me hanging, feeling rejected and confused.

"No, obviously you don't love me. Sounds more like you hate me." She dried her tears away and turned her back to me, pulling herself into a ball.

237

I closed my eyes and calmed myself. "I'm sorry, Faith. And nah, of course I don't hate ye. Ye just confuse me, that's all."

"You confuse me too," she whispered.

I thought about some way to lift her mood. "Hey, what do ye say we have some fun and make that bedframe rock? I wouldnae want my family to think I'm dating a frigid American."

With a hand on her shoulder I pulled her gently around and smiled at her. "Show me what it sounds like when Americans have sex."

She gave me a long glance, but finally sniffled and dried her eyes. "You've really never been with an American?" she asked.

I shook my head. "I'm afraid I only know what a Scottish lass sounds like."

A smile tugged at her lips. "I suspect how a woman sounds like has everything to with the man she's with."

"Good point," I nodded. "And vice versa."

Faith sat up. "So how do we do it?"

"I'm not sure. I've never faked intercourse before."

That made her laugh, and the way her cheeks blushed combined with her bed hair made her look delicious. I changed position to hide my morning wood.

"Why don't you lie down flat on your back and grab the bedframe?" she asked. "And then I'll sit here next to you and move the bed as if I was riding you."

"Riding me?" With the tent in my boxers, I wasn't receptive to that idea, so I scrunched up my face. "Nah, I prefer to be on top."

"But we're not really..."

"Get on your back, woman," I joked and pointed to the mattress. To my surprise Faith complied and lay down, arched a bit, and raised her hands to grab the iron bars of the headboard.

I rolled on to my stomach and raised my torso up, deliberately keeping my erection pressed against the mattress to hide it from her.

For a long awkward moment, we glanced at each other, waiting for the other to start.

"So how do ye like it?" I asked her. "Slow and gentle? Or hard and fast?"

"Why don't you start out slow and gentle and end it hard and fast?" she said, her eyes still moist but now full of mischief.

"This is..." I didn't finish the sentence but she nodded.

"Crazy – yes, I know."

Without taking her eyes off me she arched her back and moaned loudly. "Yes, Logan, just like that, it feels so good."

I raised a brow, butterflies taking over my body. "Like this?" I said and imitated making slow love to her.

She wiggled her butt and stretched like a cat waiting to be stroked. "Yes, babe, that's right. Give me more."

When she parted her thighs slightly and licked her lips, I felt perspiration on my forehead. *Fuck* – was the woman trying to kill me?

I looked away and focused on my movements, but rubbing against the mattress and having a gorgeous woman move her body suggestively next to me while moaning my name was the closest to real sex that I had been in years.

"Look at me, Logan," Faith moaned and when I did I was blinded by her beauty.

Don't touch her. Don't fucking touch her, I chanted in my mind.

Instead I pretended she was under me and that I was inside her.

"Ye're so beautiful," I groaned.

We continued rocking the bed, moaning and looking into each other's eyes. It was strangely intimate and I was beginning to see lust in her eyes.

Every inherited instinct told me this woman was ready for sex, but I had made an oath, and it was possible that my vision was blurred by my own lust.

"Spread your legs for me," I ordered and to my surprise she did. Faith spread her bent legs and lay completely open for me in her panties and t-shirt. I bit my lip and pushed harder against the mattress.

"Yes, yes..." she cried out and tilted her head back as if she was feeling me inside her. "God, you're so big."

I grunted, my fingers tingling with the need to touch her. *No!* I grabbed the bedsheet and curled my fingers around it, continuing my rhythmical intercourse with the pretend version of Faith under me. The bedframe was now rocking and squeaking.

I was staring at her hard nipples showing through the gray fabric, and I almost popped a vein when Faith let her hands move up under her t-shirt to play with her breasts.

My moans were real now. My balls were tightening and my reproductive system geared to breed with the woman next to me. This game between us was older than time, and it demanded every ounce of self-control from the civilized part of my brain to keep my urges in check.

I wanted to make love to her so badly! A sentence escaped from the Neanderthal inside me. "Take off your t-shirt," I ordered.

She didn't. But she did pull it up, slowly and teasingly. The sight of her belly button made me almost come. Her stomach was flat and her skin smooth.

"Yes, Logan, play with my nipples. That's right, don't bite too hard, just suckle them like I love," she whispered loudly and pulled the t-shirt high enough for me to see her perfect C-cups. Looking straight into my eyes, she sucked on two of her fingers and slid them down to play with her pink nipples.

It was the most erotic thing I'd ever seen, and I knew I wouldn't last long. We had done role-plays in the past when she pretended to be Mary, but this... this was a huge step up.

"How do you want me?" she moaned and gave me a playful smile.

I closed my eyes, wanting the moment to last. My balls were telling me they were all fired up and ready to shoot, but I wanted this sexual experience to last longer.

"From behind, I want you from behind," I said in a gruff voice.

Faith just smiled and rolled over to set herself on her knees while grabbing the iron bars again. Her t-shirt was still high up and her black silky panties marked her beautiful ass like a target to aim for.

Fuck!!!

Don't touch her... don't you fucking touch her!

I raised up on my knees next to her, not caring that she saw my huge erection in my boxers or the wet spot of pre-cum on the front, I stroked myself and almost lost it when Faith looked up at me and licked her lips.

"Do you want me to fuck you hard now?" I asked.

"Yes," she whispered and wiggled her butt.

I sat back on my heels and rocked the bed with my motions, still stroking the front of my boxers at the same time.

"Touch yourself," I told her and again she surprised me by reaching down between her legs. I couldn't see much because of her panties, but the sounds and the movements she made told me it was working for her.

"I want to fuck you so bad," I admitted.

"You are fucking me," she corrected me and gave me an aroused grin.

241

I dried my forehead. It took strength to restrain myself.

"Logan, give it to me. Harder... yes, yes, more. Oh shit, I feel you against my cervix. You're so fucking big."

She made me crazy with need, and at this point it was either ripping her pants off or mine. I didn't care when I pulled my boxers down and grabbed my cock, jerking off with my eyes closed.

"Yes, babe, yes, that's right. I want to feel all of you." She egged me on when I spilled my seed like I was the fucking Niagara Falls.

Panting, I opened my eyes to see Faith now on her back with her eyes closed, one hand still in her panties and one hand playing with her right nipple.

I sat in a trance, watching her masturbate and moan in pleasure. She had to be the sexiest woman alive.

This was the same woman who had told me I wasn't a freak just because I had dirty fantasies, and now she was making herself come in *my* bed.

God, I wished she was fantasizing about me, but more likely she was fantasizing about some stupid fictional Highlander from a book she had read.

"Yes, Logan, yes..." she moaned and that made my heart flutter.

I didn't touch her but I used my voice to coax her, just like she had done for me. "God, you're so beautiful, Faith. I love the feel of your body and your hands on me."

She lifted her hand from her breast and reached out for me, her eyes still closed.

Hesitantly I took her hand, not sure what she wanted from me. "Talk to me," she instructed and intertwined our fingers. "Tell me how good it feels to be inside me."

I swallowed hard, but did as she wanted. "You drive me crazy. You feel so tight and warm. I've wanted to fuck you for so long, Faith"

"Yes... Just take me, Logan."

Does she mean that... like really take her, or just pretend?

The sight of her made my body bounce back for round two, but touching her could mean breaking the magic and I wanted her to come too.

"Do you feel me sliding in and out of you?"

"You fit me so perfectly," she moaned.

"Do you want me to lick you?" My offer was genuine but her eyes were still closed and she just smiled and nodded. "Yes, that feels good, I love your warm tongue on me."

"You taste so good," I whispered into her ear. "Do you like it when I blow air on your clit?"

"Uh-huh," she said and arched her back. "I'm coming, Logan, yes..." Her hand squeezed mine, while her other hand made fast circular movements in her panties. "Oh yes, that feels so good "

Watching Faith come was satisfying. It might not have been my tongue, fingers, or cock that made her come, but we had still shared sex... sort of.

A minute later, she turned to look at me with a beautiful relaxed smile, her hand still merged with mine.

"That was the best sex I've had in years," she said and grinned.

"Me too."

"Does that make us pathetic?" she asked.

"Probably, but hey, at least we can be pathetic together," I joked.

Footsteps in the hallway told me we had woken up at least one of my brothers. My father and Anna slept downstairs in another part of the house. Only the guest rooms were up here.

"Did you hear that?" Faith asked and looked at me like a naughty child up to no good. "Someone is awake."

"I know," I grinned back at her. "Mission 'rocking the bedframes' accomplished."

"And we didn't even kiss," she said as an afterthought.

"No, we didn't."

Our words hung in the air, our eyes locked, and my right hand merged with her left. If I had been confused before, I was twice as confused now.

I'm crazy about Faith.

And angry at her for lying to me.

I want her, badly.

But I don't want to want her.

We're too different, and she sends more mixed signals than a traffic light with a loose connection.

"I'm hungry," she said and broke my train of thought.

"Then let's get ye some breakfast. Do ye want to shower first?"

"Aye." She laughed at her imitation of me.

"All right, then you go first while I change the sheet."

"I've never seen a man come that hard," she confessed with a nod to the sheet.

I didn't know whether to be proud or embarrassed. "Well, it's been a while so…"

She smiled. "It's probably a good thing when you decide to have children."

I frowned.

"I mean, the more sperm, the higher the chance of pregnancy, right?" she said and looked away. "Okay, that came out wrong. Anyway, I'll be in the shower." She pointed over her shoulder and spun around, leaving me with my own confused thoughts.

CHAPTER 27

Kenna

Faith

When Logan and I came down for breakfast his family were all there, Andrew and Derek with unruly bed hair and signs of hangovers.

"Guid morning," his father said and looked happy.

"Good morning," I answered politely and ignored the wolfish grins Logan received from his brothers.

"Slamming her cervix, were ye," Andrew giggled and received a reproachful glance from Anna.

"Don't you two start again, I won't have you embarrass Faith."

Logan flipped Derek his middle finger when his younger brother started moaning into his cup of coffee.

"Ye're just jealous," Logan said with a smug smile.

"Aye, we are. Can ye blame us, ye bastart?" Derek answered with a shrug.

"How come none of you are in relationships?" I asked the brothers. "How old are you, Derek?"

"Twenty-seven."

"And I suppose you must be thirty, since Logan is twenty-nine," I said to Andrew."

"Aye," Andrew confirmed.

"So, why aren't you guys married or at least in relationships?"

"I *was* married," Andrew said. "But it didnae last long."

"I'm sorry And you, Derek?" I asked.

"He has a girlfriend," Logan interjected. "Don't ye, Derek?"

"Aye," Derek confirmed and looked down the table. "I do."

"Then why isn't she here?" I asked with a smile.

He shrugged. "It's Christmas. She's with her own family."

"Do you miss her?"

He wrinkled his nose. "Nah, dinnae bother yersel, A'm fine, slainte."

"Slainte?" I asked Anna, who whispered back.

"He said, don't worry, I'm fine, thank you."

"Och, Faith." Derek rolled his eyes. "Repeat after me."

"Okay."

Derek leaned toward me and spoke slowly. "A need tae practice ma Scots."

"I need to practice my Scots," I said and felt like I really nailed the accent.

Apparently not, because they all laughed.

"So, what are you two up to today?" Anna asked.

I smiled at her. "Actually, I was hoping to go see the old castle and visit the local town. I still have some Christmas shopping to do."

"Smashing – you two do that. Maybe you can buy me a few things for the Christmas dinner tomorrow while you're in town?"

"Of course, just give us a list," Logan offered.

An hour later we were on our way.

"It's beautiful here," I said, looking out the window.

"Yes, it is. Ye should see it from above."

Silence filled the car. I knew his thoughts must have gone to his sister and the awful plane crash.

"Have you flown since that day?" I asked softly.

"Nah."

"Are you afraid of flying?"

He shrugged. "I'm afraid of water."

"Why?"

"Because we crashed in water and I almost drowned."

"So you haven't been swimming since that day?"

"Na-huh."

"Do you think about the accident often?"

"Aye, every day."

"Your family doesn't talk much about your sister. I didn't see any pictures of her in the house."

"I know. Anna is trying to stay brave." Logan's hands were holding the steering wheel tight enough to make his knuckles white.

"It's probably harder with Christmas and all," I said, and my throat tightened when I saw how moist his eyes were. "I'm sorry, Logan. I really am."

He gave a small nod, but kept his eyes on the road.

For a long time we didn't talk and then suddenly he said, "Seeing my family makes me feel the guilt heavier."

"The guilt?"

"Aye, I was the pilot."

"But it was a technical failure. That's not your fault."

"I still feel responsible," he said and gave me a small side glance.

"I don't think your sister would have wanted you to feel guilty."

He didn't answer.

"I used to feel guilty too, you know."

"Why?"

"Because that night Allan died, he was trying to get to me. He borrowed a friend's car after we spoke on the phone. I kept thinking that maybe if I hadn't told him how much I missed him and loved him, he wouldn't have gotten in that car, you know?"

"Ye dinnae know that. Ye cannae blame yerself."

"If your sister had survived and you had died, she would have felt survivor's guilt too."

"Why?"

"Because she didn't stop you from flying. Because she asked you to go. I don't know, we always find a way to blame ourselves, don't we?"

"It wasn't her fault."

"No and it wasn't yours either. I'll bet if I asked Anna, she feels guilty for not saying no to your sister's flying with you. But we can't live our lives like that. Living in fear isn't living at all."

"I know that. But Patricia was so young."

"Yes, it's not fair."

Silent agreement filled the air as we drove on for another ten minutes until we reached a small village with a cozy feel to it.

"The Christmas lights are so pretty," I said and pointed up the street.

"Aye, they are," Logan parked the car and pointed ahead. "There's a small supermarket and a few shops we can visit. What are ye looking for?"

"I don't know. What are your wishes for Christmas?"

He was silent.

"Nothing? That should be easy then," I joked.

"Aye, there is something I want, but you won't find it in any of those stores."

"Tell me, what is it?" I coaxed, but he shook his head and exited the car.

I was right on his heels. "You'd better tell me. You don't want the tickle monster to torture it out of you, do you?" I threatened with a grin and held up my fingers like claws.

He wasn't intimidated and kept walking, so I attacked and started tickling him.

"Honestly, Faith, what are ye, five?" he laughed and placed his hand on my forehead, pushing me an arm's length away from him. I couldn't reach him from this distance but I tried.

"Tell me," I said laughingly.

"All right, I'll give ye a hint." He removed his hand and my laugh died out at seeing the serious expression on his face.

"What is it?" I asked and stepped closer, observing his every move.

He looked down, kicked some gravel around, and took his time before he answered me with a wary glance. "I want an apology."

"An apology?" I repeated. Despite the cold weather I was suddenly feeling hot, as if a thousand heat lamps were zooming in on me at the same time. "For what?"

A ghost of disappointment flashed over his face and then he turned around and walked off.

Does he know I'm Mary? What else could he possibly want an apology for? He can't still be upset about the photo frame I broke weeks ago, can he?

"Wait, Logan, wait..." I ran after him on the parking lot. "There is something I've been meaning to tell you."

He stopped and turned. "Aye?"

I wet my lips and tried to find the right words. "This is hard to say, but I've wanted to tell you this for a long time." I paused to gather my courage. "Promise you won't get mad."

He shook his head. "Just say it, Faith."

"I want to apologize for not telling you tha..."

A shriek broke our connection. "Logan, is it really ye?"

He turned just in time to catch a girl flying through the air.

I stepped back and watched the scenario with mild shock. A female had her arms slung tightly around Logan's neck, her long red hair covering both his and her face.

"Sophie," he said and pulled free from her.

"I can't believe ye're here. Do ye ken how much A've missed ye?"

"I missed you too, Sophie. Wow, ye've grown up nicely," Logan complimented her and the teenage girl spun around with a large smile on her face.

"A'm seventeen, can ye believe it?"

"Nah, ye were just a wee thing, when I last saw ye."

Sophie placed her hands on her hips. "Och, Logan, ye speak differently. All American."

"Aye, I know." He laughed and turned to me. "Faith, this is Sophie, who is the younger sister of Kenna."

That name rang a bell.

"Kenna?" I asked a bit uncertain.

"His ex," Sophie explained and reached out to shake my hand. "I read about you in a magazine. Ye're very pretty." She shot Logan a proud grin. "See, I can speak American too."

"I appreciate it," I told her. "I'm having a hard time understanding Andrew and Derek."

She waved her hand through the air. "I bet they're just messing with ye. Did ye tell them to get tae fuck?"

"Get a fuck?" I said with a frown.

"Aye, to fuck off," she explained without as much as blinking.

My eyebrows flew up. She looked so young and innocent, but apparently swearing was more normal here than in Seattle. "No, I didn't tell them that."

"Ye should." She grinned and looked to Logan. "Ye should have seen Kenna when I showed her that article with you two. She says it's a PR stunt or something."

"A PR stunt?" he said.

"Aye, she says it's all bollocks. I cannae wait for her to see ye and yer girlfriend for sure. Kenna is here somewhere. Ye have to meet her."

"Kenna is here?" Logan shifted his balance and glanced around nervously. His energy changed drastically, and just from looking at him, I could tell his anxiety was taking over.

"Aye, hang on," Sophie told him and ran off shouting back to him. "I'll find Kenna for ye."

"Are you okay?" I asked.

He shook his head and started walking in the opposite direction of Sophie. "No, I'm not okay. I dinnae wish to see Kenna."

"Because she broke up with you?"

He turned so abruptly that I bumped into him. "She didn't just break up with me, she fucking tore my heart out and toasted it like a marshmallow."

"She can't be that bad. And I'm here with you."

"Ye dinnae understand. I was with Kenna for five years."

"So? I was with Allan for four years – what does that have to do with anything," I asked.

"She'll see right through our charade."

"Oh, you mean us being a couple?"

"Aye."

I looked behind him, but Sophie had disappeared. "You know what? Let's go shopping as we planned. If we meet her we'll deal with it, if we don't it's all good, but one thing is for sure, we're not running away."

He drew a heavy sigh, his eyes darting around.

"Give me your hand." I instructed and held mine out to him. "Until we're back in that car, I'm your devoted girlfriend – and don't worry; Cleo isn't the only one with a talent for acting in our family."

We walked hand in hand to the nearest shop and browsed the small place. I found some nice shirts that I bought for Andrew and Derek while Logan discreetly stayed as far away from the windows as possible.

In the next store, I found perfume for Anna and a woolen scarf for Logan's dad.

"I need to get you something too," I told him and got close enough that I had to lean my head back to look up at him.

251

"You don't have to buy me anything," he said.

I looked around the shop and pulled him to a private corner. "About that apology. This isn't the place or the time where I would have chosen to tell you, but maybe I just need to spit it out."

He nodded.

"So, remember when we first met…"

The door opened and Sophie entered with Kenna behind her.

Great!

"Here ye are, Logan. I brought ye Kenna," Sophie said excitedly and pulled Kenna with her to the corner where we stood. "Kenna has a huge surprise to share with ye."

All eyes fell to Kenna's bulging belly. Like her sister, Kenna was slim with long red hair and brown eyes. She didn't look happy to see Logan, but her naïve teenage sister, Sophie, seemed to be thinking she was being helpful.

"I already told Logan that ye didnae like the article I showed ye," Sophie babbled and turned to Logan. "That part about you being a tech wizard pissed her off." She giggled. "Kenna said you're more like a CEO, whatever that means."

"It means Chief Executive Officer, or what ye would refer to as 'the boss,'" Kenna explained to her sister in a curdled tone before turning back to Logan. "I heard ye sold the company."

Logan jaw was tense when he said, "Hello, Kenna."

"Hello, Logan."

She stroked her belly but kept pinning him with her eyes. "So is it true, did you sell the company? Derek told me ye can retire and never have to work again, is that the truth?"

Logan ignored her question. "I see ye're with child."

"Aye, I am, but ye didnae answer ma question."

He frowned and threw off nervous energy. "Because it's none of yer business."

"Maybe not, but it explains why such a bonnie lass would go out with ye." She gave me a chilly once-over.

Sophie spoke up. "Ma sister thinks yer a gold digger. She's says yer probably some poor Ukrainian lass or something."

"That's enough," Kenna bit at Sophie.

"Excuse me," I said and stepped forward. "First of all, you need to buy an atlas. The US and Ukraine may both start with U, but it's two very different countries. Second of all, I fell in love with Logan because of his humor and personality. We never discussed money, but it seems to be very important to you."

"Who's the father?" Logan asked, completely ignoring my little tantrum.

"Marcus."

"Marcus who?"

"Ma boss, remember?"

Logan wrinkled his nose. "The old guy?"

"He's only forty-nine."

"Only? That's almost twice yer age. What the hell, Kenna? Ye dumped me for an old wrinkly guy. Were ye with him while we…?"

"Of course not. It started about six months ago."

Logan looked down at her belly. "And how far along are ye?"

"About five months."

"Och."

An awkward silence filled the space. I had to do something to get Logan away from this money-hungry ex of his.

"Come on, babe," I said. "We've got a Christmas dinner to shop for, and don't forget that we have to call the captain and let him know when to have the jet ready for our return flight."

253

"You bought a *jet*?" Kenna and Sophie both asked Logan in high-pitched voices.

"Don't be ridiculous," he exclaimed as if the idea was a personal insult.

"It's my sister's jet," I explained. "You did read in the article that my twin is Cleo, right?"

"Aye, we did read that," Sophie said excitedly. "That is so cool. I looove Cleo."

"Thank you, I'll be sure to tell her that," I said. "Anyway, it was nice to meet you, Henna, and good luck with the baby."

"Kenna," she corrected me. "My name is Kenna and I'm sure you heard a lot about me from Logan."

"I dinnae think so," Sophie exclaimed. "Faith didnae know who ye were when I said yer name. I had to tell her ye're Logan's ex."

"Is that so?" Kenna looked like she had just sucked on a lemon.

"I'm sorry about that," I added sweetly. "But now that I've met you I realize I should thank you."

"Thank me for what?" Kenna asked suspiciously.

"If you hadn't broken up with Logan, I would still be looking for my soulmate." I rose up and kissed his scarred cheek. "Logan is the best part of my life."

She gaped, but found her voice again, addressing him directly. "Really, Logan, yer soulmate?"

He shrugged and looked a little overwhelmed.

"Ye told me ye didn't believe in soulmates," Kenna said and crossed her arms.

"Things change," he answered.

"But she's not even yer type," Kenna sputtered.

Logan turned to look at me and nodded. "Aye, she is. Faith is funny, and bright, kind, generous, and she's become ma best friend."

I leaned against him. "Aww, that's so sweet, babe." And then I tilted my head and gave Kenna a soft smile.

"Isn't it nice that both you and Logan found your soulmates? I'm sure you and Marcus love each other as much as Logan and I love each other..."

"Of course," she said but her words didn't match her expression.

"Well then, Merry Christmas, Kenna and Sophie."

"Merry Christmas to ye too," Sophie said and leaned in to hug me and then Logan. I heard her whisper something in his ear and him murmuring an answer

Kenna gave me a short nod and Logan a stiff hug before she and Sophie exited the shop, making a small bell above the door ring.

Next to me, Logan exhaled with relief. His shoulder visibly sank down and his tension eased. "I've been dreading meeting her for so long."

"How do you feel now?"

He lifted a hand. "Look how I'm shaking," he said and bent down, placing his hands on his knees as if he'd just sprinted a mile.

"Kenna is the one who started your issue with women, isn't she?" I asked, trying to understand why he was so affected by his meeting with Kenna.

Logan locked up at me. "Aye, she told me I was too ugly for any woman to love."

"Charming," I said dryly. "But you know she was just angry, right?"

When he didn't answer, I continued. "Logan, Kenna didn't mean it. People say hurtful things when they break up."

"She said she couldn't make love to me because my scars repulsed her."

"Oh geez, she said that?"

"Aye. And many other things like it."

I pulled him up from his bent position and hugged him. "For all it's worth, Logan, she still loves you."

He scoffed. "No, she doesn't."

"Of course she does. Couldn't you tell?"

Logan pulled back to look at me. "Tell how?"

"She was green with jealousy when you spoke about loving me. She regrets letting you go, big time."

"I dinnae think so."

"Men." I chuckled. "You really don't get women at all, do you?"

He stood quietly when I gave him a last hug and took his hand. "Come on, let's go buy Anna her groceries. I want to see the castle before it gets too late.

"All right, at this time o' day, the castle should be empty, so save your confession till we get there. That way there should be no more interruptions.

I bit my lip. "Right. But I'm warning you; you won't like my confession."

CHAPTER 28
The Christmas Gift

Faith

The castle was magnificent. Although in ruins in some parts, it was easy to see the grandness of it all.

"Was this the great hall?" I asked.

"Aye, and over here was the kitchen." Logan pointed and walked to the other end.

I excitedly took pictures with my phone. "I can't wait to show Chloe," I mumbled and gazed around in awe.

"And up here is where my great, great, great, great grandfather brought his unwilling English bride," Logan said with a grin and winked. "It was his bedroom."

"How do you know that?" I asked and followed him up the stairs.

"My father told me and his father told him and his father told..."

"Yes, I get it." I laughed and walked inside the empty room that was nothing but four stone walls with a window and a door.

"Ye want me to tell ye the story of my great, great, great, great grandfather and his bride?"

"Sure. But didn't you say that your ancestors didn't actually marry unwilling women?"

"Do ye want the story or not?" he asked.

"Okay, okay. I'll be quiet."

Logan frowned. "As the story was told to me, she was a noblewoman who despised the Scots. I don't remember why she was in Scotland to begin with, but somehow she got separated from her protectors and that's when he found her."

"What, just wandering around?"

"Nah, she was bathing in a pond close to here."

I tilted my head and narrowed my eyes. "She was bathing in a pond?"

"Aye," Logan said with a stern expression. "My forefather was completely bewitched by her beauty or maybe he was just horny, that part isn't really clear."

I stopped breathing, my heart hammering in my chest. This was the sexual fantasy Logan and I had done as a role-play a month ago.

This has to mean he knows I'm Mary.

That's why he asked for an apology.

But how did he find out?

And what if I'm wrong?

What if he doesn't know and he's just reusing the story without realizing I'm Mary?

What if the apology he asked for has nothing to do with my being Mary?

"Of course my ancestor was a rough laird." Logan puffed out his chest and took on a masculine prance as he walked around the room. "He was tall and strong, with long hair, and scars that were a badge of honor and told stories of battles and blood. That's why they called him Logan the Brave. And, aye, I'm named after him," he said with a sly smile.

I watched him closely and stood completely still when he came closer.

"His bride was a fine lady named Mary."

"Mary?"

"Aye," he said and moved so close that he could have kissed me. "She was scared when Logan sneaked up on her. At first she thought she heard an animal in the forest and hurried to come out of the water and cover herself. But that's when he grabbed hold of her." Logan grabbed my arms and held me in a firm grip. "Mary begged him to let her go, of course."

258

My eyes were wide. *Tell him you're Mary?* But before I could gather my wits, Logan gave me a devilish smile. "Ye know, Faith, it might be more fun if ye play Mary."

"What?" I said slowly, unsure what was up and down here.

"Humor me," he said. "So pretend that ye're scared, but Logan doesn't care and swings ye up on his horse and takes ye here, where he locks ye inside his bedchamber and tells his clansmen to stay away."

I nodded as Logan prowled the room like a predator.

"Don't touch me," I said in a fine British accent.

"Ohh, I will touch ye." Logan came close and pinned my wrists against the wall. "Why would I let go of such a bonnie lass?"

"You're hurting me," I exclaimed theatrically.

"Then stop fighting, and I'll make it feel guid."

"I'll never stop fighting. Get your hands off me."

"Lie down.'

I looked down at the dirty floor and frowned. "Really?" I said in my own voice.

Logan looked down too. "Never mind, ye stay here," he said and we exchanged a small smile before he found his composure again. "Are ye married?"

"No, but you *will* leave me alone," I said with my heart speeding. I had said the exact same line as Mary and by repeating it, I was giving away that I was her.

"Will I?" Logan asked with an intense glance; energy crackled between us. *He knows! But then why isn't he furious with me?*

"There's no chance of me leaving ye alone, my lady. I'm bewitched by your beauty and ye belong to me now."

I stared at him. This was surreal to me.

"We Highlanders dinnae ask permission, and I just decided ye'll be my wife," he said unaffected by my silence. "Ye didnae have anything to say, do ye?" he asked.

"You can't just decide to make me your wife. You'll need my father's consent."

Logan scoffed. "Yer father will give his consent after I've bedded ye and I tell him we're already man and wife in the eyes of God."

He leaned against me, his mouth close to my mouth, but not quite kissing me.

He's waiting for my permission, I thought and looked down when Logan slowly pulled down the zipper on my jacket. No words were exchanged but our eyes stayed locked and every nerve ending in my body was on fire.

"I *will* have ye," he said against my lips.

I turned my head. "Stop it," I whined. "You can't do this, I'm a virgin."

Logan gently pulled my chin back and looked at me, his eyes watchful as if looking for the least sign of discomfort. "Say that ye're mine," he said.

"Never," I tried to turn my chin again, but he cupped my face. "Say it or I will take ye by force."

My eyes widened. He was so dominant and sexy in this role. It was a long way from the nervous man I'd just witnessed with Kenna. Then something changed. It was like a switch got turned off and all the flirtatious, playful energy left him.

Logan leaned his forehead against mine. His eyes closed and his shoulders sagged.

"What's wrong?" I asked and reached up to touch his face. "What happened?"

"I can't do it," he whispered.

"Can't do what?"

He opened his eyes and they were wet with unshed tears. "I'm so sorry," he said in a broken voice.

"Sorry for what?"

"I shouldn't have said that. I wasn't thinking."

"Said what? Logan, talk to me, I don't understand."

"That I would take you by force. After what Niko did to you…, I'm so sorry, Faith. No woman should ever be forced against her will."

"Oh, Logan, come here." I opened my arms and held him close. The shaking of his body told me he was crying, and I let my own tears fall freely.

We cried together. Two broken people with more emotional garbage than most. But for me some of those tears were relief. Logan knew I was Mary and he had tried making it easier for me to reveal that secret, by playing out one of my fantasies.

The pain he felt just thinking about Niko's treatment of me confirmed how much he cared about me.

"Logan," I sniffled and dried away my tears.

"What?" he said and used the back of his hands to dry his own eyes.

"I'm sorry I didn't tell you I was Mary. Can you forgive me?"

"Were ye ever going to tell me?" he asked.

I nodded. "Yes. I wanted to for so long, but it wasn't easy – and you have to admit things have been crazy these past weeks."

"That's an understatement."

"How did you find out?"

"Nigel was bribed to give up information on his employees."

"That sleazeball. He promised no one would ever find out."

"A thousand dollars made him break that promise," Logan said.

"Well, I should have expected that much. My father always says, integrity isn't cheap so don't expect it from cheap people."

"Why would you work in a place like that anyway?"

I lifted my shoulders in a shrug. "They paid well, it was legal, flexible working hours, and it was supposed to be anonymous," I explained.

"Why were ye in that bar that day, Faith? That's what confuses me the most. Ye were the phone operator, why would ye come to the meeting spot? Surely ye don't do that to all the clients, do ye?"

"Of course not. I've never done it before, but you were… different."

"Why?"

"Because of your accent, and you described yourself as a fighter."

Logan took a step back. "Och, now I understand. The psychic."

"Yes, she told me to follow the fighter with the accent."

Logan blinked at me. "That's why ye were so pushy?"

"I wouldn't say I was pushy," I protested.

He raised a brow.

"Okay, so maybe I was a little pushy, but if I hadn't been, we wouldn't be here, would we?"

Logan watched me closely before he looked down. "And where exactly is that, Faith?"

I scratched my arm and tried to lighten the mood. "We're in Scotland, in a ruined castle; I thought you knew."

He pulled away and from his firmly pressed-together lips, I knew this wasn't a joking matter to him.

"Okay, sorry about that. The truth is that I have feelings for you," I admitted. "But I'm kind of a mess."

He kicked some gravel around and buried his hands in his pockets. "I guess that makes two of us."

I shook my head. "No, you don't understand. I'm so screwed up that I actually got jealous of Mary when you liked her more than me."

He frowned. "But ye *are* Mary."

"I know, but you didn't know that and you preferred Mary over me. Remember how you said I had no sense of humor, I talked to much, and you preferred your women with curves?"

He nodded.

"You said I wasn't girlfriend material, remember?" I couldn't hide the pain in my voice, and Logan pulled me into his arms and hugged me tight.

After a minute of holding me, he said, "Let's go back to the house. There's something I need to explain to ye, but I'm freezing my arse off out here."

I nodded and let him guide me back to the car. The ride to the old vicarage was only a few minutes long.

"Meet me up in our room, I'm just going to hand Anna the groceries," Logan said before we entered.

I did as he told me to, and went straight to our room, kicked off my shoes, and crawled under the duvet to get warm.

When Logan entered, he did the same and propped himself up on an elbow next to me.

"When I was eleven, I tried out for the local soccer team," he started. "I was so excited and talked of nothing else for weeks leading up to the try-out date."

"What happened?" I asked.

"I was rejected, and it was strange because I was bigger and stronger than the others."

"I'm sorry."

"When my mum told me I hadn't made the team she had tears in her eyes. I told her not to be upset and that I was happy I hadn't made the team."

"Why?"

He creased his brows. "Back then I genuinely thought I didn't want it. I would tell myself and others that the coach was an idiot, that the other players were brats, and that I would rather play golf anyway."

"But it wasn't true?" I asked.

263

"Of course not. I wanted to play soccer badly. But I think it's human nature to protect yerself against rejection by saying ye didnae want it anyway. It's a way to save pride, I guess. I only realized that after seeing a pattern with employees. Over the last seven years I've had to fire several people for various reasons. Quite a few of them told me I couldnae fire them because they quit."

"Okay, I understand, but why exactly are you telling me this?" I asked him.

"Ye tell me – aren't ye supposed to be a psychology major?"

I played with the bedsheet, thinking about what he had said. "All right, so what I'm hearing you say is that you found things that were wrong with me because you would rather reject me than feel rejected by me. Is that it?"

He nodded.

"So, when you said I talk too much, have no humor, and I'm not girlfriend material, you didn't actually mean it?"

Logan wrinkled his forehead. "At the time I meant it."

"Ohh," I said and looked down.

"Now, I see things a little different."

That made me look up again.

"First of all, I know ye much better than I thought I did. If I had known ye were Mary..." He paused. "I mean, why did ye pull that stunt on me?"

"Because I tried to talk to you as Faith, but you never relaxed around me like you did when I was Mary."

"That's because I could hide behind my phone with Mary."

"Exactly. So I used that alter ego to get you to relax and feel more confident with women, but my ultimate goal was always to get you involved with a real woman."

"With ye?" he asked softly.

"No, I honestly wasn't ready to date anyone myself."

"So ye *were* trying to fix me, like Chloe said."

"I think I was," I admitted. "I wanted you to experience love again."

"And what about ye? Ye dinnae want to experience love again?"

"Yes."

His hand touched mine. "That day at the hospital when ye kissed me. What was that about?"

"I'm not sure."

"Were ye just curious?"

"Maybe." I shrugged. "I haven't been open to love for so long and I really like you. I feel safe with you."

"Are ye still curious?" His voice was a low whisper.

"Are you?"

He nodded. "Aye, and terrified."

"Of being intimate with a woman?"

"Aye."

"But we've kinda had sex."

"Uh-huh, but not really." His hand played with my fingers, slowly intertwining them.

"Do you think we should have real sex?" I asked, my heart in my throat.

Logan gave me a quick glance and frowned. "Not after what Niko did to you. It's only been three days. I dinnae want to stir up some bad memories."

"But what if being with you could help erase some bad ones?" I argued.

He let go of my hand and moved to sit with his back against the headboard, pulling his legs up in front of him. "Why would ye even want to?" he asked, his voice full of uncertainty again.

With the way he pulled away from me, I was tempted to pull back and ask him to forget the whole thing, but I knew we were both fragile and out of our comfort zone.

"Logan, look at me."

He met my eyes.

"If I am to have sex again. I want it to be with you," I said quietly.

"But why, Faith? Ye know ye can have any man ye want, right?"

"That's not true," I protested.

"Any single man at least," he corrected himself and added, "and probably most married men as well."

"I don't want a married man!"

"Wise decision."

"Logan, have you ever cheated on a girlfriend?"

"Nah," he said without hesitation. "And I never will."

"You don't know that."

"Aye, I do. It's not something that happens to ye, it's a choice."

"Have you ever been tempted?"

"Absolutely."

"But you didn't do it?"

"Nah, I didnae."

"I like that about you."

He smiled and stretched his legs out in front of him.

I sat up, facing him, cross-legged, and with my hands resting in my lap. "Logan, I know you've fantasized about being with me."

"How could I not?" he asked and looked away.

I lifted a finger and traced it down his neck and chest. "Would you make love to me in real life if I asked you?"

He frowned at me. "What kind of daft question is that?"

"I just thought that with your anxiety maybe you wouldn't be comfortable..."

"Nah, I would be nervous as hell, but I would have to have both arms and both legs broken to say no to a request like that."

"So if I asked you to help me break my dry spell, you would be okay with it?"

For seconds we sat quietly watching each other and I got the feeling he was waiting for me to say "psyched" or something.

"Aye," he said in a soft voice. "I could be convinced for sure."

I bit my lips and lowered my eyes to his mouth.

"Are ye asking me, Faith?" he asked in that low sexy brogue of his.

"Maybe," I said slowly. "Or maybe I'm waiting for you to ask me to help you break your dry spell…"

He leaned in. "In that case, consider this an official request for yer help in the matter." With our noses tip to tip, we both broke into wide smiles like small children who just came up with a devious plan to raid the kitchen for cookies.

My heart was pumping fast when he rolled on top of me, kissing me and burying his hands in my hair.

"Wait, don't you think we should talk about what it means?" I asked. "If we sleep together, things will change between us."

He stiffened and lifted himself up on his elbows to look down at me. "What do ye mean?"

"I don't just sleep with anyone, you know. It has to mean something to you too."

"What are ye saying?"

I scrunched up my face. "Well, what do you think I'm saying? Isn't it obvious?"

Logan pulled back. "Spit it out, Faith, I cannae read yer mind. Of course it matters to me, I haven't been with anyone for two years."

"I know that, but I don't want this to be just about the sex to you. It has to mean something."

Logan frowned. "Och, woman, what is it ye want me to say?"

I hit his shoulder. "That you'll want me after you've had me, you idiot." I felt humiliated for having to actually say it aloud.

"Ahh, I see." Logan leaned his head down and placed a kiss on my collarbone. "I thought that was implied. Dinnae forget, my fine lady, that I'm a Highlander and we're a possessive lot. We dinnae share our women."

Butterflies flew around in my belly and a smile broke out on my lips.

"I think I'm in love with you, Logan," I said and weaved my hands through his thick blond hair.

"Good," he said and moved up to kiss me. "That makes the taking so much easier."

"The taking?"

"Aye," he smiled and slid his thumb over my lower lip. "Ye are in my bedchamber and I want ye."

"And Highlanders always take what they want," I said.

"Nah, modern Highlanders understand that a real man asks for consent and never uses his physical superiority to intimidate a female."

"Good to know."

"Faith." He looked me deep into my eyes. "I think ye're an amazing woman, and ye have nothing to worry about. I promise that even if ye're horrible in bed, I'll still like ye tomorrow." The wicked smile on his face told me he was joking, but I still scoffed.

"I'm not horrible in bed, that's rude."

"Well, ye are out of practice. Ye admitted that much."

I chuckled. "So are you."

"Right, so it'll probably be awkward and really bad for both of us. So maybe we should commit to at least three rounds of sex. You know, like your homemade rule about arm wrestling."

"It's an official rule."

"So ye say,' he said sarcastically. "But with a three-rounds sex rule, we'll have a rematch if we are terrible at it – what do ye say?"

"Are you asking me to have sex with you three times?"

"Minimum."

"Today?"

"If you wish. Or we could say, three times a day for three days. Or maybe three times a week for three weeks. I'm flexible; what do ye think?"

I was laughing and wrapping my legs around him. "I say we go for three times a week for three years."

"Wow, ye're into long-term commitments, aren't ye?"

"I'm the loyal type."

Logan eyes softened and he kissed me deeply before nuzzling my nose with his. "Luckily, so am I."

My whole body was tingling with desire and now that he had appeased my fear that I wouldn't be a one-night stand to him, I was done talking and wanted action.

"Please say you have a condom."

"A condom? Nah, do ye?"

"Ohhh nooo...! How typical is that? Now that we're finally ready to do it, we don't have protection."

A wide grin broke out on his face. "What do ye take me for? Of course I have a condom."

"Thank God, but it better not be some five-year-old condom that's unsafe to use."

"It's not." He got out of bed and went to his closet. "I bought them on my way to the airport."

"Really?" Propping myself on my elbow I watched him tear open a box and fish a condom from it. "And why would you buy condoms, when I specifically told you I was coming here as your friend only."

He closed the closet and winked at me. "In case there was a cute stewardess with a long layover, of course."

"As if."

269

Logan pulled his sweater off and stepped out of his jeans before he got back into bed with me.

"Ye know why I bought them," he said and rolled me onto my back, his hand lifting my thigh up to his hip.

"Hmm," I hummed as we kissed. He tasted sweet and his tongue circled mine carefully. Maybe he was afraid I would have flashbacks to Niko's treatment of me, or maybe he was afraid I would do to him what I did to Niko.

"It's okay," I whispered. "You don't have to hold back, I'm okay."

The second I said it, he began to undress me and I helped him pull off my sweater. Before it hit the floor, Logan's face was already buried between my breasts, his hands playing with my nipples.

"God, you're divine," he muttered against my skin.

I managed to get my hands down to my pants, and the sound of my zipper got his attention. His hands were almost shaking when he pulled down my pants and threw them to the floor. The way his hands slid up my inner thighs and his eyes took me in reminded me of a car commercial I had once seen. He looked like a man who had saved his whole life to buy his dream car and was finally able to touch it.

"You are so beautiful," he said and let his hands slide over my body. "I truly dinnae deserve you."

"Give me your hands," I instructed and when he did, I looked at him. "I never bought you a Christmas gift in town, so how about..." I guided his hands to the sides of my panties. "...you unpack me as your gift instead?"

His hands curled around the fabric and his breathing was ragged when he slowly pulled at my panties.

I lifted my behind to make it easy for him to slide the panties off me.

"I'm keeping these," he said and threw my blue silk panties onto his side table.

"I can give you a clean pair, wouldn't that be nicer?" I asked, but the way he arched a brow told me he wanted *that* pair.

Logan looked like a hungry man at a buffet, unsure where to start. His eyes roamed every part of my body and his hands were running down from my shoulder to my ankles and back up to push my thighs apart.

"What do ye want?" he asked.

"I'm your present, why don't you take me the way you dreamed about."

"Are ye sure?" he asked but his head was already lowering to my pelvis area.

"Uh-huh," was all I could mumble when his warm breath touched my most sensitive area and his warm tongue starting licking me."

I couldn't remember Allan licking me. It wasn't his "thing" and I never asked him to do it. Maybe that's why I wasn't prepared for the insane sensation of a man's tongue on my clit.

"Ahh…" I moaned and arched up, grabbing the iron bars of the headboard. "What are you doing?"

He didn't answer but got a firm hold around my thighs to keep me in place while he worked his magic. I couldn't lie still, and kept moving with delight.

"This is insane… you have no idea how good this is. Ohh, shit… if I had known you could do this, I would have sneaked into your bedroom every night."

His deep chuckle between my legs only made his tongue on my clit vibrate.

"I want you inside me, Logan."

"Patience," he said, but I was so hot and horny from his stimulating my breasts and pussy that I had lost my humor. I rose up and pulled on his shoulders.

"No, Logan, I mean it, I want you inside me *now*."

I stared shamelessly as he pushed off his boxers and his cock sprung out. In my state of lust, it was the most magnificent sight and with greedy hands I reached for it.

"Easy." His warning turned into a long moan when my lips closed around his hard cock.

"Geez, Faith, ye're killing me."

My slurping sounds mixed with his ragged breathing.

"Slow down, Faith... I want this to last. Fuck, ye're amazing, woman."

He had to stop me and push me back on the bed. "Ye wanted me inside ye, right?"

"Yes."

I watched him put on the condom and lower himself to my entrance. "Are ye ready?" he asked, his eyes shining with lust.

"Yes," I nodded. "Are you?"

He answered by pushing inside me. "I've wanted to do this since I saw ye in that bar."

My legs wrapped around him and my hands were around his shoulders. "You feel so good," I cried out.

His head was buried against my neck, his hands were in my hair, and he was rocking back and forth filling me up with every inch of him.

"Yes, yes... I love to feel you inside me."

He started moving faster and I slowed him down. "Fill me up and stay for a second. I just want to feel how we fit."

Logan pushed in balls deep and I cringed a bit.

"Am I hurting ye?" he asked concerned and lifted up to look at me.

"No, babe, you aren't hurting me."

"You feel really tight."

I smiled at him and let my fingers slide down over his face. "Give me time to adjust to your size."

He kissed me long and hard. "I cannae believe this is really happening. That I'm inside ye."

My eyes teared up. This is what I'd wanted for Logan all along and somehow by helping him I'd helped myself.

"What's wrong, why are ye crying," Logan asked with concern. "Are ye sure I'm not hurting ye?

"It's not that."

"Then what is it?"

I reached up my hands and weaved my fingers in with his. "It feels like coming home, doesn't it?"

Squeezing my hands, he whispered in a thick voice, "Aye, it does, beautiful It does."

My hands slid down his back.

"Merry Christmas, handsome."

He shook his head with a smile. "Dinnae call me that."

Pulling him closer. I placed kisses on his nose, chin, cheeks, and forehead. "I love every part of you," I whispered.

He started moving again, rotating his hips in a way that made me gasp. "Do ye love this part of me too?"

"I do, and I think you have to be careful," I warned him with my eyes closed. "I might get addicted to this."

Logan slammed harder against me and picked up the pace. "I would love nothing more."

"I could turn into a nymphomaniac who wants you five times a day," I teased and spread my legs wider.

"Ye wouldnae hear me complaining."

His size and movements were heaven to me, and when he pulled out of me, I made a displeased grunt.

"Come here," he said and got up from the bed. "There's something I've done with ye a million times in my fantasies."

"What?" I asked and stood naked on the bed in front of him.

"Fuck, ye're gorgeous, Faith." He spun me around and smacked my butt, which made me laugh.

"Do ye trust me?" he asked.

"Yes, of course I trust you."

"Then sit on me." First he lifted my arms and placed them around his neck. Then he slid his hands under my butt.

"What? While you stand?"

"Aye, I'll carry ye, dinnae worry."

I pursed my lips and arched a brow. "You better not drop me."

"I willnae."

Slowly, Logan lifted me up on him. Hanging with my legs around his hips and my arms around his neck, he lowered me down over his cock, closing his eyes and moaning deeply.

He was much stronger than I thought and lifted me up and down like a small doll. I tried to help by using my leg muscles, but in this position he had me spread wide and I could feel him hit my cervix, which hurt a bit.

"You're too big for me," I complained, and that only made him moan out louder.

"Maybe this is better for ye," he said and sat me down on the desk that stood up against the wall. The desk was a bit low and to meet his height, I placed my heels on the edge of the desk and lifting my butt up.

Logan didn't wait for instructions, but penetrated me again and wrapped his arms around my thighs to support my weight. The desk was rocking and squeaking as he fucked me, but he hit me in the perfect spot and I loved it.

"Yes, Logan, you're a goddamn genius at this. You can take me day and night as long as you make me feel like this."

He didn't answer but kept hammering inside me, panting and biting his lips with determination.

A wave of euphoria hit me and I wanted to laugh out loud from the joy I was feeling. "Yes, more, Logan, more. Take me harder."

He kept going in a fast pace that built up the lightheadedness I felt. "It feels sooo good."

"I'm coming, Faith, I cannae hold it back any longer."

Seeing Logan's face scrunch up into an orgasmic expression and knowing I had made him come pushed me over the edge. As he pumped inside me and ejaculated into the condom, I reached my own orgasm. My insides cramped, my clit throbbed, and a wave of heat flowed through me. "Yes, yes, I'm coming."

We were out of breath, naked, and merged together from our lovemaking when we opened our eyes and looked into each other's eyes.

No one spoke when he held on to the condom and pulled out carefully. I looked in fascination when I saw how much semen he had filled that thing with. Allan and I had always used condoms, but never had I seen anything like it.

"You should be a sperm donor," I joked when he pulled me up from the table. "I've never seen a condom that full."

He pulled it off and tied a knot and for a second there was an awkward silence between us.

"So, how do ye think we fit?" Logan asked with a small frown.

"Couldn't you tell?"

"Aye, you thought it was rubbish, didn't ye?" he said with a quick smile.

"That's right. A complete disaster. It will take a lot of training to get it right," I said and picked up my sweater from the floor. "Which is a bummer, of course, because that means we have to do it again."

Logan pulled me into his arms and kissed me hard. And then he grinned and picked me up, carrying me the four steps to the bed. "No need to get dressed just yet. I'm not done with ye."

"I'm not done with you either," I said and felt giddy inside.

"There's something I should tell ye." He smiled smugly and placed me on the bed, taking another long admiring glance at me and wrapping his arm around my waist. With me standing on the bed, his head was in line with my breasts and he tilted his head upward to meet my eyes.

"Thank ye," he said softly. "Ye are the best Christmas gift I've ever been given and I promise to treasure ye always."

Tears of joy filled my eyes and I stroked his hair.

"No, wait, what I wanted to say was..." He turned up the brogue and said, "A'm bewitched by yer beauty and ye belong t' me now."

I smacked his shoulder lovingly. "I don't *belong* to you."

"Aye, ye do, it's rude to ask for a present back, and I'm keeping ye."

"It wasn't *me* that was your present, it was having sex with me."

"Ye should have specified that – I'm certain I've got all of ye and I'm a greedy bastard, so I'm keeping my gift. Ye're mine now, end of discussion, woman." He suckled my breast and squeezed my behind.

I couldn't stop laughing at his determined expression and the happy grin on his face. He looked almost boyish with his ruffled hair and red cheeks. This Logan was a complete transformation from the man I'd first met at the bar.

"I guess I can live with that, since I'm kinda crazy about you too, but did you have to steal my panties?"

"Aye, and I'm definitely keeping those too."

CHAPTER 29
The Doll and the Troll

Logan

Andrew and Derek broke out in applause when Faith and I finally came downstairs.

"Are ye trying to break some kind of record, ye horny bastard?" Derek laughed.

Faith looked horrified to Anna, who was fiddling around in the kitchen. "I'm terribly sorry," she muttered. "We didn't realize how late it was."

"Or how loud ye were," Andrew snickered.

Anna looked up and gave Faith a huge smile. "You have nothing to apologize for, my dear. All we want is for Logan to be happy. Things haven't been easy for him, and from the sound of it, you two make each other happy."

"Aye, *very* happy." Andrew grinned and made a vulgar hand sign to Logan.

"Pooch me hame," Logan grinned at him.

"Now, I will not have that language in my house," Anna said but couldn't hide a smile.

Faith looked to me. "What ham are you talking about? Is it a Christmas ham?"

A roar of laughter broke out in the kitchen and poor Faith stood lost and confused.

I was the first to gather my wits and give her a hug. "God, ye're adorable," I said and planted a kiss on her forehead.

"What's so funny?"

"Pooch me hame is slang for kiss my arse in Scottish."

"Ohh..." she said and nodded. "I see."

"Och, I'm sure ye Americans have plenty of slang and sayings that we wouldn't understand either," my father said to cheer her up.

"Maybe, but at least you would understand the words. I feel like you speak a completely different language."

"Don't worry about it, ye'll learn now that ye're part of the family," I told her.

Complete silence fell upon the room. Anna and my father exchanged looks and then Anna clapped her hands and burst out. "Are we hearing wedding bells?"

"No, that's not what I meant," I corrected and could feel Faith look up at me. "Not yet anyway," I added.

"But soon?" Anna said excitedly and came to take Faith's hand. "You will make the most beautiful bride."

"Thank you." Faith smiled and took my breath away.

We spend that night playing board games and eating too many sweets. Faith and I sat next to each other and we constantly touched. If we weren't holding hands, we were rubbing against each other or sneaking in little kisses. It was a wonder that I didn't physically lift off from my seat with the thousands of butterflies she released in my stomach.

It's surreal.

I'm really with her.

We're a couple now.

Faith and I against the world.

Together.

I laughed more than I had in years and easily forgave my brothers for their goofy attempts at making Faith laugh. They adored her, just like I did. And how could they not?

Faith was everything a man could dream of and for some miraculous reason she wanted *me*.

I watched her profile as she rolled the dice, her tongue sticking out in concentration, her eyes full of life and laughter. The candlelight from the table illuminated her in a golden hue that only enhanced her beauty. She was like a vision from a fairytale and my fingers were drawn to her, as if I needed to feel she was real.

Gently I tucked a lock of her long blond hair behind her ear and stroked her back.

She turned her head and gave me a smile so loving that she might as well have said the words out loud.

I swallowed hard, overwhelmed with emotions of gratitude and love.

"It's yer turn," someone said, but I was entranced by Faith and didn't register it.

"Och, the poor lad is completely besotted." Derek snapped his fingers in front of my face. "Aye, she's bonnie, but it's yer turn to roll the dice."

I nodded distractedly, because despite the fact that we had already made love three times this afternoon, I was ready to take her upstairs and make love to her again. I would never get enough of Faith.

Two hours later, when we finally retired to our rooms my brothers didn't tease us with comments of rocking bedframes. Instead Andrew said, "Guid night an' sweet dreams, and Faith…"

"Yes?"

"Tell Logan to stop molesting ye, will ye?"

A smile pursed her lips. "Why would I do that when he's so good at it?"

I felt eight feet tall when I took her hand and led her upstairs.

$$\{\infty\}$$

Faith
Saying goodbye to Scotland was sad. The country had been as rugged and beautiful as described in the books.

And the people were as warm, funny, and direct as I had expected.

"Did ye like it here?" Andrew asked me when he took Logan and me to the small airport.

"Yes I loved it here," I assured him. "And I already told Logan that he has to take me to Glasgow and introduce me to your mother next time we come."

Andrew bobbed his head. "A think ye'll like Glasgow and our maw. Dae ye ken ah live in Glasgow?"

My brain was trying to decipher what he had just said and since Logan was helping the pilot from my sister's private jet with our luggage. I couldn't ask for help.

I must have looked lost, because Andrew broke into that hearty laugh of his and gave me a hug. As he was holding me close he whispered in a perfect British accent. "I said, I think you'll like Glasgow and our mom, and then I asked you if you knew I live in Glasgow too."

I was stunned and gaped at him when he released me.

"You... you've been pulling a prank on me this whole time?"

"O' course not, ye're in Scotland. We speak Scottish here!" he said with the brogue back in his voice.

Logan joined us then, reaching his hand out to Andrew and pulling him in for a masculine hug. "It was guid to see ye, brother, come visit us soon."

"In Seattle?" Andrew asked.

"Aye, ye can have the guest room since Faith sleeps with me now." Logan smiled smugly and winked at me. "And when ye come – maybe ye can bring Sophie."

"Sophie?" I asked. "You mean Kenna's sister?"

"Aye, she asked me if she could come and visit us. She's a major fan of yer sister."

"Me too," Andrew said.

"Logan, is that what Sophie was whispering in your ear the other day in the shop?" I asked.

"It was," he confirmed. "But I doubt Kenna will be okay with her going."

"Hey, Faith, just a quick question?" Andrew interjected. "Is yer sister single?"

"Yes, for the moment she is."

"Greit! Do ye think ah have a chance with her?"

"To be honest, I worry about her. She's got awful taste in men," I said.

That made Andrew laugh. "So ah *do* have a chance then."

We said our goodbyes.

Andrew kissed me too long on the cheek, which made Logan pull him off me

"Blythe yuil an a Happy New Year," Andrew shouted and waved as we entered the plane, waving back at him.

"Merry Christmas and Happy New Year to you too," we shouted back.

"I cannae wait to be back in Seattle," Logan said when we were buckled in and somewhere above the Atlantic Ocean.

"Why?"

"So I can have ye for myself," he said and kissed me.

I fished out my phone. "I have to check up on Chloe, I haven't heard from her in days and I worry about her."

"Why?"

"Because the last time I heard anything from her was the day after she got there. She's been quiet ever since."

"But didn't she say she was taking a break from all electronic devices?" Logan asked. "Wasn't that part of the program?"

"Still," I said with a frown and looked at the email again, reading it out loud.

Hey Sis,

Just checking in so you know I'm alive.

You were right, Onava is amazing and it's good for me to take a break. The forest is beautiful and I feel better already.

Onava has put me on detox from all things related to social media. I'm not even allowed to answer fan mail. But, since I'm alone and everything is quiet now, I'm sneaking a short email to you.

Just so you know, Onava was called away to Canada where her mother is dying.

She has called for her nephew to get here and "work" with me. His name is Adam Black, and according to Onava he's a respected medicine man too.

There's a picture of him on the wall, and he looks familiar to me. I hope he's not the guy I met at Christian's birthday party last January.

Take care, sweet sister, and let's get together for New Year's. By then I should be ready to go back to civilization, I hope!

Love, Chloe

PS: There are black bears here... I'm pretty freaked out about it, being alone and all. According to Onava they don't eat people, but they still kill them on occasion. So I should probably tell you that I love you, just in case...

A sound escaped me.
"What is it?" Logan asked.

282

"It's just her PS. It's so typical of Chloe to always dramatize the situation."

Logan smiled, "Let's hope she hasnae been killed by a bear. That would explain why ye havenae heard from her in a while."

"Don't say that – now I'm going to worry even more."

"I'm sure ye have nothing to worry about. What could go wrong with Chloe and a medicine man in a small cabin in the woods? I'm sure they have a lot in common."

We exchanged a long glance and then I said what we were both thinking. "Holy shit, she'll drive him crazy. Maybe it's not the bears she should fear as much as the poor man snapping when she drives him up the wall with her constant need to create drama."

Logan drummed on the armrest. "He wouldn't be the first guy to shoot her."

"Okay, that was unnecessary. Don't joke about that."

Both his hands flew up as white flags. "Sorry."

I looked out the window, biting my nail. "Now I'm really freaked out. Maybe I should go see her when we get back."

"Maybe ye should. Just don't go hiking in the woods."

"Why not?"

"Because ye can't outrun a brown bear on yer weak ankle."

"It's black bears, Logan, and although my ankle is fine, you're right. I definitely couldn't outrun a bear, but neither could you."

"I wouldnae have to," he said with a confident smile.

"What do you mean?"

"I would just have to be faster than ye."

I elbowed him. "God, you're being a jerk. I think I liked you better when you were all nervous around me."

"Och, ye still make me plenty nervous."

I laughed. "I do not."

"Aye, ye do. I'm nervous that ye'll realize how unworthy I am of ye. I'm nervous ye'll stop liking me."

"Aww, don't be. You know I'm crazy about you," I said and took his hand.

"Also," he said with a serious expression. "I'm very nervous that ye'll ask me to do chores around the house now."

I laughed out loud. "Oh, you bet I am. Things are gonna change and I'm calling for equality. You, sir, will be cooking for me when we get back."

"I'm a terrible cook, I dinnae think ye want to eat what I can cook."

"Then I'll teach you to cook."

Logan scrunched his face. "Do I have to?"

I cupped his cheeks. "How about this?" I said and lowered my voice to a sexy soft whisper. "If you come in the kitchen and cook with me, I'll wear my naughtiest lingerie the whole time."

"Nah, ye will not."

My face fell. "I thought you would love that idea."

"I do, but ye wouldnae wear it long. That's what I meant."

"Because you would undress me?"

"Aye, so unless ye want to have sex in the kitchen, dinnae dress like that."

"I could wear my cheerleader outfit just for you."

His eyes widened. "Dinnae joke about that, Faith. Seriously."

"You know we're going to live out that fantasy of yours, right?" I said with a teasing grin.

He squirmed in his seat. "Och, are ye trying to give me a heart attack, lass? My heart is pumping so fast right now. Feel." He lifted my hand and placed it on his chest.

I smiled, feeling his pulse hammering away. "I'm just trying to find ways to motivate you to start doing chores around the house."

"I'll clean for a month, if ye wear yer uniform," he said quickly.

"In that case, I'll happily wear it once a month from now on."

"Or we could hire someone to clean for us," he suggested. "That way we have more time to play."

Resting my elbow on the table in front of me and looking at him, I asked, "Is it true what Kenna said: that you sold a company and could retire?"

"Aye, I sold my company."

"Did you make a lot of money?"

"I did."

"Does that mean you don't have to work anymore?"

"That's irrelevant, as I dinnae wish to retire. It took me seven years to go from an idea to making millions on selling the company I built. I have more ideas that I want to pursue."

"Millions, huh?"

He took my hand. "Does it matter?"

"No, of course not. I'm just happy for you.

"Dinnae be happy for *me*, be happy for *us*."

"Us?"

"Aye, when ye marry me, it'll be yer money too."

My heart was running faster than the engines on the jet. "When I *marry* you?"

"Aye."

"Isn't it a bit early to talk about marriage?"

"If ye say so." He looked away.

"Logan, look at me," I insisted. "You're seriously bringing up marriage on our, what... third day as a couple?"

"Just forget it." His jaws tensed.

"No, I won't forget it. Do you realize what this means?"

He shook his head.

"It means you're cured."

"Cured of what?"

"Cured of your anxiety around women and your depressive state. You're looking ahead and being hopeful for the future, and you're ready to commit to a woman. To me."

He gave me a speculative glance. "I can see you feel really pleased with yerself. Ye think that ye fixed me, dinnae ye?"

"I do," I said and squared my shoulders.

"Aye, maybe ye did. But there's a problem with yer method."

"What problem?"

"Ye cannae replicate the treatment with yer future patients because ye already gave yerself to me, and as I told ye, I dinnae share."

"I would never sleep with a patient," I protested in a high-pitched tone.

"Good."

"But I still think I'll be a fantastic psychologist, and I already know what I'll specialize in."

"What?"

"Grief! It's something I can relate to."

"Are ye still grieving?" Logan asked and drew his brows together.

I shook my head. "No, but I'll never forget what it was like to smile brightly while crying on the inside."

"That's a noble calling. To help people in grief," Logan said and kissed my forehead. "I'm sure ye'll be wonderful at it."

"Thank you, but there's something major that we need to address."

"What's that?"

"If you're serious about being with me, you have to stay in the US. My license to practice psychology won't apply abroad"

Logan grew quiet and then he looked up at me. "That might be a problem. You see, my work visa is only valid for two years."

"Huh... well, I guess you could always find an American who would marry you."

He narrowed his eyes.

"I know one who would be interested in helping you get that green card," I said. "But she's very specific about her payment and the thing is..." I leaned closer to him. "She's a bit of a pervert."

Logan pursed his lips upwards. "Really?"

"Yes, apparently she has this fetish for role-playing and she's specifically into Scottish Highlanders. It's pathetic, really." I rolled my eyes. "You might have to enact a Highlander warrior from time to time."

Logan laughed. "That happens to be a specialty of mine, but tell me about her."

"Someone once referred to her as a Barbie doll. Are you into that sort of woman?"

"Och, looks mean little to me. Can she cook?"

"Yes, in fact, she makes a mean *sheep* pie."

Logan grinned and pulled me in for a long and deep kiss. "Say no more, she sounds like my dream girl. When can I marry her?"

"Probably sometime this summer, I'm not sure."

"All right, but just in case I get eaten by a bear or something, I think I need to tell her that I love her." Logan said and caressed my face.

I swallowed hard. "You love her?"

"Aye," he said and kissed me. "I love ye, Faith."

Emotions stuck in my throat. "I love you too, Logan."

We sat nose to nose, and then I whispered. "Look out the window."

He turned and looked out at the white cover beneath us. "It looks beautiful," he said.

"That's because we're on cloud nine."

Logan frowned. "How do you know it's number nine? Looks to me like there are thousands of clouds."

That made me laugh. "It's an American saying, it means we're in heaven or high on happiness."

"Och, ye Americans and yer crazy sayings." Logan winked at me. "Why can ye no just speak English like the rest of us?"

"I'm sorry, but you'll learn once you live with me long enough."

Logan kissed me in response and whispered. "We have that saying too, I'm just messing with ye."

We sat closely together for a minute and then I started laughing hard. "You know what I just realized?"

"No, tell me."

"Wasn't the name of that bar where we first met something like 'Trolls and Dolls'?"

"Aye."

"That's funny!"

He gave me a long glance and grinned. "Och, I get it, you mean it's funny that I brought home a troll when the bar was called 'Dolls and Trolls'?"

"No, you said I looked like a Barbie doll, remember?"

"Nah, I dinnae remember, I think ye heard wrong. With those bonnie blue eyes and that long blond hair, ye're the spitting image of a troll."

"Am not," I protested and we were both laughing.

"Aye, ye are. And besides, it's clear that I'm the doll of the two of us."

"But of course, you're my Ken."

He smacked his tongue. "Ken? Och, please dinnae offend me like that..." Puffing himself up, he made an expression of self-importance. "Obviously, I'm more like a badass action figure."

I grabbed his shirt and brought him closer with a giddy grin on my face. "Oh, for sure, so how about you take a little *action* and make me a member of the mile high club."

We kissed deep and passionately and then he whispered, "Fantasies really do come true!"

This concludes Blue, Clashing Colors #4

Thank you for reading Faith and Logan's story. If you enjoyed it, I would be grateful if you could spend just a few minutes leaving a review on Amazon. It can be as short as you like.

Thank you very much.

Want more?

In the next book we'll follow Faith's twin, Chloe, aka the famous Hollywood star "Cleo."

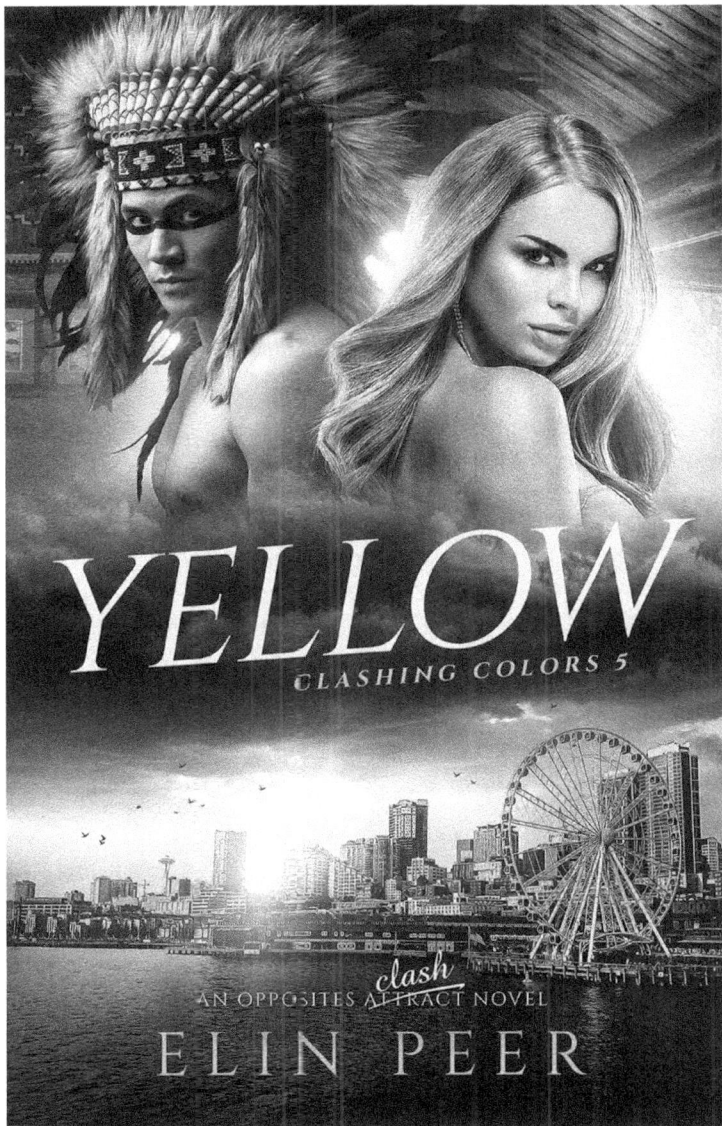

YELLOW

CLASHING COLORS 5

AN OPPOSITES ATTRACT NOVEL

ELIN PEER

1

What if you achieved your dream – and it turned out to be a nightmare?

For twenty-six years, I've chased money, fame, and beauty.
Being a movie star and dating Nick, one of the hottest pop stars in the world, should have been all I ever wanted. Except, his drugs and jealousy almost cost me my life when he shot me.

Now that Nick is on the run from the police, I promised my twin, Faith, to take a break and spend two weeks in the forest with Onava, a famous Native American healer. It was supposed to be a pleasant and relaxing detox from my crazy world of fans, social media, and paparazzi.

But my peace was over the minute Onava got called away, and her grandson Adam moved into the small cabin   instead.
Adam might be a medicine man and healer like Onava, but he's rude and shows no sympathy for my situation. What's worse is his ridiculous idea that I'm in this mess because I don't know how to set personal boundaries. I guess I'll just have to spend the remaining time practicing on Adam, which shouldn't be too hard as he gets on my nerves.

Yellow, is the fifth and last book in Elin Peer's contemporary romance series, *Clashing Colors.* Like all her books, it's fast-paced and offers both humor, wisdom, and heart. Fall in love with two flawed characters who are complete opposites and not the least bit attracted to each other, or so they say…

Buy *Yellow* today and let the last "clash" begin!

Have you read all of my books yet?

Clashing Colors:
These five contemporary romance stories dive into the theme of opposites attract.
From romantic comedy to dramatic scenes offering food for thought; these books will make you both laugh and cry.

The Slave Series:
Five intense "enemy to lovers" books portraying strong women who won't be defined as victims.
Expect some dark scenes and steamy sex.

Men of the North:
One prequel and ten romantic sci-fi stories that take place 400 years in the future where women rule the world.
These stories are unlike anything you've ever read and have made several bestselling lists on Amazon.
It's a tug of war between the crude alpha men on one side of the border and the altruistic women on the other side.
Can they find a way to integrate?

Cultivated
Set in the USA and the gorgeous Ireland, these six contemporary romance books take on the question of mind control.
They're suspenseful, fast-paced, and full of humor.
As always, they carry Elin's unique style of writing, which readers refer to as 'self-help that reads like fiction.

For a full overview of my books and to be alerted for new book releases, discounts, and give-aways, please sign up to my list at
www.elinpeer.com

About the Author

With a background in life coaching, Elin is easy to talk to and her fans rave about her unique writing style that has subtle elements of coaching mixed into fictional love stories with happy endings.

Elin is curious by nature. She likes to explore and can tell you about riding elephants through the Asian jungle, watching the sunset in the Sahara Desert from the back of a camel, sailing down the Nile in Egypt, kayaking in Alaska, river rafting in Indonesia, and flying over Greenland in a helicopter.

After traveling the world and living in different countries, Elin is currently residing outside Seattle in the US with her husband, daughters, and her black Labrador, Lucky, who follows her everywhere.

Want to connect with Elin? Great – she loves to hear from her readers.

Find her on Facebook: facebook.com/AuthorElinPeer
Or look her up on Goodreads, Amazon, Bookbub or simply go to elinpeer.com

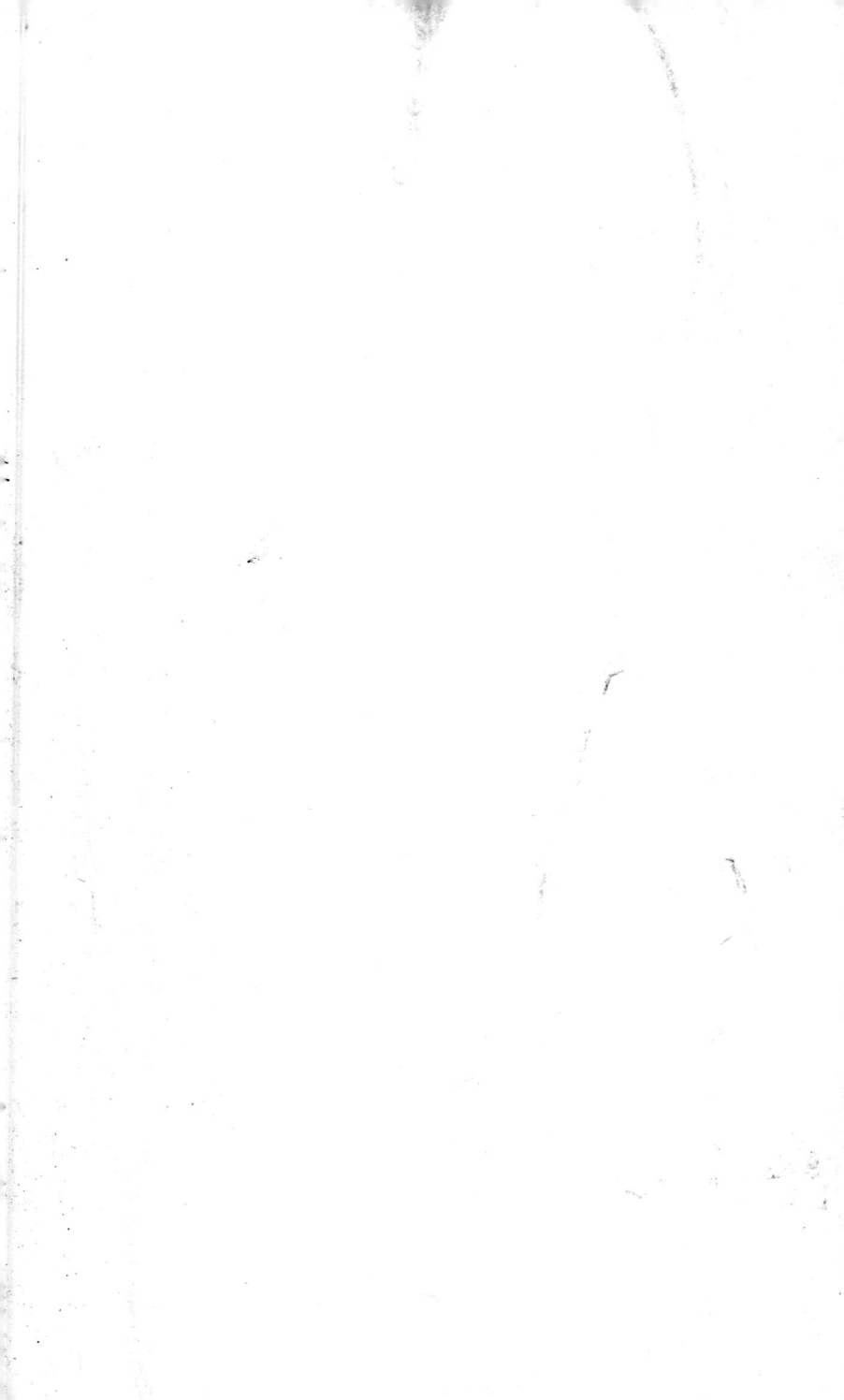

www.ingramcontent.com/pod-product-compliance
Lightning Source LLC
Chambersburg PA
CBHW052238050525
26234CB00040B/1456